TRAMPLED TO DEATH

"Eleanor!" Walter shouted.

If she heard him at all, she mistook his warning for another attempt to dictate her actions. Stubborn to the last, she continued on.

Time slowed to a crawl. Walter began to run, but he was too far away to avert disaster.

At the last instant, Eleanor glanced over her shoulder and saw her doom approaching. Her terrified scream drowned out all other sound until it broke off with horrifying abruptness. There was no room for the draft horse to veer around her in the narrow thoroughfare. As Walter watched in disbelief and horror, his wife was knocked down and trampled by the runaway. Flashing hooves struck her. Then the wagon's heavy load passed over her prostrate form with a sickening series of thumps . . .

Books by Kathy Lynn Emerson

FACE DOWN IN THE MARROW-BONE PIE

FACE DOWN UPON AN HERBAL

FACE DOWN AMONG THE WINCHESTER GEESE

FACE DOWN BENEATH THE ELEANOR CROSS

FACE DOWN UNDER THE WYCH ELM

FACE DOWN BEFORE REBEL HOOVES

Published by Kensington Publishing Corporation

FACE DOWN
BEFORE
REBEL HOOVES

Kathy Lynn Emerson

KENSINGTON BOOKS
Kensington Publishing Corp.
http://www.kensingtonbooks.com

KENSINGTON BOOKS are published by

Kensington Publishing Corp.
850 Third Avenue
New York, NY 10022

All Kensington titles, Imprints, and Distributed Lines are available at special quantity discounts for bulk purchases for sales promotions, premiums, fund-raising, and educational or institutional use. Special book excerpts or customized printings can also be created to fit specific needs. For details, write or phone the office of the Kensington special sales manager: Kensington Publishing Corp., 850 Third Avenue, New York, NY 10022, attn: Special Sales Department, Phone: 1-800-221-2647.

Kensington and the K logo Reg. U.S. Pat. & TM Off.

First Kensington Paperback Printing: April 2003

10 9 8 7 6 5 4 3 2 1

Printed in the United States of America

WHO'S WHO IN THE REBELLION OF 1569
(*real people are marked with**)

FROM AUGSBURG, HAMBURG, AND ANTWERP

Sir Walter Pendennis, diplomat and former intelligence gatherer

Eleanor, Lady Pendennis, his wife

Susanna, Lady Appleton, herbalist and sleuth; widow of Sir Robert Appleton

Lionel Hubble, her henchman

Nick Baldwin, merchant; Susanna's lover

Toby, his manservant

Warnaar Garartssonne van Horenbeeck, merchant of Antwerp

Lucius Dartnall, clerk at Haug and Company of Augsburg

IN YORKSHIRE

*Thomas Percy, seventh earl of Northumberland, not to be confused with John Dudley, duke of Northumberland, who was Susanna's guardian after her father's death. The duke (a Protestant) was executed for treason in 1554, after which the Northumberland title was restored to the Percy family (which favored the Catholic religion).

*Anne, countess of Northumberland, his wife

Sir John, a priest

Guy Carnaby, Northumberland's secretary

Joan Lascelles, Cecily Carnaby, Margaret Heron—waiting gentlewomen to the countess of Northumberland

Bess Kelke and Meggy Lamplugh—chamberers at Topcliffe

*Sir George Bowes, steward of Barnard Castle

Marion Standbridge, Eleanor Pendennis's cousin and a waiting gentlewoman to the countess of Westmorland; Carnaby's mistress

*Charles Neville, sixth earl of Westmorland

*Jane, countess of Westmorland, his wife; sister to the duke of Norfolk

*Leonard Dacre, thoroughgoing villain; younger brother of the first husband of the duke of Norfolk's third wife, who died in 1567

FROM LEIGH ABBEY AND LONDON

Jennet Jaffrey, housekeeper at Leigh Abbey

Mark Jaffrey, Jennet's husband; steward at Leigh Abbey

Rosamond Appleton, the late Sir Robert Appleton's illegitimate daughter by Eleanor Pendennis

Susan, Kate, and Rob (aka Mole) Jaffrey, Jennet and Mark's children

Fulke Rowley, horsemaster at Leigh Abbey

Hester Peacock, Rosamond's nursery maid

Catherine, Lady Glenelg, half sister of the late Sir Robert Appleton

Gilbert, ninth Baron Glenelg, her husband

OTHER REAL PEOPLE (WHO ARE MENTIONED IN THE STORY BUT DO NOT ACTUALLY APPEAR IN IT)

Elizabeth, queen of England

Mary, queen of Scots until her abdication; Elizabeth's prisoner in England

Christopher Norton, a handsome young man sent to infiltrate Mary's household

the duke of Alba, governor of the Netherlands for Spain

Thomas Howard, fourth duke of Norfolk, a prisoner in the Tower of London

Thomas Radcliffe, third earl of Sussex, lord president of the queen's council in the North

Pope Pius V, who has the power to excommunicate Elizabeth, thus freeing her Roman Catholic subjects to rebel against her

1

IMPERIAL FREE CITY OF AUGSBURG—
SEPTEMBER 1569

Muttering invective, Eleanor Pendennis stormed out of the bedchamber. Sir Walter watched her go with a mixture of irritation and regret. Ill temper would build into a towering rage before the day was out. The fury in his wife's wide hazel eyes already flashed brighter than the gold clasp fastening her new velvet cloak.

The scent of sweet marjoram lingered after her departure. Once upon a time, he would have said it was his favorite perfume. Now he found it cloying, and Eleanor more so.

She was a strong-minded woman. In the general way of things, he admired the quality, especially when it was combined with feminine grace and fierce passion, but during the last four months Eleanor's willfulness had tried his patience. When she recovered from this latest heat, he'd have to remind her, in a calm and reasonable way, of the vow she had taken to obey her husband in all things.

Now that he'd succeeded in negotiating a secret loan from the bankers of Augsburg to Elizabeth of England, Walter meant to return home. He would not go to London, where he'd lodged for many years, but to his estate in Cornwall, there to rusticate and renew relations with his brothers—it had been years since he'd seen any of them—and sire sons of his own to raise up into country gentlemen.

Eleanor had not been happy with his plan when she'd first heard of it. She'd wanted him to accept another ambassadorship. When he'd refused to consider that alternative, she'd reviled him, complaining that he no longer loved her. He wondered if she had the right of it. Of late it seemed as if they could not be in the same room together without quarreling.

Walter donned his warm, dark green wool cloak, resigned to the fact that the interior of the church was always damnably cold. As he'd expected, Eleanor had left the house without waiting for him to escort her to the small stone edifice used by Augsburg's English congregation. She was well ahead of him, striding along the cobbled street at a rapid pace and paying no attention to her surroundings. He suspected she was still mumbling epithets under her breath.

Out of habit, Walter paused a moment longer before he left cover. Most passersby were on their way to divine worship, dressed in their somber best, but he did spot a pickpocket in the crowd, and a whore making her way home after a long night's work. There was no one who presented any threat to him, but he could not help but be glad he'd soon be able to leave crowded cities and their dangers behind.

Walter had always intended his present assignment to be his last. Eleanor would have to accept that he had lost his desire to fight dragons for the queen. After years of service to the Crown, first as an intelligence gatherer and then as a diplomat, he was ready to retire.

Thinking of the clean, bracing air of home, he inhaled deeply, then choked on the reek of offal from a nearby butcher's stall. Only a bit less powerful was the rich aroma of a pile of horse dung so fresh it was still steaming. Shaking his head, he set out after his wife.

The babble of churchgoers calling out greetings to one another vied with the clatter of hooves and the rattle of wheels on cobblestones. A cheerful cacophony, Walter thought, just as a farm wagon hurtled past him at breakneck speed, scattering the crowd in its wake. It had seemed to appear out of nowhere, and pedestrians up ahead were still oblivious to the danger bearing down on them.

"Eleanor!" Walter shouted. "To me!"

If she heard him at all, she mistook his warning for another attempt to dictate her actions. Stubborn to the last, she continued on.

Time slowed to a crawl. Walter began to run, but he was too far away to avert disaster.

At the last instant, Eleanor glanced over her shoulder and saw her doom approaching. Her terrified scream drowned out all other sound until it broke off with horrifying abruptness. There was no room for the draft horse to veer around her in the narrow thoroughfare. As Walter watched in disbelief and horror, his wife was knocked down and trampled by the runaway. Flashing hooves struck her. Then the wagon's heavy load passed over her prostrate form with a sickening series of thumps.

Stunned, Walter skidded to a halt. The wildly careening wagon continued on, leaving Eleanor behind. Unmoving, she lay face down on the cobbles. Her once bright crimson cloak was mud stained and blood streaked, the lace trim torn. Her limbs splayed at unnatural angles beneath the folds of her finery.

Walter's legs refused to function. His mind struggled to deny what his eyes saw. The landmarks around him faded, buildings and people alike becoming a blur. He tasted bile.

"Eleanor."

On the heels of his own anguished whisper, Walter

began to run again, frantic now to reach her. Already fearing the worst, his stomach twisted as he flung himself to his knees by her side. He reached out, intending to turn her over, to gather her into his arms. He stopped himself just in time.

He had been in battle, seen men injured, seen them hurt more terribly still by rough handling afterward. If Eleanor, by some chance, was still alive . . .

Many hours later, Walter sat by his wife's bedside. He wanted to pray for her recovery. Instead his thoughts churned restlessly, struggling to come to terms with a bleak future.

Eleanor's injuries were dreadful. One hip had been broken, and the opposite leg. She had sustained horrible bruises and a number of deep cuts. Bandages swathed one side of her face. One shoulder had been dislocated. The physician, a man well respected in Augsburg for his knowledge of medicine, did not expect her to survive. He warned that if by some miracle she did recover, she would never walk again. She'd spend the rest of her life crippled and disfigured.

Could she live with that?

Could he stand to see her suffer?

He had no answers. He did not even know which outcome to pray for. A short, bitter laugh escaped him as he recalled that they'd been on their way to church when the accident occurred.

"Walter?"

Eleanor's voice was so faint that he thought at first he'd imagined the sound. Her eyes remained closed. Her breathing was still ragged and shallow.

"My dear?"

"Forgive me?"

"There's naught to forgive."

A little sob escaped her. Although it obviously pained her to do so, she raised her eyelids sufficient to peer up at him. He leaned closer, taking her cold hand in his. His heart ached for her . . . and for himself.

"Rest, Eleanor. You have grave injuries."

"Am I nigh unto death?"

He could not bring himself to choke out an answer, but she must have read the seriousness of her condition in his expression.

"I have done a terrible thing," she whispered.

"Eleanor—"

"No!" Her voice grew stronger. Determination gleamed in the hazel depths of her slitted, agony-filled eyes. "Hear me out. You must."

"As you wish."

He expected to be told she'd spent the household money on fine fabric, or, at most, that she'd gone behind his back and written to someone at the English court to inquire about his prospects for employment there.

"I have betrayed you, Walter. And England. The proof of it is in my little cypress box, beneath the false bottom."

Although every word of her confession was painful to them both, she soldiered on, unfolding a story that first hurt, then shocked, then angered him. He could scarce fail to believe her. Not only was this a deathbed declaration, but she offered evidence of her perfidy.

Eleanor had lapsed into unconsciousness by the time he'd deciphered the damning document he found in her hiding place. With grim precision, he slid it back into its oilskin pouch, replaced the packet in the cypress box, and snapped the false bottom into place.

Did he know his wife at all? Had he ever? He'd never guessed that she would go to such lengths to avoid retiring to Cornwall.

With the clarity of hindsight, he realized Eleanor had

been the one who'd urged him to request that first appointment as an ambassador. Newly married, they'd been sent to the court of Sigismund Augustus of Poland. Later he'd been appointed an envoy to Sweden's king Erik. Apparently, Eleanor loved the excitement of life at court so much that she'd been unable to give it up. Instead, she'd involved herself in a plot to overthrow Elizabeth of England, gambling that the queen's successor would reward her with a place in the royal household.

She had turned traitor.

Hands curled into fists, Walter avoided looking at her still form on the bed. He could not bear to go near her, knowing that she had betrayed him and all he stood for.

Hardening his heart against Eleanor, resolved to waste no more pity on someone who had so foully abused his trust, Walter examined the letters she'd kept in the top compartment of her cypress box. He found nothing in any of them to alarm him, but the most recent communication from their mutual friend Lady Appleton, which Eleanor had not seen fit to show him, did contain surprising news.

By the time Walter left his wife's chamber, his thoughts had turned to how he could best use the information she had given him. Before their marriage, he had devoted himself to ferreting out and thwarting plots against the Crown. This was familiar territory. He'd send a warning to the queen first, but there was also much more he could do to protect the realm.

He called the servants together and gave terse instructions in a voice that brooked no disobedience. That done, he extracted enough Hungarian ducats, Rhenish gulder, rose nobles, and crona from his money chest to fill a substantial pouch, sufficient to ensure that the physician who'd treated Eleanor would swear to any who inquired that her injuries had been minor, her recovery imminent.

On the morrow, Walter intended to take his wife, dead or alive, out of the city in a covered carriage. Her tiring maid had been hired during their sojourn in Cracow. He'd send the woman home from the first city they passed through on their way north. Then, with the help of his manservant, Jacob, who had been with him for years and was unquestionably loyal, he'd be able to bury Eleanor in secret.

Conspirators in England expected her to deliver a packet to them when she returned home. Walter did not mean to disappoint them. A substitution would be made, not only of its contents but of its messenger.

He permitted himself a small, grim smile as he contemplated the single stroke of good luck in all this. The person most ideally suited to take Eleanor's place was also on the Continent, in Hamburg. He'd appeal first, he decided, to Susanna Appleton's loyalty to Queen Elizabeth, but if that did not work, he'd not hesitate to compel her cooperation by reminding her that she owed him her life.

2

Nineteen Days Later

Burying a dead Englishman in hallowed ground in Hamburg required tact, patience, and resourcefulness. The city's Lutheran ministers had little tolerance for those who practiced the rites of the Church of England. "Heretic" services could only be held at the headquarters of the Merchant Adventurers. When Nick Baldwin went off to attend the funeral of one of that company, a careless apprentice who had drowned in the Bleichen Fleth, the outermost canal among many that traversed the city, Susanna, Lady Appleton, remained behind in his comfortable little house and considered how best to break the news that she would soon be leaving.

If she wished to avoid being trapped for the winter, when sailing back home became not only hazardous but foolhardy, she must leave before the end of October. The previous winter, ice had clogged the Elbe all the way from Hamburg to Ritzbuttel, near the river's mouth.

A sigh escaped her. They'd have another week together, two at the most. It had been wonderful to be with Nick again. Since he'd first become involved in readying the Hamburg market for regular English trade, more than two years earlier, he'd been able to return to England only twice. He continued to have responsibilities here, to the Company of Merchant Adventurers and to his own business interests. Susanna, likewise, had obligations that required her presence at Leigh Abbey in Kent.

Chief among them was Rosamond, her late husband's daughter by another woman.

The little girl, who would soon celebrate her seventh birthday, greatly resembled her father. She was the bane of Susanna's existence . . . and her greatest delight. Quick-witted, Rosamond devoured the lessons Susanna gave her. She'd shown an early flair for herbal lore, and she was far more advanced than most children her age, even boys, in reading, writing, and mathematics.

Unfortunately, Rosamond had inherited more than Sir Robert Appleton's dark hair and eyes, narrow face, and high forehead. He had also bequeathed her his temper, his stubbornness, and his infuriating self-assurance.

And his charm. That made up for a good deal.

Susanna's marriage to Sir Robert had lasted more than twelve years, most of them acrimonious, and had ended badly, but as the direct result of being widowed, she had acquired three good things—a greater knowledge of herself, Rosamond's guardianship, and the freedom to do as she wished with the rest of her life.

Just now, she wanted to go home.

Taking up paper and quill, Susanna began to list the arrangements she'd need to make beforehand. She had scarce completed half of it when Nick's man Toby interrupted her.

"You have a visitor, madam. Sir Walter Pendennis."

"Walter!" Delighted by the prospect of a reunion with one of her oldest and dearest friends, Susanna rose from the writing table with such alacrity that she overset her stool. "Show him in, Toby."

She resisted a temptation to rush to her mirror, and settled for smoothing her skirts and poking a stray wisp of brown hair back up under her coif. Even that small amount of primping made her smile at her own foolishness. Although Walter had once asked her to be his bride, she'd never thought of him as a potential lover. Walter was more like the older brother she'd never had, as well as a good and loyal friend. She was heartily glad to welcome him to Hamburg.

At first glance, Walter looked much the same as she remembered, a tall man with shoulders nearly broad enough to touch either side of the carved doorway. The slight paunch he'd had when they first met was a bit more obvious, and his sand-colored hair was thinner, but his love of bright colors remained undimmed. A vivid green satin doublet gleamed in the sunlight pouring through the chamber window. Over one arm he carried a short cape of scarlet wool.

For a moment they just stared at one another. Awash with memories, Susanna lacked the words to express what she felt. The months just before Walter left England had been emotional ones for both of them. He'd risked his reputation to help her, a commodity she knew was of more value to him than life itself.

Walter found his voice first. "My dear, it is good to see you."

"And you, Walter. But where is Eleanor? Surely you did not leave her behind in Augsburg." The moment she mentioned Eleanor's name, Susanna sensed something was wrong.

"Tell me first how you came to be here." Pulling off his gloves, Walter entered the room. He greeted Susanna with a brief kiss, then turned to survey their surroundings.

Susanna frowned. She trusted her instincts, but if Walter was in distress of mind, it did not show in his face. Then again, he'd had years of practice at keeping his expression a careful blank.

"The last letter you wrote to us said you were bound for Hamburg, but you did not explain why you decided to make such a long and difficult journey. Now that the duke of Alba's Spanish infantrymen are at large in the Low Countries and England has declared an embargo on trade with them, 'tis scarce the best time for an Englishwoman to travel abroad alone." His stance was a little too stiff and his mien a bit too forbidding, both subtle indicators that he struggled to contain some strong emotion.

"But I am not alone, Walter," Susanna said in mild tones. "I am with Nick Baldwin."

The look Walter gave her was sharp enough to puncture the skin. When he'd last been in England, she and Nick had been neighbors and no more than casual friends. Their relationship had changed a good deal since then.

She had to clear her throat before she could continue. "We were, I assure you, most careful when passing through the Netherlands." She motioned Walter toward a small armchair with a semicircular seat and arms, the most comfortable piece of furniture in the room. When he sat, she perched on the edge of the window seat.

"Are you his mistress?"

The bluntness of Walter's question took Susanna aback. She could feel her chin lifting, jutting out as her father's had been wont to do when he was called upon to defend his actions. "That term implies he controls my actions."

"What would you call yourself then?"

"In private, Nick calls me his *mitgeselle*." The German word, when used to describe a wife or mistress, meant both helpmate and companion. As an endearment, Susanna found it pleasing.

Walter's expression revealed none of his thoughts. He appeared, however, to be contemplating her statement, examining all aspects of it. It required more self-control on her part than Susanna had expected to keep from blurting out excuses for her behavior. No matter what

Walter had done for her in the past, she owed him no explanations. On the other hand, she did want him to understand that she saw no cause for shame.

"Why have you not married him?"

Drawing her legs up onto the window seat, she wrapped her arms around her knees, hugging them tightly to her chest. "For the same reason I would not marry you when you asked me. I have no desire to lose everything I own to a husband, no matter how good a man he seems."

After marriage, a woman no longer controlled either her own person or her possessions but became mere chattel. The man she wed assumed absolute power.

Susanna hoped Walter would let the matter drop. She did not want to wound his feelings, but if he persisted he would soon realize that her love for Nick was far stronger than any attachment she had formed with him. Although she had a deep and abiding affection for Walter, she would never have invited him into her bed. Indeed, she had wholeheartedly encouraged him to marry Eleanor.

"What business has Baldwin in Hamburg?" Walter asked.

"Nick is a merchant. When Hamburg granted the Merchant Adventurers of London a ten-year charter, including in it wide-ranging privileges to settle here and trade, Nick was one of the first to arrive. Now Hamburg is poised to replace Antwerp as the principal gateway for English trade with Germany and the Baltics." With no small amount of pride, she added, "Two fleets, each consisting of thirty ships, made the voyage from the Thames this year, sailing up the Elbe to unload cargoes of broadcloth."

"That does not explain why you came here. You are not a merchant."

Exasperated by Walter's inquisition, she answered with the simple truth. "Letters were a poor substitute for having Nick at my side and in my bed."

Walter slumped in the chair in an attitude of utter dejection. After studying him for a few moments, Susanna left her cushioned bench to fetch an angster of the local wine. Most people drank direct from the long-necked bottle, but in the hope of reviving Walter's spirits, Susanna poured the liquid into a glazed, earthenware cup, then spiced it with honey and cloves.

After a few sips, he managed a faint smile. "Wine, Susanna, when Hamburg is called the city of beer?"

"Robert always used to say your mind was a storehouse of trivial information." The name of her late husband, his onetime friend, hung heavy in the air between them. Before she'd married Walter, Eleanor had been Robert's mistress. She was Rosamond's mother. "Tell me what troubles you, Walter, and how I may help."

"I do need your assistance." He took another swallow of the wine.

"You know I will do anything I can for you. You need only ask."

"I hope you mean that." He drained the goblet but continued to hold it in both hands. "There was an accident, nearly three weeks ago now. Eleanor was run down by a horse and wagon. Her injuries were most grievous. There was naught anyone could do for her."

"Oh, my dear!" Sinking to her knees at his side, she touched his velvet sleeve in an instinctive gesture of comfort.

Eleanor dead? She could scarce believe it. Even though they had not known each other well, they had spent several weeks together at Appleton Manor in Lancashire. They'd made candles and traded recipes and developed a certain liking, in spite of the suspicions they'd entertained about each other at the time.

"I am sorry for your loss." The words seemed inadequate.

"She made no provision for Rosamond."

To Susanna's dismay, relief flooded through her. Eleanor's death meant she would never try to reclaim her daughter. Rosamond would continue to live at Leigh Abbey, continue to call Susanna "Mama."

"I have made provision for her, Walter. In time she will inherit her father's estate and all I own, as well."

"Few women would be so generous to a husband's by-blow."

Frowning, Susanna tried to peer into Walter's down-cast eyes. How odd his behavior was. Walter did not comport himself like any new-made widower she'd ever seen. If he grieved, he hid it well. But then, he would. She knew better than anyone what his history was. Until his marriage, he had been one of the queen of England's most dedicated intelligence gatherers, over-seeing a squadron of spies that had once included her late husband.

"You did not travel here to Hamburg to discuss Rosamond." She realized how tightly she was gripping Walter's arm and relaxed her hold. "Nor did you come here for the sole purpose of telling me of your wife's death. A letter would have sufficed for either purpose." She plucked at the bright-hued fabric of his sleeve. "Why do you not wear mourning?"

Walter chuckled as if her comment pleased him. "Sharp-eyed and sharp-witted. I was right to choose you."

"You speak in riddles."

"I act to confuse. My intent is to give the impression that Eleanor is alive and well. For that reason, we left Augsburg in a closed coach on the day after the accident. Anyone who watched us go must believe Eleanor suffered only minor injuries."

Regarding Walter with wary eyes, Susanna digested this information and came to the conclusion that Eleanor had died at some point during the 450-mile journey. She could only imagine the agony he must have endured, forced to increase a doomed woman's suffering in order to . . . what?

Nothing less than the fate of the realm could be at stake. Numbed by that realization, Susanna's fingers slipped from Walter's arm. She sat back on her heels and braced herself for the revelations to come. "What do you want from me, Walter?"

A brief softening of his harsh features accompanied his answer. "I require a wife."

3

"Damned popinjay!" Nick Baldwin fought a near over-whelming urge to lay violent hands on Sir Walter Pendennis. "Who does he think he is? If you marry any-one, Susanna, you will marry me!"

Nick had come home to find his domestic bliss shat-tered. Pendennis had needed only to snap his fingers and Susanna had agreed to do his bidding. She'd al-ready sent some of her belongings to the ship he had waiting. If the weather held and the wind was right, they'd sail on tomorrow's tide.

"He does not want to marry me." Susanna sounded flustered, although she continued to fold sleeves and kir-tles in an efficient manner, arranging them in neat piles on the bed. "And I have no plans to wed anyone. Walter wants me to *pretend* to be his wife."

"Worse and worse! Bad enough he'd propose mar-riage to you, but if he does not even mean to offer you his name—"

Dropping a wrist ruff and whirling around to face him, Susanna struck him, hard, on the chest. "Bodykins! You sound like a dog about to fight over a bone!" She glared at him in annoyance. Since she was a trifle taller than he was, their eyes were level.

"Where would he go with you that you needs must pretend to be his wife?"

"I cannot tell you that."

"Dragon water!" he bellowed, seizing her about the waist and lifting her off her feet. "Do you think I'll allow you to go haring off on some secret mission, no matter how noble the cause, without—"

"*Allow* me?" Her voice was dangerously soft as she glared down into his face.

Nick lowered his volume to finish what he'd been about to say, but continued to hold Susanna aloft. "Without knowing where you're bound or how much danger you'll be in? You do not know me as well as you think if you believe I can stand aside while you risk your life!"

Susanna's expression mellowed. The hands that had curled into fists on his shoulders relaxed and administered soothing strokes. "There is little danger. Put me down, Nick, and I will tell you what I know."

When he set her on her feet again, she relocated a stack of white linen shifts, scrambled up onto the bed, and patted the coverlet beside her.

"You'd betray Pendennis's secrets?" he asked.

"There is no need for sarcasm." She waited for Nick to join her.

After a moment, he relented. He never could resist her when she looked at him with equal parts love and exasperation in those keen blue eyes.

"I told Walter that I trust you with my life and that anything he had to say to me he could tell you as well."

"My thanks for that." He kissed her soft cheek and slung an arm around her waist, tugging her tight against him and relishing her unique scent, an appealing blend of soap and ink and mint.

She rested her head against his shoulder. "Even so, Walter insists that secrecy is important. Indeed, he did not tell me many details, only those he felt he must in order to convince me to help him."

He would not have had to say much. Susanna was the most intelligent woman Nick knew, but she could also be surpassing foolish when it came to doing favors for those she cared about.

He felt her draw in a deep, strengthening breath, and he tried to prepare himself for what he was about to hear. He doubted he'd like any of it.

"I have known Walter Pendennis for a long time. Only once has he disappointed me, and even then he acted for the best of reasons. He put the good of England ahead of his personal feelings."

"He was a spy. Is he still?"

"No. But there is intrigue afoot, and likely it involves overly complex plots and secret codes." He heard the note of resignation in her voice. "Robert's schemes always did. For all that, I had no choice but to agree."

Nick's already sagging hopes dipped lower. Every word she uttered felt like another nail being driven into his coffin. "Agree to what?"

"Walter does not want just any wife. He needs must convince the world that I am the one he had. I am to pretend to be Eleanor."

Nick shifted their positions until he could see her face. "You look nothing like Lady Pendennis."

"We both have brown hair, although Eleanor's tresses were of a darker hue."

"That is passing little resemblance." He'd encountered Eleanor Pendennis only once, years before. He could not recall the color of her eyes, but he did remember a turned-up nose in a delicate oval countenance. Susanna was decidedly square-jawed. "You are tall for a woman and sturdily built. Pendennis's wife was small and slender. The substitution will never work."

"Walter says it is unlikely anyone who knew Eleanor, except perhaps as a small child, will be found among the conspirators."

Conspirators? Nick mistrusted the term. Nor was "unlikely" a word that inspired confidence.

"What conspiracy does Pendennis seek to thwart?" Some plot against the English throne. That was clear enough. But Nick could not imagine how Pendennis's wife came into it. "You said you trusted me," he prompted when Susanna hesitated to reply.

"Aye. I do. But how do I explain when Walter revealed so few details to me? All I know is that a certain English nobleman expects Eleanor to arrive in Yorkshire carrying a dispatch from someone with power and influence on the Continent."

"What nobleman?"

"Thomas Percy, seventh earl of Northumberland." Susanna managed a wry smile. "Ironic, is it not? Yet another treasonous plot seems to have attached itself to the name Northumberland."

She did not need to explain her comment. Nick knew that two separate families had connections to the title. The Percys, *earls* of Northumberland, had been attainted for treason during the reign of Henry VIII and had regained their place in the peerage only recently. In the interim, the title of *duke* of Northumberland had been granted to John Dudley, the man who had been Susanna's guardian after her father's death. Dudley had arranged Susanna's disastrous marriage to Robert Appleton, and later been executed for his treasonous attempt to put the lady Jane Grey on the throne of England.

"Why would Lady Pendennis serve as a courier to the earl?" Nick asked.

"According to Walter, Eleanor stumbled into the plot during their sojourn in Augsburg."

"If Pendennis was sent there to negotiate a loan," Nick mused aloud, "he'd have gone to the Fuggers, the richest banking family in the city. If the Crown's interest concerned mining, he'd have consulted with Haug and Company. They are already extracting copper and lead from English mines for the queen."

"I know naught of Walter's original mission, but it brought Eleanor into contact with an Englishman named Dartnall. Lucius Dartnall. When he discovered that Eleanor had a distant family connection to the earl of Westmorland, who is hand in glove with Northumberland in this conspiracy, he approached her about carrying a packet back to England. Walter says she came to him at once with Dartnall's request. Then she pretended to be in sympathy with the plight of Catholics in England, encouraging further confidences about the treasonous plot now being hatched. Dartnall told her there is a plan afoot to funnel money and information into the north of England from Catholic interests on the Continent."

Any number of things about this situation disturbed Nick, not the least of which was the faraway look in Susanna's eyes. When she frowned, he smoothed one finger over the furrow in her brow and eased the line away. "What is it that most troubles you?"

She shook her head. "I wish I could explain. I lack the words to describe the . . . strangeness in Walter's voice when he spoke of events in Augsburg."

"Grief? The man just lost his beloved wife."

"Something else."

"I do not understand how any man who professes to love a woman can ask her to put herself in danger. Mayhap Pendennis had less affection for his wife than you believe. Certes, he has little care for your safety, if he can substitute you for her." A sudden fear turned his blood to ice. "How did Lady Pendennis die?"

"No one murdered her, if that is what you mean." Irritated by his denunciation of Pendennis, she rearranged herself in the middle of the bed, sitting tailor-fashion.

Accepting her need for a small separation, Nick tucked a bolster behind his back and leaned against the headboard. "You can scarce blame me for wondering. Those who spy for a living put themselves and their families at risk of being stabbed or bludgeoned or poisoned or—"

"It was an accident. A tragic mishap like that apprentice's drowning in the Bleichen Fleth. A runaway wagon struck Eleanor. Its driver was killed, too, thrown from his seat. He cracked his skull open on the pavement."

Nick winced. "Was she killed instantly?"

"She lingered. I do not know how long. Time enough to take her out of Augsburg."

"Tell me more about this connection between Lady Pendennis and the earl of Westmorland."

"Westmorland's father married three times. The second and third brides were sisters from the Cholmeley family. Eleanor's mother is also a Cholmeley, from a cadet branch. The kinship is remote, useful to convince the conspirators to accept Eleanor as one of them but no threat to me when I assume her identity. Walter seems certain no one I will meet in Yorkshire knew Eleanor."

"Do any of the conspirators know you?"

She shook her head. "I do much doubt it, for Yorkshire is well away from Kent. Besides, why would anyone question my identity when I bring with me the packet Master Dartnall gave to Eleanor? That should suffice to prove I am who I say I am. Simply serving as their courier demonstrates my dedication to their cause."

"Are you to deliver this packet, then, and leave?"

"Eleanor intended to remain, in the hope of discovering details of the conspirators' plans."

"She was going to spy for him."

"Yes."

"And you mean to take her place."

"Yes. Nick, they want to depose Queen Elizabeth. They must be stopped."

"What if word of the accident in Augsburg gets back to England? What if they learn that the real Lady Pendennis is dead?"

"Walter gave out that she was not badly hurt. That man, Dartnall, who is the conspirators' contact in Augsburg, can have no reason to doubt the story."

"Pendennis must have concocted the plan to substitute you for his wife within hours of her accident. While she lay dying." Cold-blooded bastard!

"What other choice did he have?" Susanna's expressive eyes begged him to understand not only Pendennis's actions but her own decision to go along with his plans. "I am the only one he can trust to take Eleanor's place. If I refuse, England may well be plunged into civil war. That is too great a burden to have on my conscience, not when I can do something to prevent it."

Nick felt a giant fist curl around his heart and squeeze. Pendennis had played upon Susanna's loyalty to the queen and her faith in his honesty to convince her she must undertake this hazardous mission. No argument Nick could offer would change her mind. She already knew the dangers she would face and was not swayed by them.

"Let me come with you, to keep you safe. I can pretend to be your servant."

"Oh, my dear. I would like nothing better, but I could not hide my affection for you. Everyone would think Lady Pendennis unfaithful to her husband." She tried to smile and failed. "Besides, you have obligations here."

"I can delegate my duties to others, for as long as a few months if need be."

Susanna leaned toward him, forcing him to meet her eyes, to see the pain and longing there, as well as the determination. "Nick, I would have left here soon, even if Walter had not come to Hamburg. And you would have stayed behind. Can we not pretend our parting is no more than that?"

Her words were gently spoken, but they pierced like arrows.

With exquisite care, he gathered her into his arms. "Well then," he whispered as he began to kiss her, "if this is to be our last night together, let us make it one we will both remember for a very long time."

4

LONDON—OCTOBER 11, 1569

Only in the stable attached to her husband's London house did Catherine Glenelg find a measure of peace. She was happy grooming Vanguard, her favorite horse, in the company of two dogs, a cat, and a falcon with a broken wing. She wished she could stay with them instead of returning to young Gavin, who was teething, and Gilbert's mother, whose greatest delight was criticizing her daughter-in-law.

"Shall I come and live here with you?" she whispered into a velvet ear. Vanguard butted her, as if to express understanding and sympathy, and gazed at her with large, sleepy eyes. All black, except for a white blaze on his forehead, the courser was getting on in years. He had once belonged to Catherine's half brother, Sir Robert Appleton.

Most people, Catherine thought, would say she had no cause to complain. She was the wife of a charming, handsome, titled man. Although his estate was in Scotland, he made his principal residence in London to please her. Moreover, Gilbert did not desert her to hang about the fringes of the royal court, presently at Windsor, as so many noblemen did. Oh, he spent time there, had been there, certes, for the last week, but only on behalf of the earl of Moray, who ruled Scotland as regent in the name of the infant King James. Unlike most husbands, her Gilbert came home as often as possible. He was devoted to Catherine and faithful to their wedding vows.

But he refused to send his mother away. That formidable Scotswoman, who insisted the servants address her as Lady Russell, even though her English husband had never been knighted, was slowly driving Catherine to madness.

Vanguard nickered in protest when Catherine wielded a hedgehog skin brush with too much force. She set it aside, using a wisp and her hand to continue currying. So lost was she in her task that she did not hear Gilbert enter the stable. He was right behind her before she became aware of his presence and turned, smiling, to greet him with mock formality. "Lord Glenelg! Well met!"

"Lady Glenelg." He bowed, then swept her into his arms, banishing the last of her discontent in a most satisfactory way.

Breathless and much restored in spirit, Catherine emerged from the embrace a few minutes later. She noted that they were alone in the stable. "Did any see you come in?"

"Temptress. Would you lie with me in the straw?" Eyes the color of the sky in summer laughed at her, then darkened with sudden heat.

"Is that a question, my lord . . . or an invitation?"

Unlike so many husbands, who grew fat and complacent once they wed, Gilbert had changed little in seven years of marriage. He was straight and tall, and his thick red-brown hair, which he wore a bit longer now than when she'd first met him, was as abundant as ever. When he pulled her into his arms, she combed her fingers through it, delighting in the texture . . . and in his growl of response.

In the empty stall next to Vanguard's, freshly strewn with sweet-smelling hay brought in from the country, Lord and Lady Glenelg moved a wooden-tined pitchfork out of their way and disported themselves without further speech for the best part of the next hour. Eventually, sated, wrapped in each other's arms, Catherine encouraged Gilbert to tell her about his latest visit to the English court. It helped relax him, she had discovered, to unburden himself and from early in their marriage he had paid her the supreme compliment of trusting her not to repeat anything he told her in private.

"I scarce know where to begin."

He tucked a dark brown lock behind Catherine's ear and bent to touch his lips to the lobe. She shivered in delight and might have been persuaded to abandon talk for a repetition of other, more pleasurable activities, had he not pulled away from her.

When he sat up, his expression was grim. "The duke of Norfolk has been arrested."

Catherine was not surprised. Queen Elizabeth had little tolerance for those who thought they knew better than she did what was best for the realm. Norfolk had long been among the most vocal of her critics.

Gilbert assumed the role of tiring woman and began to reattach various pieces of Catherine's clothing. "More than a month past, the queen had a private audience with the duke at which she forbade him to pursue any match with Mary of Scotland."

"And he disregarded her wishes?"

"Aye, he did."

At second hand, Catherine knew a great deal about the struggle for power and influence among the courtiers surrounding Queen Elizabeth and about the rival claimants for England's throne. When Mary, queen of Scots, had fled her own country the previous year, seeking sanctuary in her cousin Elizabeth's kingdom, Elizabeth had wisely ordered her imprisoned. Some in the government felt Mary should be executed, as she would provide a rallying point for rebels whilst she lived.

To Catholics, Elizabeth was a bastard and a heretic who had no right to England's throne. For them, Scotland's deposed queen, the granddaughter of old King Henry's elder sister, was the legitimate heir. As England's only duke and highest ranking peer, Norfolk, already thrice a widower, had been put forward as a possible spouse for Mary. One faction at court argued that marrying him to the queen of Scots would assure that she caused Elizabeth no more trouble. Norfolk, these men claimed, knew how to control a woman. And should Elizabeth die childless, then Norfolk, English and a man, would rule England, making decisions on behalf of his foreign-born wife.

It gave Catherine headaches every time she attempted to sort out all the whys and wherefores of machinations at court, but she did understand two unalterable facts. One was that religious issues always got tangled up with matters political. The other was that Scotland, the country to which Gilbert owed his allegiance, had of late declared it treason for any Scot to support Queen Mary.

Catherine tried to lighten Gilbert's mood as she helped him with the points on his shirt and doublet. "I do most heartily wish someone would devise a better way to fasten sections of clothing together," she grumbled. "To be able to remove and reassume garments, all of a piece, would be a great boon to lovers everywhere."

Gilbert did not respond to her teasing. "'Tis said Queen Elizabeth told Norfolk that she reckoned she would be removed from her throne within four months of the wedding if she allowed him to wed Mary."

Catherine's hands stilled. "She was that sure there would be rebellion?"

"She fears an uprising in the North. That is why she acted against Norfolk when new rumors reached her from abroad. She had Norfolk detained for questioning. It was a loose captivity at a gentleman's house, allowing him to place a note inside a bottle and attempt to smuggle this message to the earl of Westmorland, his brother-in-law. The missive was intercepted. It revealed that Westmorland, Norfolk, and others had planned to muster their men on the sixth day of this month."

"Five days ago." Catherine felt her face pale. "What is happening in the North?"

"All seems quiet. Since Norfolk's message begged Westmorland to call off the rebellion, it was sent on to him. As a precaution, however, the queen closed all English ports and put the militia on alert. And she sent Norfolk to the Tower. There will be no more smuggled messages. As befits his rank, his grace is allowed two personal servants but he is forbidden the use of either pen or paper."

Catherine's fingers trembled as she put her hair and headdress to rights. She had lived in the North until she was fourteen. She knew well the forces at work there, and the passions of the people. On her estates in Lancashire, many still clung to the old religion, in spite of the law against hearing Mass. They were encouraged in their disobedience by the persistent rumor that Pope Pius V planned to excommunicate Queen Elizabeth, bestowing on her subjects the blessing of mother church to rise up against the heretic queen and put a Catholic monarch on the throne in her place.

Dismayed by the brooding expression on Gilbert's face, she attempted to hide her own worries. "Well, then, it appears the crisis is past. Come, *caro sposo*. Let us go in to our son."

Gilbert slung an affectionate arm around her shoulders and dropped a kiss on her forehead. "A far more pleasant topic. What remarkable new feats has he accomplished since I last saw him?"

"He's acquiring teeth." Catherine grimaced.

"So that is why you hid yourself in the stable."

They walked together toward the house and a reunion with their fussy baby and an old woman determined to find fault with everything Catherine did. The blithe plotting of acts of rebellion, she thought, had a certain appeal. She indulged in a brief satisfying fantasy in which Gilbert's mother was abducted by pirates and carried off to be sold into slavery on the Barbary Coast. A harmless pastime, she assured herself, as long as no one tried to turn a diabolical daydream into reality.

5

Walter Pendennis paused in the act of scooping watery oatmeal pottage into his mouth to study his supper companion. Lionel Hubble had grown into a lean and well-muscled young man. No longer the gangly lad Walter remembered, the gardener's boy at Leigh Abbey until he was promoted to second gardener, Lionel had for some years now been able to take on the additional duty of bodyguard when his mistress traveled.

The two men ate standing up, near a brick firebox positioned amidships in their small merchant vessel. Walter appreciated the warmth, and the savory aromas wafting upward from two large copper cooking cauldrons with wide leaded rims, but the smoke did not vent properly. For every three or four swallows of the pottage, he had to stop and cough.

They had been at sea for more than a week but were less than halfway back to England. He'd not seen Susanna since they first set foot aboard ship in Hamburg. Her face an unhealthy shade of green, she'd mumbled something about ginger and peppermint and disappeared into the master's cabin reserved for her use.

"Was she as ill as this on the voyage over?" Walter asked.

Mopping away a mushy bit of parsnip that had dribbled into the deep cleft in his chin, Lionel thought about the question before he answered. "Worse, Sir Walter. Spewing the whole way, she was."

Susanna had said that she'd suffered greatly from seasickness on the journey from England and spent the entire crossing from Gravesend to Dordrecht "wretchedly ill," but he'd thought she must be exaggerating.

"Canals bothered her, too," Lionel said. "The one to Amsterdam and the rest of them."

This was a side of Susanna that Walter had not encountered before. She'd always been strong, blooming with good health. He'd seen her discouraged, and consumed by guilt and grief but never had he imagined she could be laid low by a mere physical ailment.

Reminded by his thoughts of the last journey he'd undertaken in company with Susanna and Lionel, Walter grew curious. "Why is Fulke not with you on this trip?" He was accustomed to thinking of Susanna's two henchmen as a pair. Fulke was only a year or two older than Lionel. At one time, he'd been much taller and bulkier, but the younger man had caught up as he'd matured.

After chewing and swallowing a chunk of ship's biscuit—plain, poor food, but blessedly free of weevils—Lionel answered. "Fulke grew tired of travel. He did not want to come. He'd been to the Continent before, he said, when Sir Robert was alive. Lady Appleton did not insist he accompany us. She said there was no need when she had me to protect her. And Master Baldwin and his man."

"This Baldwin . . . what do you know about him?"

Lionel's grin showed off teeth that lapped over one another. "He's more widely traveled than Fulke and has been to far more interesting places. He tells the most wonderful stories, all of them true."

"I have traveled to a goodly number of exotic places myself. Italy and—"

"Master Baldwin has been to Muscovy. And Persia." He named the latter place in an awed whisper.

"Is Lady Appleton also impressed by travel narratives?"

Oblivious to Walter's growing irritation, Lionel nodded. "She loves to listen to him tell his tales."

Walter all but threw his empty bowl into the stack of dirty dishes and stalked toward the nearest hatch. Lionel, still talking, unaware that his praise of Baldwin affected Walter's self-control, dogged his steps.

"I'd not care to go to Persia, but I like to travel, and 'twas much more pleasant to make the journey to Hamburg than to stay at Leigh Abbey."

Arrested by an odd note in Lionel's voice, Walter gave him a sharp look. "Why do you say so?"

"There is a woman there. Hester Peacock, Mistress Rosamond's nursery maid. She fancies me."

A great many women, Walter imagined, would fancy Lionel. He had grown into a handsome man. "Ugly, is she?"

Color seeped into Lionel's face. "She is overtall and no beauty, that much is certain. But 'twas not her appearance made me want to flee. 'Twas the way she'd look at me, all calf-eyed, as if I could do no wrong."

Several hours later, after the sun had set, Lionel's words still lingered in Walter's thoughts. Eleanor had looked at him "all calf-eyed" once upon a time.

Fabric rustled behind him. One hand on his knife, Walter turned to confront a potential attacker and instead beheld a familiar face lit by the bright beams of a moon at the half. "Susanna!"

"Good evening, Walter."

"How do you feel, my dear?"

"To mine own surprise, much steadier on my feet than I have been."

"You will forgive me, my dear, but you do not appear to be all that steady."

"By comparison to what came before, I am a rock."

"Mayhap the fresh sea air will do you some good, then." He offered her his arm.

After a slight hesitation, she took it and allowed him to lead her to the waist-high rail. She inhaled a few cautious breaths, then seemed to relax. "Perhaps I should not have stayed in the cabin so long, or relied upon mine herbs. This bracing breeze and the scent of brine do appear to be salubrious."

"I have often observed that after a few days at sea, many of those who at first cast up their accounts find their stomachs settling and their spirits restored."

"I have never seen the moon look quite so large," she murmured.

"Distances are deceiving at sea."

"Which way is England?"

He studied the sky for a moment, finding navigation a challenge at sea. He'd just oriented himself using the North Star and pointed west when the ship changed course, veering away from their destination. Walter glanced at the great squares of canvas above them. While a half-dozen barefooted seamen controlled the sails with the use of lines, others swarmed into the rigging in response to the boatswain's whistle. Their coarse white linen trousers flapped in the wind as they climbed higher.

"Would we not get there much sooner," Susanna asked, "if we went in a straight line?"

He shook his head. "A ship must travel in a zigzag pattern because it is dependent on the wind to fill the sails. That is why it takes so long to cross only a few score miles of water, and why storms delay so many journeys by driving ships off course."

"How, then, do we manage to land at our chosen destination?"

"A well-trained crew knows how to trim the sails to match the speed and direction of the wind."

After a short silence, during which they watched the activity overhead, she changed the subject. "You said the rebels are in Yorkshire. Why that county when their leaders are the earls of Northumberland and Westmorland?"

"Both earls also have strongholds there." Walter paused to gather his thoughts. This seemed as good a time as any to part with the few additional details he meant to give Susanna. "The city of York is some seventy miles north of Wingfield Manor, where, at last report, the queen of Scots was imprisoned. I believe the rebels' intent is to free her and place her on Elizabeth's throne."

"Last report?"

"Only after we make landfall will I have means of getting news of recent developments at home. Information that reached me in Augsburg is already more than two months old."

"Then it is possible the plan for rebellion has already been discovered. My impersonation of Eleanor may not be necessary."

"In the North, there are always more treasons to unearth."

She frowned. "On land, where there is no need to zigzag, why do men still choose the most roundabout route to a goal?"

Unable to think of an adequate response, Walter let that question pass unanswered. "Shall we adjourn to your cabin?" he asked instead. "If you are to succeed in your mission, it will be useful for you to understand the intricate relationships that bind the rebels together. For generations, the earls of Westmorland and Northumberland have ruled in their respective shires like petty kings. And in the North, more than anywhere else in England, both politics and religion take second place to the old feudal loyalties."

6

Engrossed in studying the notes she'd made two days earlier, following what she privately thought of as Walter's lesson in genealogy, Susanna did not realize he had entered her cabin until he made a sound low in his throat and snatched a paper away from her.

"What is this? How could you be so foolish as to write down such incriminating information?"

"Calm yourself Walter." She did not rise from the stool she'd drawn up to a small table. "You know it helps me organize my thoughts to make lists, and since fully half the conspirators you told me about have the same three or four surnames, I wish to avoid confusing them." She sent a bright smile in his direction. "Never fear. I will burn all these scraps of paper just as soon as we sight land."

Too tall to stand upright in the cabin, he glowered at her from a stooped position before relinquishing her writing. She waved him toward the box bed, the only other place to sit.

"I understand your concern. Documents have a nasty habit of coming back to haunt their creator. But would you rather I mix up the players?" In a gentle, teasing tone, she added, "Think what disastrous results might ensue from mistaking one of Westmorland's uncles for the other."

Walter would not be cajoled. "Better to destroy it now."

"Not yet. Rereading my notes has raised more questions. And writing them down helps occupy my mind."

She'd sought distraction to help her forget she was at sea, no easy task when every breath reminded her. This was a sweet-smelling ship compared to most, used to carry wine and spices, but the odor of tar permeated everything. The constant movement of the ship continued to make her queasy, and she could never forget that the undulating waters of the North Sea lay just beyond her cabin's three small square windows. At that thought, Susanna reached for the infusion of ginger and rosewater she'd prepared earlier. Sipping the soothing liquid, she indicated the first name on her list.

"The earl of Northumberland. What more do you know of him, Walter?" That he was a ringleader of rebellion was no longer enough.

Given Walter's years in intelligence gathering, Susanna was certain he knew a great deal about everyone she would encounter in the course of her mission. For some reason, however, he had so far been reluctant to volunteer more than the most superficial information. Extracting a tooth from a mastiff would have been easier than persuading Sir Walter Pendennis to part with his secrets.

He reached for her goblet and sniffed. "Ginger?"

"It settles the stomach."

"Why do you smile?"

"I was remembering that Catherine cannot abide the taste, not even in sweets." Her sister-in-law was as dear to Susanna as anyone in the world. The two years she had lived at Leigh Abbey had been happy ones.

"Lady Glenelg is well?" Walter asked. He'd met Catherine at the same time he and Susanna first crossed paths. He had, she recalled, asked a favor of her on behalf of the queen on that occasion, too.

"She is not only well, but the mother of a young son.

Gilbert managed a post in London shortly after you left England. I believe they are much happier there than in Edinburgh. But you are trying to distract me, Walter, and it will not work." She reached across the short distance between her stool and his perch and retrieved her posset. The feel of the goblet, cool and smooth beneath her hand, was soothing in itself. "I want information about Northumberland. If I am to join his household, I must know something of the man himself."

"I've never met him."

She waited.

"He was warden of the East and Middle Marches for a time but is no longer."

"Removed for improprieties?"

"For suspicion of having Catholic sympathies."

"And his wife?"

"She is said to be beautiful and spirited and by all accounts is devoted to her husband. I do not anticipate you will experience any difficulty convincing him to let you join her household. Make of me as vile a husband as you will. Say I beat you. Better yet, tell them I returned to England to argue for the execution of the queen of Scots. That should win you sympathy."

"Deception does not come easily to me. It will be challenge enough to cross myself and manage a rosary." She'd been practicing with the beads Walter provided, but still felt fumble fingered and awkward. "Nor do I understand why I am to throw myself on the Northumberlands' mercy rather than go to Eleanor's kinsman."

"The packet you carry is meant for Northumberland."

"The two earls are allies. No doubt I will come in contact with Lady Westmorland at some point. What more can you tell me about her? All you've said to date is that she is the duke of Norfolk's sister. Which one? The duke, I recall, has three." Susanna ran one thumb over the length of her quill, finding it hard to resist the urge to make notes. "It seems most strange to me that any of them should be at the heart of a Catholic plot. They were raised and educated by ardent supporters of the New Religion."

"Lady Westmorland is Jane, the eldest. Do you know her? More to the point, does she know you?" Walter levered himself off the berth and braced his hands on the table. Concern escaped, for a moment, from behind the mask he wore to conceal his emotions.

"We've never met, but I've heard of her scholarship. My father was part of the same forward-thinking circle as her tutor. Both advocated educating daughters with as much thoroughness as sons." Susanna stopped fiddling with her pen and set it aside. "Does it matter? Even if you have the right of it and the two earls raise the North, they'll doubtless follow tradition and leave their wives at home."

Walter ignored the question, distracted by another name on her list. "Leonard Dacre." He grimaced. "Avoid him if you can. I had dealings with him some years ago and found him most untrustworthy. He provides intelligence to the queen when it serves his purpose but does not quibble at betrayal if there is profit in it."

"Tell me more about Eleanor's family," Susanna said. If there was any danger of being recognized as an imposter, it would come from them.

"We have been over this before," Walter complained. "You have it all writ down. Eleanor's mother was born Philippa Cholmeley. She married Sir Eustace Lowell, who died impoverished when Eleanor, their only child, was very young. Lady Lowell married second Sir Giles Gillingham. At that time she sent her daughter to be fostered by Lady Quarles, a distant connection of the Lowells."

Walter's clipped sentences increased Susanna's certainty that he did not wish to be pressed on the subject of his late wife. She wondered what lay at the core of his distress, but he allowed her no opening to probe.

"You do not need to worry about encountering Lady Quarles. She died two years ago."

"What about Lady Gillingham's side of the family?"

"There are Cholmeleys throughout the North. So many that no one would expect Eleanor to keep them all straight in her mind."

"She'd know her own mother. Where is Lady Gillingham now?"

"Nowhere near where you'll be, and she'll make no effort to contact you. Eleanor had naught to do with her after she went to Lady Quarles. She never forgave her mother for sending her into servitude."

"How sad to be estranged from her closest kin." And it troubled Susanna that Eleanor's mother could not be told of her child's death.

"She rarely spoke of her family, and never fondly. There was one cousin who plagued her as a girl. Mary? Marion?" He shrugged. "No matter. I doubt you'll encounter her in Northumberland's household. She lives on the bounty of an uncle who likes to keep her close to home." Walter rubbed the bridge of his nose, as if a headache threatened.

Susanna took up her quill to add the name Mary to her chart of Eleanor's kin.

Another low growl issued from Walter's throat. Before Susanna could prevent him, he seized her lists, opened the lantern hanging overhead, and thrust the papers into the candle flame.

7

"A handful of Englishmen still reside here," Nick's companion informed him, "and others return from time to time to conduct business."

"The Merchant Adventurers have been expelled, their merchandise seized." Nick spoke quietly, in Low German.

"Those who profess to be Catholics may still prosper."

Nick grunted. The city was no longer friendly to heretics from across the German Ocean, as locals called the North Sea. That was why he'd taken the precaution of arriving in the guise of a Bavarian draper, hiding his true nationality.

Several hours earlier, when Nick and his manservant had walked into the mercer's shop, Warnaar Garartssonne van Horenbeeck had asked no questions. Instead, he'd invited both Nick and Toby to lodge with him for the duration of their visit. The two merchants now sat in a dark, quiet corner of the Sign of the Golden Angel, long a favorite haunt of Englishmen living in Antwerp. Nick was curious to see who among his countrymen remained in residence. So far he'd recognized no one, and no one knew him.

"Those who are cooperative with the current political and military leaders do well enough," Horenbeeck said.

Nick frowned. His old friend had used the word

waicher. A more accurate translation than "cooperative" would be "pliant."

A look of concern creased Horenbeeck's broad, flat face. "Why did you risk coming here, Nick? You are no partisan of Spanish rule."

"To collect debts owed me."

"A bill of exchange could have been sent to you in Hamburg to settle those."

"Perhaps I am curious to see how Antwerp fares under the duke of Alba's control."

"Curiosity?" Horenbeeck sounded doubtful.

"I did live here for three years. I am interested in what has changed since I left."

Nick spoke the truth, as far as it went, but he'd had another, more personal reason for leaving Hamburg the day after Susanna sailed for England. Although he had lived there alone before her arrival, one night without her in the house they'd shared had convinced him he needed a change of scene. He'd chosen Antwerp because the overland journey would take at least two weeks and provide him with a goodly number of distractions. He'd been right about that. There had been Spanish troops everywhere. He'd been wrong, however, to think he could so easily put Susanna Appleton out of his mind.

"And have you found changes?" Horenbeeck sipped his beer and watched the door. They'd both taken stools that put their backs to the wall and gave them an unobstructed view of new arrivals.

Nick grinned. "Seventeen years have passed since I first saw this city. I was a young sprig of twenty back then." He'd been sent by his father, who'd been in the business of exporting wool from England. "How could I not find differences?"

"This is still the greatest port and richest market in the world," Horenbeeck declared. "The Bourse remains a meeting place for merchants of all sorts, and the center for the distribution of spices, and the hub of an international money market."

"True. All true."

But where, at one time, more than a thousand foreign businesses had carried on transactions worth, by one calculation, two and a half million golden ducats a year, now Antwerp had as many enemies abroad as friends. English privateers had been given leave to prey on merchant ships trading here. In the countryside of the Netherlands, as in England, rebellion stirred.

"The streets, squares, and those homes built of stone are much as I remember them." Nick tried to sound casual. "And the two towers of the Cathedral of Notre-Dame continue to dominate the skyline. But there has been an addition, a new structure incorporated into the southern wall of the city between the Kronenbourg and St. Joris gates." The pentagonal fortification had a bastion at each star point and was fronted by an expanse of open ground across which nothing could move without being seen from the ramparts.

"The Citadel." Horenbeeck looked grim. "Built on the orders of the duke of Alba. Is that why you've come? To study our defenses?"

"I can think of no reason why England should involve herself in a civil war in the Low Countries."

"Pray God it will not come to war."

"Amen to that." Nick signaled for more beer.

"Do you know that fellow?" Horenbeeck asked as the door opened to admit a young man in a dark blue cloak. "He is English."

The newcomer had the stoop-shouldered, slightly squint-eyed look of a clerk. "He is unknown to me."

"Name's Dartnall," Horenbeeck supplied. "Works for Haug and Company."

Nick's eyes narrowed. Here was a coincidence. The very man who'd approached Eleanor Pendennis in Augsburg was now in Antwerp. Haug and Company had branches in both cities, he remembered, and in many other places besides, but why was Dartnall here at just this moment? The most logical answer to that question alarmed him. Antwerp was some distance from the sea, but it was located on a large, easily navigable estuary of the Scheldt and was thus a logical point of embarkation for England. Even with the embargo, a quick crossing was possible. If Dartnall was bound for Yorkshire on business with the earl of Northumberland, he could wreck all Pendennis's carefully laid plans. Should Dartnall catch sight of Susanna, he'd recognize her at once as an imposter.

"Can you devise a way to let Dartnall know I am an Englishman in disguise?" Nick asked Horenbeeck. "And somehow make him think me a papist, as well?"

With an air of gloomy resignation, Horenbeeck assured Nick that he could.

The undertaking required the consumption of copious quantities of beer, both before and after Horenbeeck's departure. In the end it was Nick's commiseration on the subject of the unreasonable expectations of employers that won Dartnall's trust, that and the drink and Dartnall's delight at being able to speak English to a fellow countryman. Much of what he said concerned petty complaints against people whose names Nick did not know, but eventually he asked if Nick had ever heard of a fellow named Pendennis. Nick denied it.

"Cannot abide the idea of a Catholic on the throne," Dartnall declared. "Spoilt some fine plans over the years."

"There are many people in England who seem content with things as they are."

"And a great number who are not." Dartnall slung a companionable arm around Nick's shoulders and breathed beer fumes into his face.

They were the only Englishmen in the common room and no one else was near enough to overhear their conversation. In addition, although Dartnall's German showed no trace of an accent, his English had the flavor of Yorkshire. It grew more pronounced with every swallow of beer. That alone, Nick suspected, would make the fellow's words difficult for an eavesdropper to translate.

"Powerful folks," Dartnall muttered. "Peers."

"What's this Pendennis to them?"

A smirk appeared on Dartnall's pale face. "A spelk toon frey hissen."

For a moment, Nick was unsure what language Dartnall spoke. *"Spelk?"*

"Splinter."

A splinter took from himself. Even translated, the Yorkshireman's statement made no sense. The fellow was cup shot, and no mistake. "What splinter?"

"Why his wife, friend. His rib." Dartnall chortled. "He daren't trouble her. I do think he be afeared of her. E'en the devil would not take her."

Dartnall's sputtering laughter had Nick tightening his grip on his tankard. Assuming a bit of the pattern of Yorkshire speech himself, the better to lull his drunken companion into further confidences, Nick wagged an admonishing finger at Dartnall. "Thou hast been up to summat."

Belatedly, a cautious look came into Dartnall's eyes. "I do not see how any can blame me. 'Twas their mistake." Worry replaced the wariness.

"A mistake about Lady Pendennis?" Nick had difficulty curbing his impatience. If Dartnall knew what had really befallen her and told the conspirators in England she was dead, Susanna would be in danger.

Dartnall was deep in his cups, muttering incoherently. "Wast sure they could rely upon the woman."

"What woman?"

"Sent word she was not to be trusted. Because of her husband, see thou so? But she did not die, and none have come after me, so how can they have had the right of it? When she does deliver up the packet, all will know her to be loyal to the cause, just as they thought at first."

Nick did not have to feign confusion as Dartnall emptied his tankard and called for a refill. His desire to beat the story out of the beer-soaked lout grew stronger. "At first you were to trust this Eleanor Pendennis?"

Dartnall's nod was so vigorous that his bonnet fell off. "She toon a packet I had for England."

"Took a packet," Nick repeated, translating.

"Fair jumped at the chance." Chuckling, growing more inebriated with every passing moment, Dartnall rambled on.

In with the dross was gold. Although it sore tried Nick's patience to extract information at such a slow rate, over the course of the next hour he heard enough to formulate a surmise. At first, thinking Pendennis no more than a simple diplomat, the conspirators welcomed the chance to use his wife as a courier. Then someone must have belatedly discovered Pendennis's past as an intelligence gatherer and Dartnall had received word that it was dangerous to deal with the wife of such a man.

The clerk yawned and blinked at Nick with sleepy eyes. "Ordered me to arrange an accident, they did."

Nick felt a chill course through him. His fingers clenched hard on his empty tankard.

"Followed her," Dartnall mumbled.

"You followed Lady Pendennis, waiting for an opportunity to stage an accident?"

"Aye. Simple matter when it came to it." Dartnall chuckled. "Clout on the head for the farmer who owned the wagon. Sharp blow on the flank of the horse that pulled it."

A vivid picture filled Nick's mind and made him wish he'd not drunk so much beer. Closing his eyes did not banish the image, nor could it blunt the impact of Dartnall's words.

Eleanor Pendennis had been murdered.

Too cup-shotten to notice Nick's reaction, Dartnall kept talking. Nick forced himself to listen, even managed to ask a question or two, although part of his mind continued to reel in shock.

Dartnall had killed two people, Eleanor Pendennis and the driver of the runaway wagon, and he showed not a bit of remorse. That he'd been fooled by Pendennis's deception and believed Lady Pendennis was still alive did not excuse him. He was still responsible for the death of an innocent countryman. Split his skull open on the cobbles? Was that what Pendennis had told Susanna? Nick wondered if he believed it.

"Who gave the order for Eleanor Pendennis's death?"

"'Thumberland." Dartnall mumbled. "His seal."

Nick had thought Susanna's greatest danger lay in being unmasked as Lady Appleton. Now he feared she would be in deadly peril if the rebels believed her claim to be Sir Walter's wife. When she landed in Yorkshire, calling herself Lady Pendennis, the earl of Northumberland could well authorize another attempt to kill her. Dartnall might have convinced himself that she was one of them, but Dartnall was a fool. Others more clever than he were sure to be suspicious of their new recruit.

Abandoning any idea of returning to Hamburg, Nick fixed his mind on practical matters. If he could get to England quickly enough, he might still be able to stop Susanna from walking blind into a nest of vipers. He knew people in Vlissingen, a little seaport at the mouth of the Scheldt, who could find him a fast ship with a captain willing to run the embargo. Given fair winds, he'd be in Yorkshire in less than a week. He might even arrive there ahead of the *Green Rose*.

8

Waves breaking near shore made the short distance Susanna had to cover in the ship's boat the most harrowing of the entire voyage. Driven by a powerful northeast wind, icy spray pelted her, drenching her clothing in the frigid air.

As the tiny craft plunged and rose again, she caught an enticing glimpse of bold overhangs and a projecting headland. The sea surged halfway up an opening in the cliffs.

The bay through which they lurched and bucked seemed entirely open to the force of the gale. Susanna wondered that the *Green Rose* had not been lost on the rocks. Someone had told her it was high tide. As if to prove it, another huge wall of water rose up, obscuring her view and convincing her she was about to drown within sight of shore. She would never set foot on English soil again.

"Almost there!" Walter shouted to be heard over the crash of the surf.

Their little boat dipped downward again, causing Susanna to grip the sides more tightly and close her eyes. She could not help but remember that similar circumstances, years before, had cost her father his life.

"Time to go, Sir Walter," yelled one of the rowers.

Susanna heard a mighty splash as Walter left the boat.

She let out a little yelp of protest as she was scooped from her precarious perch. No one paid her any heed. A crewman swung her over the side as if she were no more burden to him than a sack of wool. Seconds later she dropped into Walter's outstretched arms.

He staggered a bit but kept his footing. "Hold on," he instructed.

With her arms wound tightly around his neck, he waded through knee-deep water. Another wave almost knocked them both flat, but somehow he remained upright, reached the shore, and began to climb a narrow path.

Hidden away behind the rocky landscape, the village remained invisible until they were almost upon it. A cluster of buildings clung to the high-water mark, nestled in a deep gully between two cliffs that protected the little settlement from the force of the wind.

"We're safe now." Walter lowered her to her feet.

"And to think," she murmured, testing the strength of her legs and finding them capable of a few stiff steps, "that for a few days I thought I could enjoy being on the water."

Chuckling, he glanced over his shoulder to chart Lionel's progress. Susanna's gaze followed his. Coming after them, her loyal henchman and one of the seamen carried their baggage, holding the cases and bags high above their heads. They plowed through the undertow at a steady pace, untroubled by the choppy water.

As Susanna watched, the sun came out from behind the clouds, at once transforming the color of the sea from gray to a jewel-toned blue edged with white. When she turned to study the rocky coastline, she was treated to another striking display of color. Bright greens and umbers streaked the deep purple of the escarpment.

"Home," she whispered. "England." She did not think she had ever seen anything more beautiful.

* * *

An hour after they set foot on land, wearing garments that felt dry only in comparison to the kirtle and bodice she'd had on when they arrived, Susanna huddled close to the hearth in the common room of an inn called the Boar's Head. She shared its warmth with Lionel, who had gotten thoroughly soaked when he'd twice returned to the rowing boat to collect the rest of their belongings. Walter never traveled without numerous changes of clothing, and Susanna, in addition to the necessities, had brought along her own saddle.

Walter joined them by the fire a few minutes later. Shoving aside the heavy cloak Susanna had hung over a bench to dry, he seated himself and extended his booted feet toward the glowing embers.

"Did you deal with the port commissioner?" Susanna expected to have to pay a duty on the value of any possessions she'd brought into the country.

"No need. This village supports free trade. That is why I chose to disembark here rather than wait until the ship reached Hull."

In its entirety, the settlement consisted of only a dozen dwellings, a chapel, and the inn. "The residents make their living by smuggling?"

"And by fishing. Both are time-honored professions along this section of the coast. A third is provisioning travelers."

In other words, Walter had paid good coin to insure that none of the villagers mentioned their arrival to the authorities. Until that moment, Susanna had not considered that he might wish to hide their return from government officials. She supposed the precaution made sense. At this stage, there was no way to tell an enemy from a friend. Anyone might be in league with the conspirators.

"I took the liberty," Walter added, "of paying the vicar to spare us the obligation to attend this morning's service of divine worship."

"Is it Sunday?" Susanna frowned, wondering how she could have lost track of time to that extent. "By my reckoning, it should be a Tuesday."

"Aye. But also All Saints' Day."

The door to the common room creaked open to admit the innkeeper. "Here thou is." With a gap-toothed smile, he placed the tray he was carrying on the small folding table he'd set up earlier. "Hot mutton pies to take away the chill." A mouthwatering aroma joined the smell of wet wool.

"Lady Pendennis and I thank you, my good man."

Although Lionel had been warned that Susanna meant to assume the identity of Sir Walter's wife, he made a startled sound.

Walter waited until the innkeeper returned to his kitchen, then rounded on the younger man. "Do you want to get her killed? God's blood, man! Remember to play your part."

Susanna placed a restraining hand on Walter's arm. The fabric beneath her hand was still damp and encrusted with brine. "No harm done, my dear. Lionel will remember my new name the next time."

They devoured the meat pies in silence. Only after the last morsel had been consumed did Walter return to the business that had brought them to Yorkshire. He withdrew several long, tightly rolled strips of paper from concealment inside his doublet. Maps. Placed end to end, they showed the route she must follow, with landmarks such as bridges, fords, and ferries sketched in. It appeared to Susanna that a great number of rivers and streams wound through this part of England, bisecting the road at regular intervals.

"A guide will take us across the moors and the Hambleton Hills as far as Thirsk." Walter stabbed at a section of the curling paper to indicate that town. "There I will turn northwest toward Streatlam while you and Lionel go south to Topcliffe, Northumberland's Yorkshire seat."

"We will need horses."

"I have already seen to that. These villagers do a steady business in selling mounts to newcomers who, as far as the customs agents know, never arrived at all."

"What news of the rebellion?" she asked.

"There are, as yet, no troops on the move, but rumors of unrest abound."

"Have you a way to discover more? Should we go to York first? The queen's council in the North—"

"A waste of time. The packet you carry must be delivered as soon as possible. Indeed, getting it this far has already taken longer than it should have. You will have to tell them that we landed in London. That should account for the delay."

"And lead them to believe I'd have heard the latest news of court and country on my way to Yorkshire."

"Not if you seized your first opportunity to flee from your husband and were obliged to hide from possible pursuit as you traveled north."

Filled with sudden misgiving, Susanna studied her old friend. She was keenly aware of Lionel's silent presence just a few feet away. He was the most loyal of servants and she felt responsible for his safety. It was one thing to risk her own neck, quite another to ask one of her retainers to do so.

She was prepared to enter the household of the earl of Northumberland as a spy. She had given her word and would not go back on it. But she did have to wonder if Walter had told her everything she needed to know. "What is in the packet?"

"A letter." He rolled the maps and tucked them back inside his doublet.

"From whom? And what does it say?"

"Eleanor would not have been able to break the code. It will be best if I do not tell you."

The mere hint of a secret cipher made her uneasy, reminding her of the many schemes in which her late husband had been involved.

"Ignorance will protect you," Walter insisted, just as Robert had once said. "You must trust me, Susanna."

"I do, Walter, but I would feel more confident of success if I knew—"

"You have said yourself that deception is not easy for you. 'Tis true. You lack skill as a liar. This way you can truthfully answer that you do not know what is in the packet."

"If I am so unsuited for this task, mayhap I should leave Topcliffe as soon as I have delivered it."

A darkening of Walter's features warned Susanna he did not like that suggestion. "Getting this letter into Northumberland's hands is the most important thing," he agreed, "but since they know already that you agreed to be a courier, and your arrival proves your loyalty, it should not be difficult to convince them you wish to stay on at Topcliffe rather than return to your husband."

"And then?"

"Mayhap nothing. If the conspiracy comes to naught, I will turn up at Topcliffe myself and pretend to beg my lady wife's forgiveness. You will come away with me and that will be the end of it. But if there is an uprising, you will be in a position to overhear information vital to putting it down. Listen and remember, and send word of all you learn to me."

"How am I to do that without arousing suspicion?"

"Within a day or two I will have my old contacts in place. I will dispatch someone to infiltrate Topcliffe."

"How will I know him? And how do you know whom

to trust? You have been out of England for years. Allegiances change. Men turn traitor."

They had been conversing in low tones, sharing the bench before the hearth, heads close together. Susanna felt Walter stiffen at her suggestion. Although his expression remained enigmatic, she suspected she had touched on a sensitive point. He must have doubts of his own.

"The man I send will have this ring." He showed her the agate he wore on his left hand, a black stone with a distinctive banded pattern of milky opaline layers.

She smiled. "A pity I did not realize earlier that you had that stone. I'd have asked to borrow it. Agates, it is said, are a sovereign remedy against seasickness."

The answering smile she'd hoped for did not appear. "Trust no one else, except Lionel." Walter glanced at the young man, who had fallen asleep by the fire. "If you have information for me that cannot wait, if you should, for example, come upon incriminating documents or letters proving the queen of Scots plotted with the conspirators, send Lionel to Streatlam, the manor belonging to Sir George Bowes. If I am not there, Bowes will know where to find me."

"Bowes," she mused. "Why does that name sound familiar?"

Belatedly, the fleeting sign of humor she'd hoped for earlier appeared on Walter's features. "We spoke on the ship of the way family connections link people together. There are times when the fate of the entire kingdom seems to depend less upon noble ideals than it does on the ties of kinship."

"True. And heralds are not the only ones who need to pay attention to genealogy." She was here, she reminded herself, because Eleanor claimed a distant kinship with the earl of Westmorland. "But what has that to do with Sir George Bowes?"

"He had a sister who married a Scot."

"Not so uncommon this close to the border."

"This is a particularly opinionated Scot by the name of Knox. John Knox. You may recall his work, my dear." Walter went so far as to chuckle. "You once had several copies of his book in your possession."

"*The First Blast of the Trumpet Against the Monstrous Regiment of Women,*" Susanna murmured.

Walter might find the coincidence laughable, but neither the content of that polemic against government by women nor the use to which Susanna had once put it, using its text to send coded messages to her late husband, provoked any mirth in her. Rather, she was reminded yet again of the many hidden pitfalls ahead.

How, she wondered, had Eleanor ever found the courage to volunteer to go into the enemy camp alone? She must have believed implicitly in Walter's ability to rescue her.

That was the key, Susanna supposed. Walter had asked her to trust him, and she did.

She only wished he had it in him to return that trust.

9

Streatlam was sturdily if unimaginatively built of large blocks of stone. It stood in county Durham, poised between the high, desolate moorland of Yorkshire and the Pennine Uplands. To Walter's surprise and pleasure, what he discovered inside did not echo the manor house's stark and uninviting exterior. Remarkable oak paneling and rich plaster work decorated the rooms. In the great hall the ceiling had a variety of curved surfaces. On one side a spreading vine filled in the panels that supported the ceiling ribs. The other side was balanced by an oak tree that seemed to spring from the angle of the room. In its branches, the artist had sculpted a squirrel eating a nut.

"Magnificent," he told Sir George.

"I seem to recall that as a young man you were sent to Italy to study architecture," Bowes replied, "therefore I take your praise as a high compliment indeed. But you have not come here to admire my ceilings, Sir Walter. What does bring you to Yorkshire?"

"I heard rumors abroad that the earls of Northumberland and Westmorland are fomenting rebellion. That they plan to marry the duke of Norfolk to Mary of Scotland and put him on the throne in Elizabeth's place."

Sir George, a lean, hard man with small eyes and a full beard, grinned at him with undisguised glee. "They may have planned to do just that, but they've not much hope of success. The duke of Norfolk was clapt into the Tower of London more than three weeks ago and is like to remain there for some time to come."

Walter returned the smile. Whether the queen had acted on the warning he'd sent from Augsburg or some other intelligence, she'd successfully removed one of the two most serious threats to England's security. "What has been done about the two earls?"

"The queen," Bowes related, "wrote to a third, the earl of Sussex, who serves as lord president of her council in the North, ordering him to summon Northumberland and Westmorland to the royal court, there to give account of themselves and their recent activities. Instead, Sussex advised her to leave well enough alone and sent her a list of other men he deems more dangerous to the safety of the realm. Crookback Dacre, for one." Bowes grimaced when he spoke the name. Like Walter, he had crossed paths . . . and swords . . . with Leonard Dacre before. "Old Norton and his sons are also on the list."

"Is he yet living? The man must be close to ninety by now."

"Aye, and like to reach a hundred. He served as sheriff of Yorkshire last year and executed his duties as well as a man half his age."

"Should the earl of Sussex have included himself among potential rebels? It calls his loyalty into question when he gives the queen such unsound advice."

"His reasoning makes some sense. 'Tis already November. Who would be mad enough to leave a warm fireside and wage war in the north of England in winter?"

"You feel Sussex can be trusted, then? That he will not betray the queen?"

Bowes shrugged. "In his tenure as lord president of the council in the North, he has shown himself a fair man. And just."

"But is he sound on matters of religion? If he has secret Catholic leanings, he might well be disposed to join the rebellion."

"As sound as any man whose wife's family supported the New Religion from the start."

"What of the queen of Scots? Is her prison secure?"

"She was moved to Tutbury Castle at the first hint of trouble. 'Tis well defended."

Bowes went on to confirm most of the other rumors Walter had heard as he passed through the Yorkshire countryside, but the latest news to reach Streatlam from London had come by way of York and was now more than a week old.

"I will go to York on the morrow," Walter said, "there to confer with Sussex. But first I need pen and paper and the services of a dependable messenger."

If he knew court politics, the queen's advisers would be bogged down in endless debate, accomplishing nothing. For that reason he intended to communicate directly with Queen Elizabeth. He'd take his authority only from her. He was certain Her Majesty would grant it, once he'd revealed the contents of the letter Susanna had taken to Topcliffe.

No one, not Susanna, not even the queen, would ever know he'd switched one message for another. If his gamble succeeded, if that substitution provoked an ill-conceived uprising now, when it could be defeated, instead of later, when a well-planned rebellion might succeed in toppling the throne, he'd have the satisfaction of knowing he'd saved England from civil war.

10

"There." Lionel pointed to what was clearly the tower of a fortified manor house.

Much as Susanna had expected from its name, the earl of Northumberland's stronghold, Topcliffe, was situated on an escarpment. Built of sandstone, with a slate roof and mullioned windows, it looked down upon the rushing water of the fast- flowing River Swale.

A guard armed with a halberd stopped them at the gatehouse. Susanna met his cold gray stare with an imperious manner designed to send him scurrying for his superior. With both feet resting comfortably in a velvet sling, one knee in the hollow purpose-cut in her pommeled saddle, Susanna knew she gave an impression of confidence. Court ladies rode so, rather than on a pillion behind a man. Even mounted on a strange horse, one inclined to nip at anyone who came too close, she felt she had some control over her volatile situation.

Within a quarter of an hour, Lady Pendennis was announced in the great hall of Topcliffe, where the earl of Northumberland presided in regal splendor. His surroundings spoke of wealth and comfort. The hall was hung with a multitude of tapestries. His chair, which stood on the same dais that would, at mealtimes, hold a table, resembled a throne.

The earl's attire created an equally impressive effect. Attached to a black velvet jerkin edged with strands of gold bullion were sleeves of rose-colored satin. Hose, cap feather, and breeches all matched that shade. The latter were fashionably slashed, the cuts bound with gold to emphasize the white satin puffed out through the openings.

As Susanna approached, the earl turned large, close-set eyes her way, staring at her down his beak of a nose. Although a bevy of household officials and servants, some in Northumberland livery, others dressed in the fashion of the day, fluttered and squawked in his vicinity, the nobleman ignored them to goggle at her.

Susanna met his gaze with more boldness than she felt, and as she continued to study him, she realized that his bearing did not match his trappings. His shoulders stooped. The expression on his face was vacuous rather than probing. He looked more like the lord of misrule at a Christmas feast than a true leader of men.

At his right hand was a short, fat tight-lipped man in priest's garb. The censorious look he sent Susanna made her far more uneasy than Northumberland's fixed stare. Would her impersonation be exposed before she'd begun? The prospect of being thrown out into the cold Yorkshire night was unappealing. Even more so was the possibility she might be tossed into a makeshift gaol.

It was the man on Northumberland's left, rather than the priest, to whom the earl finally turned. "Deal with this woman, Carnaby."

A golden-haired giant of a man with hamlike hands, Carnaby had an air of insolence about him. He wore no livery but was clearly in the earl's service. Without hesitation, he stepped down from the dais and seized Susanna's elbow, forcing her to accompany him in the direction of an inner door.

Lionel attempted to intervene but was prevented by two sturdy henchmen. Fighting panic, Susanna dug in with her heels. She was no weakling. Halfway across the great hall, Carnaby abruptly abandoned the effort to remove her from the earl's presence. Thrusting his face close to hers, he growled a command. "State your business, madam. Then leave."

"I came here to deliver a packet to the earl." Susanna's chin lifted.

Her voice contained a betraying tremor but by a supreme effort of will she managed to achieve a haughty tone. "I will not leave until I have given it into his hands."

"I will take it."

"You will not."

His grip on her elbow tightened to bruising force, but she thought she detected a gleam of reluctant admiration in his eyes. A moment later he was towing her toward a window alcove with ground-eating strides. She went with less unwillingness this time, although his rapid pace made her stumble when she took an awkward step on the leg she'd injured years before. Cold, damp, and long hours in the saddle had aggravated the old wound.

Susanna told herself it made good sense to retreat to a place where they could talk privily. Catching Lionel's eye, she managed to send him a smile of reassurance, but she felt far from confident.

"What manner of man chose you as his courier?" Carnaby demanded.

"Master Dartnall of Haug and Company."

A flicker of recognition greeted the name.

Susanna gave Carnaby's hand a pointed look. When he released her, she had to fight the urge to rub her tender elbow.

"How long since Dartnall entrusted you with this packet?"

"Some two months past." Susanna hoped Walter was wrong about her ability to lie. She'd not expected this particular question and was uncertain just how much before her accident Eleanor *had* been given the letter.

"It has taken you a great length of time to deliver, madam."

"Have you traveled abroad of late, sirrah? It is no short journey from Augsburg to the sea, and I was more than three weeks aboard a ship, after which it was another considerable undertaking to reach here from London."

His eyes widened at the mention of that city, then narrowed again with renewed suspicion. "Tell me, Lady Pendennis, where is your husband?" His hand strayed to the hilt of the dagger he wore at his waist. "I vow, he is a man I would like to meet."

"I do not know, nor do I care." Susanna's determination not to let Carnaby succeed in his blatant attempt to browbeat her put a snap in her voice.

"Indeed?"

"I have left my husband, Master Carnaby. How could I remain with a man who has gone to court to advocate the immediate execution of the queen of Scots?"

Apparently, this was the right thing to say. Within minutes, Susanna stood once more before the earl. At Carnaby's prompting, she produced the oilskin-wrapped parcel Dartnall had given to Eleanor. She had carried it, since leaving Walter's company, in a placket hidden in the folds of her cloak.

With a wave of one beringed hand, Northumberland sent a livery-clad page scurrying forward to retrieve it. A badge, the Percy lion engraved on a metal plate, was fastened to one of the hanging sleeves attached to the back of the armhole of his doublet.

As Susanna watched, breathless in anticipation, the earl opened the packet and extracted a letter. His face fell. "In code." He thrust it at the rotund priest. "Translate it."

"What are we to do with Lady Pendennis?" Carnaby asked.

The earl's air of indecision increased. He toyed with the ends of his broad red-brown beard for a time, then offered up a tentative suggestion. "We offer you hospitality for the night, Lady Pendennis, and outriders when you continue on your way on the morrow."

"Your pardon, my lord, but I have nowhere to go if I leave here."

Carnaby whispered something in the earl's ear.

"Ah. Good." Northumberland turned back to Susanna. "I shall send you to my wife, Lady Pendennis. She will know what to do with you." Clapping his hands for the page, he instructed the boy to escort her to the countess.

Susanna bobbed a curtsey and hoped her relief did not show. Walking swiftly, she followed the lad out of the hall, along a narrow corridor, and up a flight of stairs that had been built into the outer wall of the three-story tower. A large bedchamber occupied the top floor, an imposing room dominated by a square-headed fireplace ornamented with more Percy lions.

The countess and her ladies were within, clustered about a woman sitting on a bench on the far side of the room. Her face was buried in her hands and she was sobbing. Preoccupied, no one paid any attention to Susanna, giving her an opportunity to study them.

Even from the back, there was no question which one was the countess. Her mode of dress was as distinctive as her husband's. A tube of finest silk trailed behind her French hood, concealing her hair and most of the ruff at her throat. Wide sleeves had been gathered up to reveal their lining of white damask. A Spanish farthingale displayed the rich brocade of her skirt to advantage. When the countess turned, Susanna's gaze followed the Kendall green fabric, admiring the way the overskirt divided down the front and folded back on itself to reveal a heavily embroidered cream-colored underskirt beneath.

"What do you know of diseases of the eye?" The countess's face above a partlet of fine lawn and a carcanet of emeralds and pearls was dominated by high, aristocratic cheekbones and a small, perfectly shaped mouth.

"What is it you require, my lady?" Susanna was a skilled herbalist, but Eleanor had not been. She'd used her still-room to produce scented waters.

"Something to stay a rheum's defluction. Naught we have tried has alleviated Mistress Carnaby's discomfort or restored her sight."

Carnaby? Was this the wife of the brutish man she'd encountered in the great hall? Her sympathy already engaged, Susanna stepped closer, but what she saw when she got her first good look at the woman's affliction was not encouraging. The rheum was mixed with phlegm and had produced cataract films, pins, and webs.

Susanna had always read widely, devouring in particular any book that dealt with herbal lore or medicine. She had also talked to countless cunning women, adding their recipes and their wisdom, handed down from mother to daughter, to her own store of knowledge. But she was neither physician nor surgeon, and some things could not be cured even by one of those learned men.

"What remedies have you tried?" she asked Mistress Carnaby, hoping Eleanor's lack of expertise on the subject was not widely known.

"I washed mine eye with a water made of a gallon of strong ale, a handful of cumin, and as much salt."

Susanna had to strain to hear the soft-spoken words. "Distilled in a limbeck?"

"Aye." Mistress Carnaby attempted a smile. "It did sting mightily."

"What else?"

Another of the waiting gentlewomen spoke up.

"Celandine, rue, chervil, plantain, anise, and fennel, stamped all together. We let the mixture stand all night and anointed her eye with it this morning."

"Such remedies are all very well for bleared eyes," Susanna murmured, "but for the pin and web in the eye, where a film spreads from a central point, stronger medicine is needed, and even that may not help."

With a gentle touch, she lifted the eyelid, tilting Mistress Carnaby's head so that the light from the window fell onto the afflicted area.

"A simple drying medicine, comfortable to the eye itself, may give some relief. I can make one from the white of a roasted egg and a little white copperas. A drop at a time, the liquid produced when those two ingredients have been violently strained through a fine cloth, is put into the eye."

Mistress Carnaby winced, but the countess had no qualms about proceeding. "Roast an egg, Kelke," she commanded one of her chamberers.

While her order was being carried out, Lady Northumberland drew Susanna apart from the others.

"Who are you, madam?"

"Eleanor Pendennis, my lady. I brought a message to the earl. From Augsburg."

"Ah! Lady Pendennis." From her tone of voice, the countess not only knew who Eleanor was but was unsurprised by her arrival. "I had all but given up on you, madam."

"There were . . . delays."

"But you did bring something to us from the Continent?"

"Aye, my lady. The earl has it. Or, rather, he gave it to the priest to decode."

"Do you know what message it contains?"

"Oh, no, my lady. How could I? Indeed, I was instructed not to open the packet."

"In other words, you did open it, only to discover that you could not break the code."

Susanna started to deny the charge, then thought better of doing so. Certes, anyone in her position would have been tempted to look. There was no harm in admitting to this particular frailty. "'Twas most galling," she confided. "I should like, someday, to know what it was I carried, for in serving as a courier, I abandoned my old life. I cannot return to my husband after this."

"Egg's ready, my lady," Kelke announced.

While Susanna prepared the medicine, the countess left the chamber. By the time she returned an hour later, Susanna had learned that Mistress Carnaby was the widow of Guy Carnaby's brother, Ranulf, and that Carnaby was one of the earl's secretaries.

"You brought tidings from the duke of Alba, Spanish military leader in the Netherlands," the countess informed Susanna. "Excellent tidings."

"I am pleased to hear it, my lady."

So that was it, she thought. The conspirators must plan to orchestrate an invasion that would coincide with their uprising. Walter had been right. The Crown was in danger.

"You will also be pleased, I hope, to join my household as a waiting gentlewoman. As such, you may stay with us as long as you like."

Susanna *was* pleased, and said so. Yet she was also plagued by the thought that there were a great many more questions she should have asked Walter before she agreed to spy for him.

11

"Damned popinjay!"

"Interfering merchant!"

In one of the stables attached to the house called the King's Manor, headquarters of the queen's council in the North, two men stood glowering at each other. Nick Baldwin fair seethed with rage. He could feel the veins in his neck bulge as he controlled a desire to lay violent hands on the jackass who'd sent Susanna into mortal danger. The fact that Pendennis was taller might give him the advantage in a sword fight, but in a wrestling match or hand-to-hand combat—

"Why are you here, Baldwin?"

"I must speak with Susanna."

"Impossible."

"Where is she?"

A Dutch bottom smuggling goods from Vlissingen had brought Nick as far as Hull, the port that had been Susanna's destination when she left Hamburg, but the *Green Rose* had already been and gone by the time he landed. He'd set off at once for York, assuming Pendennis would make contact with the authorities before taking action. He still clung to the faint hope he'd arrived in time to stop Susanna from leaving the city.

If Pendennis had been a basilisk, his glare would have struck Nick dead. "We cannot speak of this here."

Nick's eyes narrowed. The only other person in sight

was the stable boy leading a piebald mare out to be watered. Was this some trick to get rid of him? Nick's fingers itched to draw the knife sheathed in the top of one of his thigh-high riding boots.

Pendennis gestured toward the saddle room between the stable and the grooms' lodgings, where tack and tools were stored. "There we can be more private."

Still suspicious, Nick followed him. Their footsteps on the paved floor were the only sounds save the snufflings and rustlings of the horses. The moment Pendennis closed the saddle room door behind them, Nick went on the offensive. "I find it strange," he drawled, "that the earl of Sussex knows nothing of your return to England with your wife."

"You talked to Sussex?" All but choking on the question, Pendennis looked as if he'd like to follow it with a string of curses.

Nick had to admit that Thomas Radcliffe, third earl of Sussex, was not an imposing figure. His features—large ears, a receding hairline, a trailing brown mustache and small, wispy beard—were ordinary. But as lord president of the queen's council in the North, he was the supreme authority here, answerable only to Her Majesty. Pendennis ought to have reported to him immediately upon his arrival in Yorkshire.

"I told him nothing." There had been precious little he could say. "You do not trust him. Why?"

"I owe you no explanations, merchant."

"Not even if I tell you your wife was murdered?"

Pendennis's face revealed both surprise and disbelief before he could mask his initial reaction to Nick's blunt revelation.

"That was no accident in Augsburg. Lucius Dartnall made a deliberate attempt to kill Lady Pendennis on orders from England. To my mind, that means the conspirators will try again."

"You must be mistaken."

"Must I? Someone who knows your history warned the earl. Dartnall was told to stop her before she could betray their conspiracy to you."

Pendennis had gone pale, but in no other way did he reveal that he was shocked by what Nick told him.

"It is not safe to let Susanna meet with the conspirators."

"She is already at Topcliffe."

Nick felt his jaw tighten and his hands curl into fists. "Then we must get her out."

"Start at the beginning. Tell me all you know."

The last thing Nick wanted was to waste time talking. Tersely, he summarized his chance encounter with Dartnall in Antwerp. "He believed Lady Pendennis suffered naught but a few scratches," he said at the end of his account. "Since no manhunt or arrests followed her narrow escape, Dartnall concluded that no one suspects the mishap was planned, and further that she must have held her peace about what she knew. Even when he is not cup shot, the fellow lacks wit. He has talked himself into accepting that the earl made not one, but two errors in judgment. He is convinced Lady Pendennis is loyal to their cause, in spite of her connection to you."

"'Tis a logical conclusion."

"I see little logic in it, and less sense." If Dartnall represented the caliber of henchman the conspirators depended upon, Nick thought their rebellion doomed from the start, but that scarce made Susanna's position any less precarious.

"Dartnall's orders—were they written in code?" Pendennis's voice was uninflected.

Nick eyed a row of buckets, some wooden and some leathern, and wondered if he could provoke a reaction by throwing one at him. Where was the man's anger? His grief? He seemed to have no interest in avenging his wife's death. "I did not ask. Dartnall said the missive was sealed with Northumberland's ring."

"Why would the earl use a cipher to hide his identity, then reveal it by using his own signet?" Pendennis displayed nothing more volatile than annoyance, with perhaps a bit of impatience thrown in.

"The more crucial question is who told Northumberland about your past? A conspirator aware of your activities as an intelligence gatherer might also know what the real Lady Pendennis looked like."

"There is no reason to think that. I am certain Susanna is safe. No doubt Northumberland will come to the same conclusion Dartnall did, that extreme measures were unnecessary. In arriving at Topcliffe, fleeing from me and bringing with her a certain packet, Susanna proved her loyalty to their cause." Pendennis's smile was very nearly a smirk. "And what that packet contains will put an end, once and for all, to infamous plots such as this one."

Nick seized the front of the bright-hued doublet near the neck ruff and jerked hard, pulling Pendennis's face level with his own. "What have you done?"

"Unhand me!"

"Answer me!" But he could guess. "You substituted another message for the one Dartnall sent."

For the second time that day, the other man's expression betrayed him. Nick's fist connected with his jaw in a blow powerful enough to snap Pendennis's head back. He staggered but did not fall. Lifting one expensively gloved hand to his mouth, he wiped away a trickle of blood.

"If you have a specific reason to be concerned about the content of the message, merchant, reveal it now."

"Cold-blooded bastard! Susanna—"

"Is safe, I tell you! She is a clever and resourceful woman. There is no reason to suppose that—"

"Dartnall is accustomed to the ways of merchants," Nick cut in.

"What of that?" Disdain dripped from the words.

"It is the practice of every merchant to send duplicate messages, to assure that at least one of them reaches its destination. It is common to make two, sometimes three copies. If one of those arrives and is compared to the letter Susanna brought, the conspirators will know she lied to them."

When Pendennis said nothing, Nick knew he'd been right to worry.

"Dartnall is no professional spy. He's a clerk employed by Haug and Company who discovered he could earn extra income by providing certain services to English Catholics and their allies abroad. Entries in the company books hide most transfers of information and money to the earl of Northumberland, but this packet you are so concerned about has some special import. He had to recruit a courier who would be above suspicion to take the original. He entrusted it to your wife, but at his first opportunity, he set out himself with a duplicate." Nick reached inside his doublet and withdrew a small, oilskin-wrapped parcel, the twin of the one Pendennis had given Susanna.

Pendennis seized and opened it and read its contents.

"I offered to deliver this," Nick told him. "Dartnall, bemused by drink, thought that a fine plan, since it spared him the necessity of a journey to England."

"Excellent. I will prepare a second substitute message."

"If you can get another message in, then you can get Susanna out."

"No need. Once this arrives, she will be in an unassailable position. She can continue her work for me without fear of exposure."

"She will be in an ideal position to be murdered. Spies are not popular, Pendennis. Do you think they will spare her because she is a woman?"

"She is in no danger, I tell you! Do you think I would risk her life?"

"Yes, if it served your purpose. You have already sacrificed your own wife."

"It can scarce benefit Susanna if we work at cross-purposes." Pendennis's voice contained a note of warning.

"And if there is a third copy of this message? What then? Damn you, Pendennis!" Nick had never begged for anything in his life, but he was close to it now. "Let me go to Topcliffe."

"I have my own agent ready."

"No one you send can protect her as I will."

Pendennis regarded Nick with calculating ice blue eyes. "You are untrained and unpredictable, merchant. I cannot take the risk of using you. By your very presence, you could increase the danger she faces."

Nick saw his point. His sudden appearance in England would startle Susanna. She might give herself away. But he did not like the contemptuous way Pendennis dismissed him. "I did you good service to deal with Dartnall in Antwerp. He was on the verge of bringing that letter to England. The moment he saw Susanna, he'd have realized she was an imposter."

"And how did you deal with him, after you offered to take his place as messenger?"

"Why, I saw him off to Augsburg before I left Antwerp."

"Then you have already made one grave mistake," Pendennis said. "You let Dartnall live."

12

"Lionel?" Susanna whispered. Just before dusk, gloomy shadows abounded in Topcliffe's small garden. "Lionel?" she called again, a bit louder this time. She had not had so much as a glimpse of her henchman since shortly after they'd arrived two days earlier, but they'd agreed, before reaching the earl of Northumberland's stronghold, to meet at this time and in this place—every country house had a garden—if they'd found no other opportunity to exchange information.

"Here, mistress." Lionel emerged from behind a scraggly yew, looking over his shoulder and moving with extreme caution.

"Were you followed?"

"I do not think so. Best to be certain."

She waited while he inspected the four corners of what had once been a pleasant little walled-in space. Now it was much overgrown and had a desolate air about it.

"The earl has no gardener," Lionel informed her. "They say he is too impoverished to afford one."

"He seems able to purchase fine clothing." And his household at Topcliffe numbered at least sixty. She had been endeavoring to learn all their names and the connections that bound them together.

"All bought on credit. So is food and drink. He owes hundreds of pounds for Malvoisie and Muscadel and

Rhenish wine sent from London through Newcastle and transported here by carriage."

Susanna drew Lionel with her into a sheltered corner where they could sit close together on a stone bench and talk without fear of being overheard. "What have you heard of rebellion?"

"A pursuivant from the earl of Sussex arrived yesterday to summon Northumberland to York. I've seen no sign he means to obey. He may fear arrest. The duke of Norfolk is already in the Tower of London."

That was news to Susanna. Although she had done her best to listen and observe during her short tenure as Lady Northumberland's newest waiting gentlewoman, she'd heard not a single word to indicate there was a rebellion afoot. Nor had anything further been said of the letter from the duke of Alba. Instead, Lady Northumberland had asked about the time Walter and Eleanor spent abroad. This had led to a few awkward moments, since Susanna had not traveled nearly as much on the Continent as the real Lady Pendennis. Fortunately, the countess was a gregarious, entertaining woman who enjoyed recounting her own adventures as much as she liked hearing about the exploits of others.

"Are they all traitors here, madam?" Worry put grooves in Lionel's forehead and an earnest look in his eyes. "They do not seem evil. Everyone has been most welcoming."

"Everyone? Even Master Carnaby?" Remembering later how Carnaby had fondled his knife when he'd asked her about Walter, Susanna had begun to wonder if she'd misinterpreted the gesture. She'd seen it then as an attempt to intimidate her, but what if there was some old enmity between the two men?

"He's an odd one, right enough," Lionel agreed. "All the grooms dislike him and they say he takes liberties above his station."

"Find out more about Carnaby if you can, Lionel, and the priest, too, but have a care to arouse no suspicion."

Puffed with pride at being trusted with so delicate an assignment, Lionel continued his report, including in it the curious story of a mule kept in the stables and treated like royalty by the grooms. "In a special stall, it is," he said.

Susanna frowned. Very few people in England had firsthand knowledge of mule breeding, which had become a lost art since the break with Rome, but she had once read a treatise on the subject and could not ignore the possibility that the beast in question might have been bred out of an Andalusian mare by a Catalan jackass specifically to be ridden by a high-ranking prelate. Was it there in the hope that the Church of Rome would soon be restored in these parts?

Lionel's somber expression came from pondering a different dilemma. "Since the pursuivant's departure, no other strangers have been allowed to enter Topcliffe. What if Sir Walter's man is not able to get in?"

Susanna sent a reassuring smile his way. "If I need to contact Sir Walter I shall send you to him, Lionel. I have found the perfect excuse. Northumberland's young daughters live at Wressel, another of his Yorkshire estates, where they are looked after by nursemaids and tutors. What more natural than for me to ask that my child join them? To have Rosamond brought up with a nobleman's children would be a great honor. Lady Northumberland can have no possible reason to deny such a reasonable request. Indeed, some here would deem it a golden opportunity to save a child's soul from heresy. On the pretext of traveling to Leigh Abbey to fetch her, you will be allowed to leave Topcliffe."

Lionel's countenance brightened. "But instead of going south, I will turn north at Topcliffe village and ride hard for Streatlam." Cheered by the prospect, he returned to his newly assigned duties in the earl's stables.

Susanna remained a little longer in the gathering darkness, thinking about her situation and the task Walter had set for her. Was there any chance he was mistaken in his belief there was a plot to overthrow the queen? Susanna liked the countess, with her lively recollections of an energetic youth. To hear her tell it, Lady Northumberland had been as much a rumpscuttle as Rosamond was, always climbing trees to rescue cats and borrowing the fastest horse in the stable to race her male cousins across the countryside.

The countess's waiting gentlewomen, Joan Lascelles, Margaret Heron, and Cecily Carnaby, had enjoyed less adventurous girlhoods. Like their mistress, however, they'd made Susanna feel welcome here. Mistress Carnaby could not do enough for her. Although her vision remained impaired, she was grateful to Susanna for the greater comfort she now enjoyed.

At first Susanna had been careful around the two chamberers, Kelke and Lamplugh, concerned that they would resent the added burden of serving a fourth gentlewoman. Contrary to her expectations, they had not only been willing to clean every garment she'd brought with her, but Kelke had also offered to embellish the plainest of the sleeves. She'd added decorative crossbars and braiding in the latest fashion.

Jennet would get on well with Bess Kelke, Susanna decided, and wished her old friend was not so far away. She missed Jennet's company and could have done with her assistance.

The birth of three children had not done much to slow Jennet down. She might be a bit more plump than in their early years together, when she'd been Susanna's tiring maid, but she was just as adventuresome now that she was housekeeper at Leigh Abbey. She'd always been more than a servant, but it was in her role as a loyal family retainer that she'd acquired a number of useful skills. Jennet had a remarkable ability to make herself all but invisible in the presence of her betters, a talent that often allowed her to eavesdrop on private conversations.

Susanna wondered if her own position at Topcliffe, that of a simple waiting gentlewoman in the service of a noblewoman, might not provide similar protective coloring. Servants were unobtrusive. Anonymous. Could she become equally inconspicuous? Certes, it was worth the attempt, for if she was able to blend in well enough to go unnoticed, she might even overhear talk of a conspiracy.

13

A housekeeper's keys were the symbol of her position. The more of them she wore suspended from her waist, the greater her responsibility. Jennet's keys unlocked everything from the manor's great oak door to the little casket Lady Appleton used to store her supply of ginger. They jangled and clashed as she paced the confines of her mistress's study, the sharp ring of metal against metal underscoring every word she read aloud from Master Baldwin's letter.

"This makes no sense at all!" she exclaimed, fixing Baldwin's man Toby with a formidable glower.

Toby said nothing. The lad was worn out, as well he should be after traveling all the way from Antwerp. But Lady Appleton was supposed to be in Hamburg. Jennet stopped in front of the *mappa mundi* on the wall. Those two cities were farther apart than London was from York, which was where Master Baldwin wanted Jennet to meet him. "Is Lady Appleton in Yorkshire?"

"Ought to be by now. That's where she and Sir Walter meant to go."

"Sir Walter Pendennis?"

Nodding, Toby wrung the cap clutched nervously between his hands until it lost all semblance to headgear. There was a worried expression on his beardless face.

"Start at the beginning," Jennet suggested.

"Sir Walter came to Hamburg and took Lady Appleton and Lionel away with him because his wife had died."

"Faith! Lady Pendennis dead?" Jennet was so startled she almost dropped the letter. It had said nothing about that. "When? How?"

"In Augsburg. As to how, well that's the problem, you see. Sir Walter told us she was killed in an accident, but that he'd lied to everyone and said she was scarce hurt. Then he came for Lady Appleton because he needed a wife to go back to England with him."

Jennet sank into Lady Appleton's favorite chair and stared at Toby in bewilderment. "He asked Lady Appleton to marry him?" And just what did Master Baldwin think Jennet could do about that?

"Oh, no," Toby corrected her. "Sir Walter wanted her to pretend to be the wife he had."

That made even less sense, Jennet thought.

"Master Baldwin did not like the idea," Toby added. "He swore most foully the day they left. And then we went to Antwerp, and there Master Baldwin learned that Lady Pendennis's death was no accident after all. 'Twas murder."

"What?"

"Murder."

"I heard the word. 'Tis the meaning of it confounds me. Why would anyone murder Lady Pendennis?"

And who, she wondered, was to tell Mistress Rosamond her mother was dead? Then again, mayhap the child would not grieve too much. She'd not seen Lady Pendennis since she was two. It was Lady Appleton she called "Mama."

"Master Baldwin says Lady Appleton may be in danger. That's why he went to York and sent me here to fetch you."

Jennet reread the letter Toby had brought. It was terse

to the point of rudeness. Master Baldwin all but commanded her immediate departure for York. This was all most mysterious, and alarming, but the words "Lady Appleton needs your help," underscored twice, could not be ignored.

"You must tell no one that the real Lady Pendennis is dead," Toby warned. "Master Baldwin bade me be sure to tell you that."

"Certes, the news must be kept from her daughter."

"Poor little mite," Toby said.

"Never mind Rosamond. Why did Lady Appleton go to York? And why does Master Baldwin think she needs my help? Why does she not ask for it herself?"

"She does not know she is in danger. Master Baldwin did not tell me much, but I think it must have something to do with Sir Walter having once been an intelligence gatherer."

A knock at the door heralded the arrival of Jennet's husband, Mark, who served as Leigh Abbey's steward. He took one look at Toby and reached for the aqua vitae. "The lad's reeling with exhaustion," he chided her.

"I have more questions for him."

"They can wait until he has food in his belly."

Jennet let him fuss while she ruminated further. Not long ago, Dover and Rye, and likely other English ports, as well, had suddenly and inexplicably been closed. Rumors had flown about the countryside until they reopened, wild tales of imminent invasion, of rebellion . . . of unquiet in the North.

When Toby had been fed, Jennet made him repeat everything he'd told her, including the claim that Lady Pendennis had been murdered. When he'd finished, Mark and Jennet exchanged troubled looks.

"I do not like the sound of this," he said.

"Nor do I, but if Lady Appleton needs me, I must go."

"She has Lionel and, by now, Master Baldwin, too."

Jennet gave a derisive snort. She liked Lionel well enough, and he was useful when heads needed bashing, but for cleverness she made two of him. As for Master Baldwin, if he'd thought he could rescue Lady Appleton on his own, he'd not have sent for her. There had never been any love lost between them.

"You have no idea what is going on." Mark ran one hand through his mole brown hair in exasperation. "The only thing Toby knows is that Lady Pendennis is dead and Lady Appleton is pretending to be Sir Walter's wife."

"Not just dead. Murdered. There's cause enough to take action. And it appears that Master Baldwin has some plan in mind. Why else send for me?"

If he did not, Jennet would devise one of her own. In truth, she'd already had a most excellent idea. When they passed through London on the way north, she would act upon it.

Sensing her determination, Mark stopped trying to talk her out of leaving. "Do you want me to go with you?"

Jennet shook her head. "The children need you here." In case something did happen to her.

"Take Fulke, then."

Tears filled her eyes as she nodded. She had married a most remarkable man. He might have forbidden her to go. Legally, he could have enforced his will. Instead he paid her the supreme compliment of letting her decide what was best to do.

14

By the fifth time Susanna took a morning constitutional on the leads, the guards at Topcliffe had grown as accustomed to seeing Lady Pendennis circle the wall walk at roof level as they were to watching the other gentlewomen practice with longbows at the archery butts. If she paused now and again to admire the view, they paid no attention to her.

Susanna had discovered she did not need to become a nameless, faceless servant in order to be invisible. What people were in the habit of seeing, they soon learned to ignore. Armed with her capcase full of medicines, supplemented with ingredients from Topcliffe's stillroom, she was free to roam all over the fortified house to minister to the dozens of small ailments common among a large number of people packed close together as cold weather came on.

As she stared down at the hall-and-chamber block and the range of lodgings at ground level, Susanna reviewed the progress she'd made in the last few days. A tonic of fennel root mixed with wine had been highly successful for alleviating the catarrh and had given her an excuse to mistake a separate door in the end wall of the ground floor for a way to the kitchen. The storeroom she'd stumbled into had been full of weapons, but they'd all been rusty and ill cared for. An air of neglect hung about the place. That the room had been unlocked and unguarded also seemed to argue that the earl had no intention of mounting a rebellion.

She'd made opportunities to talk with almost everyone in the residential tower and the annex built against it to the east. A poultice to reduce the pain of gout—rue and lovage pounded with preservative honey and applied hot—had even won her the gratitude of Sir John, the priest. She'd also suggested several remedies for the temporary relief of the pesky quartain ague suffered by a number of the earl's henchmen. If cinquefoil did not help, meadowsweet would.

As in many households, people here grumbled about the government, ever ready to describe the woes and calamities the kingdom suffered under its present monarch. They lamented the loss of the way things had been in the good old days. Various remarks also gave credence to the rumor Lionel had repeated—that the earl was desperate for funds to satisfy his lavish tastes. But no one, at least in Susanna's hearing, had proposed rebelling against the queen as a way to cancel his debts.

Still, there was that mule. Had it been imported in anticipation of the needs of a new Catholic archbishop in the North? Susanna paused in her circle of the wall walk, catching sight of approaching riders. No prelates appeared to be among them, but they carried the earl of Westmorland's banner. More interesting still, they were led by a woman.

Half hidden behind a large, heraldic lion hewn out of stone, Susanna watched the newcomers arrive at Topcliffe's gatehouse. At first, seeing the deference with which their leader was treated by the most menial servants at Topcliffe, she thought the countess of Westmorland herself might have come to call. She reassessed that conclusion when Northumberland's secretary, Guy Carnaby, crossed to the still-mounted woman, swung her out of her saddle, and engulfed her in a passionate embrace. By the time he released her, her hood had been knocked askew to reveal hair as black and glossy as a raven's wings.

The wall walk had direct access to Lady Northumberland's chamber. When Susanna descended the narrow stairs from the roof, the countess was the only person there. She had just opened the large, German-made blanket chest that occupied pride of place in one corner of the room. Something in her demeanor made Susanna pause in the shadows. Willing herself to stillness, she watched the noblewoman work the latch on an inner compartment, reach inside, and retrieve a roll of parchment. Taking it with her, she went into the privy attached to her chamber.

Susanna hesitated only a moment. There would be no better time to investigate. The other waiting women had doubtless gone to greet the new arrival. The countess, whether she was reading the document or throwing it down the jakes, would be occupied for a few more minutes.

The ornately carved chest stood about two feet high, its dark wood gleaming in the sunlight streaming through a nearby window. Both lid and compartment stood open. Within were more rolls of parchment. They were maps, similar to the one Walter Pendennis had used to show Susanna the route to Topcliffe. Unsure what this meant, she retreated to the window and was innocently gazing into the courtyard when the countess emerged from the privy.

"Ah, Eleanor! Good. I was about to send for you." Her dark eyes twinkled, as if she had a secret to share. "You will be pleased, I think, to learn that Lady Westmorland has sent one of her women from Brancepeth Castle with messages. Her name is Marion Standbridge."

Walter's dismissive words echoed in Susanna's mind: *Mary? Marion? No matter. I doubt you'll encounter her in Northumberland's household.*

"Marion? My . . . cousin?" Eleanor's cousin. What was she doing here? For one giddy moment, Susanna wondered if *she* could be Walter's agent. Then she remembered what she'd seen from the wall walk. Marion Standbridge was no stranger here. Moreover, she was passing friendly with Guy Carnaby, the person at Topcliffe Susanna trusted least.

The shuffle of leather-shod feet on the stone steps warned them of the newcomer's imminent arrival, together with the countess's three waiting gentlewomen. Susanna turned to greet them, forcing a smile.

"Nell?" Marion's voice, airy as thistledown, expressed delight. Her eyes, which were faintly almond shaped, giving her an exotic look, warmed as she tripped lightly across the chamber, arms extended toward the woman she assumed to be her cousin. She had restored her headdress to order, concealing most of her midnight hair.

Unable to evade either Marion or the cloud of musky perfume emanating from her, Susanna allowed the much smaller woman to engulf her in a delicate embrace. As she endured the intimacy, she could not help but think the heavy scent an odd choice for one so fragile.

Stepping back, Marion flashed a brilliant smile that showed off a great many remarkably straight teeth. "Why, coz, do you not remember the imp who tagged along after you when you were twelve and I was five?"

Susanna breathed a little easier. She'd been afraid Marion had known Eleanor later in life. Before she had time to feel complacent, however, Marion introduced another subject fraught with pitfalls.

"I bring greetings from your lady mother."

Susanna tensed. "Is she here in Yorkshire?" So much for Walter's assurances!

A trill of laughter greeted that question. "Oh, no. She remains at Gillingham Place."

"Is she in good health? She and her husband both?"

Susanna wondered how far away Gillingham Place might be. She'd never heard of it and did not dare assume it was in Westmorland, where Eleanor had lived until she went to Lady Quarles.

"Oh, aye," Marion assured her.

"I am glad to hear it. But, I vow, I am surprised she should bother to send a message to me. We have been estranged for many years, as you must know." Susanna hoped she'd injected just the right note of aggrieved resentment into her words. Eleanor *had* been shabbily treated by her kinfolk.

Marion seemed amused by Susanna's comment. "She speaks of you often."

The countess of Northumberland cleared her throat, recalling Marion to her duties. The real reason she was at Topcliffe was to deliver messages from the countess of Westmorland.

Susanna and the other waiting gentlewomen took up their embroidery at the other side of the room, but they had a clear view of all that transpired. After she read her sister countess's letter, Lady Northumberland produced the map she'd retrieved earlier. She and Marion pored over it for some time, making Susanna wonder if she'd been mistaken. She'd begun to think the queen had naught to fear. After all, the earl of Northumberland fell far short of what was required in an impassioned rebel leader. Even his own tenants referred to him, behind his back, as "Simple Tom."

But Anne, countess of Northumberland, possessed all the boldness, cleverness, and ruthlessness her spouse lacked. She even had experience in the art of command. She was the absolute ruler of her household, alternately charming and bullying its large domestic staff. In the last few days, Susanna had seen ample evidence that the youthful impulsiveness the countess had bragged about had not lessened as she grew older. She'd ordered a huge bonfire built the previous night, just so she could enjoy watching it burn. She'd only been dissuaded from tossing gunpowder into the flames by Guy Carnaby's warning that it took more than that to produce fireworks.

Needle poised over a rosebud, Susanna paused, her uneven stitches forgotten. Carnaby? Was he the key? Lady Northumberland conferred with him on a regular basis. Susanna had assumed they met so often because he carried orders to the countess from the earl. But what if the chain of command went in the other direction?

"Nell?"

Belatedly, Susanna realized Marion meant her.

"Your pardon, coz. I was wool-gathering."

"The countess has given us leave to continue our reminiscences. Shall we find a more private place to talk?"

A short time later, at Susanna's suggestion, they walked together in the same chilly garden she'd used four days earlier for her assignation with Lionel. Marion's conversation contained references to dozens of relatives Susanna had never heard of, let alone met, but she nodded and smiled and prayed that Eleanor had not been familiar with most of them either.

Abruptly, Marion halted beneath a trellis and gave Susanna a sharp look. "Your letter was most welcome, Nell."

Susanna hid a sudden burst of anxiety with a laugh. "Which letter?" If Walter had been mistaken about Eleanor's total estrangement from her family, this masquerade was about to fall apart.

"Did you write more than one?" Marion's eyes narrowed to slits.

Susanna's sense of impending danger became almost palpable in the crisp November air. She sank down onto the same stone bench she'd occupied on her previous visit to this garden and buried her face in her hands. Making every effort to sound as pathetic as possible, she put a hitch in her voice. "There is something I have not told anyone. Something terrible."

At once, Marion was all sympathy. She sat beside Susanna and slipped one arm around her waist. "What is it, cousin? Tell me. Let me help."

The bench was as hard and cold beneath her as Susanna remembered, but she found Marion's perfume less overpowering in the open air. Drawing in a deep, strengthening breath, she plunged into the only tale she could think of that might allay suspicion. "I was injured just before I left Augsburg." The first of what she intended to be carefully orchestrated sobs broke the narration. "A runaway horse." Susanna sniffed and risked a peek at Marion through her fingers. The other woman's face wore a frown. "I was struck down. I was unconscious for hours. Ever since, there have been gaps in my memory." She gripped Marion's arm and dared to meet her eyes. "I cannot recall some things clearly, and others not at all. I fear I have no recollection of writing any letters to England from the Continent."

A look of patent disbelief greeted this claim, but Susanna found it easy to sound earnest with so much at stake. If Lady Northumberland was behind the plans for rebellion and had been corresponding with Lady Westmorland through Marion, then Eleanor's cousin was as committed to the uprising as they were. Any hint that "Nell" was an imposter, even the suspicion that she did not share their dedication, would force them to take steps to ensure her silence. Susanna did not care to contemplate just how they might achieve this goal. For all she admired Lady Northumberland, she knew that anyone willing to contemplate treason would be prepared to risk her own life and would not hesitate to do away with an unimportant gentlewoman who stood in her way.

"I have never heard of such a thing," Marion said.

"Nor had I, but a doctor Walter took me to in London

told me of a similar case, a man struck in the head by a falling rock. Afterward, he was unable to recall anything about himself, although in time he recovered some of his memories." She let go of Marion's arm to fumble for a handkerchief and noisily blew her nose.

"You did not remember me, did you?"

Susanna shook her head. "There are great, gaping holes in my past. I remember why I fled my husband's lodgings, but not how I came to meet Master Dartnall. I know that I have a daughter I've not seen for more than four years, but I have no clear recollection of how I came to leave her behind in Kent."

"Your letter bragged of your husband's importance."

"I have no memory of any letter," Susanna insisted. "Not to whom I sent it nor what I said. Where was I at the time I wrote it?"

"Poland."

Dabbing at her eyes, in the hope Marion would believe she shed tears of despair, Susanna tried to think what to say next. From Poland, Eleanor would have written of her new husband's recent appointment as ambassador. She had been pleased, Susanna remembered, although she'd been disappointed to discover that the post would earn Walter only eight hundred pounds per annum, far less than the stipend paid to the ambassador to France.

Of what else, Susanna wondered, would Eleanor have boasted? Had she said something, even that long ago, to make the conspirators believe she would help them? Susanna could not imagine what it might have been. It was possible there was no connection at all between this letter and the uprising. Perhaps Eleanor had simply been in the right place at the right time to meet Dartnall and reveal, in all innocence, that she had ties to Westmorland.

Marion broke a long silence. "It must be most annoying to lose part of your past."

Susanna managed a rueful laugh. "In particular when there is no rhyme or reason to which things I remember and which things I cannot recall. Why, I might easily encounter someone I've met before and have no memory of him. Think of the embarrassment!"

"Do you remember Uncle Roger? Sir Roger Cholmeley?"

"Roger is a common name in our family." There had been at least three in the genealogy Walter had sketched for her.

"I mean your mother's uncle, who is my mother's, too. He is very wealthy, Nell, in case you have forgotten that."

"And I wrote to him?"

"Yes. You announced your marriage." For a moment resentment simmered in Marion's unusual eyes. "According to Uncle Roger, a good marriage erases all manner of past mistakes."

And Marion was still unwed. Susanna wondered why Guy Carnaby did not take her to wife, but she could not inquire without revealing she'd spied on them from the wall walk. "Marion," she said instead, "I have left my husband. When he hears that, Uncle Roger is unlikely to think well of me."

Marion did not look convinced, but she again enfolded "Nell" in her musky embrace. "I am heartily glad you have come back to us, coz. Welcome home."

Several hours later, Susanna returned to the garden. She expected to find Lionel there, but her stomach clenched at the sight of him . . . walking arm in arm with Marion Standbridge. When Lionel leaned down to speak to her, Marion's laughter rippled forth, a light trill that put Susanna in mind of stories about the fairy folk.

Piskies were said to bemuse the mind and seduce the unwary. Certes, Lionel looked as if he'd fallen under some sort of spell! He appeared transfixed by Marion's every word. Worse, he seemed to be answering questions she put to him.

Susanna had thought Marion accepted "Nell," both as long-lost cousin and as fellow conspirator. Had she been hasty in coming to that conclusion? Praying Lionel had not already let something slip, she went in search of the countess of Northumberland. Susanna's impersonation would be safer if Lionel left Topcliffe, and since none of Walter's agents had communicated with her, she told herself she had every reason to send her man to him.

"I came here to free myself from the worst excesses of the queen's new men," she explained to Lady Northumberland, after she requested that Rosamond be added to the household at Wressel. "I would have my child safe, too. If I leave her where she is, it may occur to my husband to use her against me."

"Children are often hostages to fortune," the countess agreed. "Send your man to fetch her and advise him to make haste. Soon it will no longer be safe to travel to the North."

"Winter *is* almost upon us."

Lady Northumberland's smile was arch. "Aye. That, too."

No more than an hour after Lionel left Topcliffe, having sworn to Susanna that he'd said nothing to make Marion suspect that her cousin was an imposter, the earl of Northumberland burst into his wife's chamber. "Another messenger from the earl of Sussex has arrived!" he blurted. "I am once again summoned to York."

The countess took one look at his pale face and dispatched Marion to fetch Guy Carnaby. Then she confiscated the piece of parchment her husband had been waving in her face. "From the lord president of the council in the North," she muttered as she skimmed its contents. "I care little for the tone of this." She read a portion aloud: "Look not to escape the plague in this world that God hath appointed to disobedience, and in the world to come the punishment that He hath promised to be due for it."

"What shall I do, Anne?" the earl twisted his beringed hands together and looked to his wife for guidance.

Her waiting gentlewomen gave up all pretense of continuing their game of primero to listen for her answer. Susanna held her breath. If she had wanted proof of the countess's position in this household, she had it now.

"Sussex wishes to force your hand, to push you into making a choice. Submit and go to York and you place yourself at the mercy of the queen. That is no choice at all."

"What else is there to do?"

"Delay."

"I have delayed all I can. The pursuivant Sussex sent last week made the same demand. I promised then to come within a few days. Now Sussex insists that I fulfill that promise."

"What have you done with his latest messenger?"

"Sent him to wait in the village while I compose an answer."

"Better to have told him no outright, as the earl of Westmorland has already done."

Marion returned with Carnaby and Sir John, the priest, and a servant to light more tapers. As the chamber filled with the scent of beeswax, Sir John added his support to the countess's plan, but the earl continued to balk.

"What if Sussex sends a force to seize me? What if one is already on the way? We must flee. We must hide." He fiddled with his beard, knotting the red-brown strands around his fingers. "We can spend the night in the keeper's house. None would think to look for us there. Then at first light we will go north. I've fortified castles there. Alnwick. Or Warkworth."

Lady Northumberland contained her impatience with

visible effort. "Will you abandon everything at this late date? You know that Westmorland has already written to the pope, asking His Holiness for aid."

The priest's look of alarm darted from the earl and countess to her women, still clustered around the hearth with their cards. "My lady! Have a care. Send your attendants away that we may speak freely."

"They are as concerned in this as I am," she told him. "Any decision made here affects them, too."

Sir John reluctantly bowed his acceptance of her decree.

"All will be well, my lord." Carnaby ignored the priest to address the earl. "You have promises of help from both de Spes and the duke of Alba."

The earl's hand dropped to the front of his doublet. Something he had beneath the velvet made a crinkling noise. "Yes. I have both letters here, and the second copy of the one Lady Pendennis brought."

His reference puzzled Susanna, but as long as they did not seem to mistrust her, she was not concerned by it. Alba had written the letter she'd brought to Topcliffe. Guerau de Spes, she recalled, was the current Spanish ambassador. Since he lived in London, she did not imagine his support would be of much practical use in the North.

"Is it wise to carry those about with you?" Lady Northumberland tapped the front of her husband's doublet with one slender finger.

"Both are in a safe cipher."

Not when Walter Pendennis had been in possession of the duke of Alba's letter, Susanna thought. She had no doubt he'd broken whatever secret code the conspirators used.

"I will wall myself up at Alnwick," the earl declared. "They'll not come after me there."

"It is futile to flee unless you mean to leave the realm."

"Live in exile?" Appalled by the suggestion, he goggled at her.

"Submit. Live in exile. Or stand and fight." As her husband grew ever more uncertain what he wanted to do, Lady Northumberland's confidence increased. "Alba promised help."

Susanna held her breath, waiting for someone to rein in her reckless enthusiasm. The countess's avid expression gave her away. She enjoyed being the center of attention and reveled in the prospect of more excitement to come.

"It is too early," the earl complained in a petulant voice.

"Declare for rebellion," his wife urged him. "Do it now."

"I needs must think." Without another word, he left the room.

Carnaby would have followed him had the countess not caught his arm. "Let him go. We do not need him."

"If he flees, all is lost."

"He will neither flee nor falter. I'll not give him time to panic to that extent. And if he cannot be brought round by other means, I will trick him into declaring himself."

No one dared ask what she had in mind.

"Here is what you must do," she continued. "When midnight comes, ring the bells in Topcliffe church in reverse order."

"But madam, that is the call to arms. The duke of Alba is not yet here. The earl—"

"Do not tell me how to deal with the earl!"

Her dark eyes blazed, and Susanna, in her mind's eye, imagined the countess holding a pistol to her husband's head, forcing him to commit himself to rebellion. She shook her head to dispel the image. For all Lady Northumberland's ambition, she was fond of her bumbling spouse.

She was also determined upon her course. Calling to her women, she ordered them to begin packing. "On the morrow, we will go to Brancepeth," she declared, "there to join forces with the earl of Westmorland."

15

Sir Walter Pendennis's step was jaunty in spite of the condition of York's narrow, unpaved streets. The center of the city was so strewn with rubble that it put him in mind of the aftermath of a siege. The smell from the river encouraged that impression. Being tidal, it did little to carry away the noxious refuse discharged into it. In truth, however, the devastation was the result of a wholesale tearing down of churches. The destruction had begun with the dissolution of the monasteries and was still ongoing.

Walter wondered idly if York would be a target for the rebels. He doubted it. Logic dictated that they march direct to Tutbury Castle in an attempt to free the captive queen of Scots. He hoped they would. A quick ending to an ill-conceived uprising would suit him well.

The message Dartnall had entrusted to Eleanor had advised the conspirators to delay any action until spring, by which time the pope would have issued a bull of excommunication against the queen and the duke of Alba would be justified in invading England. The missive Susanna had taken to Topcliffe had said something quite different. Thanks to Walter, Northumberland believed an armada would arrive off Hartlepool by mid-November, ready to invade at his signal.

Walter's lips curved into a self-satisfied smile as he reached the George in Coney Street, the inn where Nick

Baldwin lodged. Hartlepool's harbor went dry at low tide. An extra precaution. Walter felt confident he'd left little to chance.

Baldwin did not look pleased to find Walter at his door. He offered him no refreshment, nor was there anywhere to sit in his small room under the eaves, save upon the bed. Both men remained standing.

"You have heard the rumors?" Walter asked.

"More than rumors, I do think."

"Aye. The rebels are up in arms. Sussex sent a messenger to Topcliffe yesterday. He was still in the village when the signal was given—church bells rung in reverse order at midnight. He left at once and hid in the woods till dawn, then set out again at first light."

"What news of Susanna?"

"She remains at Topcliffe, and you, Master Baldwin, must not interfere with her there." Walter did not trust the merchant's promise to stay away. It was only his fear of endangering Susanna that had restrained him thus far.

Baldwin ducked as he passed, pacing, under the low eaves. The expression on his face was not pleasant. "What happened when your man took the second copy of Dartnall's packet to Topcliffe? Did he see her?"

"He was not allowed past the gate, but there is no reason to think they mistrust Eleanor. The order for her death was a mistake. They know that now. Once she left me, any reason to harm her vanished."

But to Walter's annoyance, his conscience had been troubled ever since Baldwin turned up in York. Had he kept more from Susanna than he should have? She'd faced danger before, he reminded himself. And once before, because he'd failed to protect her, she'd almost lost her life.

She'd forgiven him for that. She'd forgiven him again, two years later, for holding back the truth about her husband. By then, Walter had thought himself in love with her. He'd worked up his courage, proposed marriage, and been turned down. A short time afterward, he'd met Eleanor. The bitter truth, he now acknowledged, was that he'd wed Eleanor more because he believed he had no chance to win Susanna than because he preferred Eleanor.

Did he still want to wed Susanna? Walter could not be certain; Eleanor's betrayal had left a cold void in the place where his heart had once been.

"What do you plan to do about Dartnall?" Baldwin's demand for information jerked Walter's wandering thoughts back to the present.

"I will deal with him when the time is right. As for Northumberland, execution for treason will also serve as his punishment for ordering my wife's death. Listen well, merchant. I say again that you will help Susanna most by doing nothing. This rebellion will be put down within a few days. Once Sussex musters his troops, they will attack the rebels and capture their leaders." Once and for all time, they would put an end to the threat to Queen Elizabeth's throne. "As soon as we have the conspirators in custody, Susanna can walk away."

Baldwin bit back a retort, but his skepticism was obvious.

"You are an enigma to me, Master Baldwin." Walter came at last to the real point of his visit. He did not like loose ends, and this merchant dangled like a thick length of rope. "How is it you were able to trade in Persia without the sanction of the Muscovy Company? And keep your profits from being confiscated by the Crown when you returned home?"

"Have you wasted time investigating me when civil war is about to begin?"

"I like to know the nature of any man I am obliged to deal with. I wondered, too, who it was that told you someone at Leigh Abbey could be trusted in that business of the queen's gift. Susanna once let slip that she assumed I was the one who'd vouched for her, but I was unaware of your existence until she introduced us. For whom do you work, Master Baldwin?"

"Do you think I am an intelligence gatherer, too, Pendennis?" That seemed to amuse him. "I am what I seem. No more."

"How did you succeed in Persia, then? Those who came after you were unable to convince the Great Sophy to deal with them."

"They did not trouble to learn the local language and customs. The men who went back this year will have fared better, but their success or failure is of little importance to me. My only concern is Susanna's welfare."

Before Walter could press his inquiry, a familiar voice hailed them from the other side of the door. "Master Baldwin? Sir Walter? Are you within?"

Baldwin lost no time admitting Susanna's henchman. "Where is Lady Appleton?" he demanded.

"Why, at Topcliffe," Lionel answered. "Where else should she be?"

"She is well? Safe?"

"Oh, yes, Master Baldwin. Or at least she was yesterday afternoon when she sent me to Streatlam with a message for Sir Walter."

"Streatlam? Of all the—"

"It makes no difference," Walter interrupted.

"No difference? Topcliffe is only fifteen miles from York. Lionel went more than thirty miles in the wrong direction before turning back."

Walter ignored him. "Why did Lady Appleton send you to me, Lionel? Have you news?"

Every word Lionel spoke made it more plain he'd left Topcliffe before the uprising began and had no notion troops were gathering even now. He brought details of Topcliffe's defenses but seemed to know little else of value. "Lady Appleton said to tell you that the earls are not the ones who need watching," he said at the conclusion of his report. "She says their wives are far more likely leaders for any rebellion."

"Woman warriors? What nonsense!"

"Remember Boadicea," Baldwin said softly, referring to the ancient queen who'd defied Roman invaders of Britain.

"She was defeated."

"Isabella of Castile was not. She drove the Moors out of Spain. And the Jews. A good model for devout Catholics, some would say." Baldwin turned back to Lionel. "Does anyone at Topcliffe suspect Lady Appleton is not Lady Pendennis?"

"Oh, no, Master Baldwin. And they all like her there, too. She's been using her skill with herbs to treat the sick."

"Eleanor could never tell a poultice from an infusion." Walter was unsure if that was cause for concern or not.

"Northumberland's folk do not know that," Lionel pointed out.

"There is no ill will toward her? No one seems to resent the arrival of Lady Pendennis? No one was surprised to see her turn up alive and well?"

"No, Master Baldwin. And I've let nothing slip. I swear it! Not even when Mistress Standbridge cooed questions at me about Sir Walter."

16

The town consisted of one long street. Its church, town hall, and inn all had an air of decay about them, and off to the west Susanna could just make out the ruins of a crumbling castle. "What is this place?" she asked, uncertain if they were still in Yorkshire or had passed into Durham.

They'd been riding since dawn, but with a household the size of Northumberland's, even rebellion had been obliged to wait upon provisioning. They were an entire day later in starting than Lady Northumberland had intended. Susanna reckoned the entire distance to Brancepeth at some thirty miles, and they'd traveled no more than a third of the way. They rode in a long double line with carts following behind to carry their belongings.

Cecily Carnaby closed one eye and squinted through the other, although she claimed she saw a hundred times better now than she had before Susanna suggested roasting an egg. "Northallerton," she answered in her soft, mellifluous voice.

Susanna recognized the name and envisioned in her mind the map Walter had shown her. He'd have passed through here on his way to Streatlam. Could she locate Sir George Bowes's house if she slipped away from the cavalcade and went off on her own? She doubted it. Such an attempt would also be most foolhardy. To be brought back a prisoner would benefit no one.

"A pity we are not here on a Wednesday." Susanna had to strain to catch Cecily's murmured comment. "Wednesday is market day in Northallerton. A stirring speech from the market cross and we'd have roused the rabble to join our cause."

Leaving the village behind, they crossed over a bridge with one stone arch and continued along the center of a vale, passing between a range of hills and a river over gently undulating land. Rabble? Susanna turned the word over in her mind. Did the rebels mean to rely upon untrained farmers and shepherds? 'Twas true she'd seen no sign of an army, but how could any cause hope to succeed without a well-trained band of soldiers?

Cecily sighed. "I wish we were to pass through Giggleswich on this journey. Water from St. Alkelda's holy well is said to aid those whose vision is impaired."

"Nonsense." Susanna spoke before she remembered that belief in the healing powers of saints, particularly local martyrs, was a tenet of Roman Catholic faith.

"I am sure you have the right of it." Cecily looked resigned. "If every shrine worked miracles, no one would ever die."

"You've had a difficult time of it. Losing your sight. Your husband."

A soft laugh answered this probing remark. "Ranulf made little difference in my life dead or alive." With that enigmatic comment, she closed her eyes against the glare of the sun and said nothing more.

Susanna shifted her attention to Marion Standbridge and Guy Carnaby, who rode just ahead. Next to his bulk, she looked fragile as a flower, but she did not seem intimidated by his greater size. For his part, Carnaby behaved with great gentleness toward her. When the two of them had shared a trencher at supper the night before, he'd taken care to present Marion with the tenderest morsels.

After a time, Carnaby was called away to deal with a

problem elsewhere in the cavalcade and Marion dropped back in the line. Susanna's mare, the horse Walter had procured for her in that village on the coast, shied nervously at the change in position.

"You should have named her Skittish." Marion eyed the roan with wary eyes.

"Turmeric suits her. Both have a tendency to bite." Susanna had learned that the hard way when she'd attempted to make friends with her new mount.

"Turmeric?"

"A spice." It was Nick's favorite, a taste he'd picked up during his travels. "It must be pleasant," she commented after a bit, "to return to Brancepeth and not be obliged to leave Master Carnaby behind."

Marion gave Susanna a sharp look, then sent a pointed one in Cecily's direction before spurring her horse forward. Had she chosen the animal for its satiny black coat, Susanna wondered, to match her own fine mane? Clucking to Turmeric, she caught up with Eleanor's cousin, putting Cecily and the others out of earshot.

"Have I misspoke, coz? 'Tis plain he cares for you."

"Uncle Roger will not permit me to marry Guy."

"Are you betrothed to someone else?"

"No."

"Then how can Uncle Roger prevent your marriage? You are old enough to make your own decision."

"Uncle Roger controls my dowry."

Injustice always made Susanna angry. She wondered if there was some way she could help Eleanor's cousin. "Is Uncle Roger at Brancepeth?"

"Uncle Roger is too old and frail to leave his home in Westmorland."

"I am sorry to hear it." Musing aloud, she continued. "Perhaps I will pay him a visit there after this business is finished."

Marion's laugh sounded forced. "This *business*? Rebellion, do you mean? Oh, it will not take long to transact. All the North will rise up to support us. We will gather our troops, free Queen Mary, and topple that usurper from the throne by Christmas."

"So, Mary of Scotland *is* part of the plan. I'd begun to wonder." At present they were riding away from the place where she was being held.

"She is the key." Marion could not seem to resist the opportunity to boast. "I may not have made what our uncle would consider a good marriage, but I *am* in the confidence of the countess of Westmorland. For months now she has carried on a secret correspondence with Queen Mary. Your countess and mine and the queen of Scots have among them conceived a plan that cannot fail."

Susanna's stomach tightened. Just as Walter had surmised, all those she'd met and liked at Topcliffe, especially Lady Northumberland, were traitors. And there *were* letters. Proof of treason. If she could lay hands on them when she reached Brancepeth, Walter would have the evidence he needed to remove forever the threat Mary of Scotland posed to the realm. With a new sense of purpose, she rode on.

Joan Lascelles, a plump, cheerful young woman who tended to find a silver lining in the darkest cloud, urged her pretty little dapple-gray palfrey forward. "I heard you mention Queen Mary," she gushed at Marion. "Do you think she will need more ladies to serve her?" Joan fair vibrated with excitement at the thought that she might have a chance to become one of them.

"She has ladies sufficient to her needs." Marion sounded irritated. "Scots ladies."

"She'll need English ladies when she's England's queen," Joan protested. "Besides, some of those Scots are no better than they should be. Mary Seton, for one. They say Christopher Norton had no trouble seducing her."

"Oh, that!" Disdain filled Marion's voice. "'Tis but a ploy to establish contact between our party and the queen of Scots. Norton only pretended to pay court to Mistress Seton."

"Who is Christopher Norton?" Susanna asked.

"One of Old Norton's sons. No doubt he will be at Brancepeth with his father and all his brothers."

Susanna tried to remember what Walter had told her about the Nortons but could only recall that there were a great many of them.

"He's the handsome one," Joan whispered.

Marion laughed. "Nell has high standards in that regard. Norton's not so fine as her manservant. What was his name again?"

"Lionel Hubble," Susanna said. "He's naught but a lowly groom, Marion."

"I do not want to marry him, Nell. Only flirt with him awhile. 'Twill keep Guy from becoming complacent. Do you think this Lionel will return soon with your daughter?"

Susanna replied, with depressing honesty, that she had no idea when she might see Lionel again.

It was dusk before the entourage stopped in Darlington for the night. They claimed every bed the town had to offer. It was Cecily Carnaby's turn to attend the countess. Susanna, Marion, Joan, and Margaret Heron shared cramped quarters in the room adjoining hers. They'd scarce fallen asleep when a great to-do awoke them. Susanna was first through the connecting door.

"Kill it! Kill it!" the countess screamed.

Cecily was attempting to obey, slashing at a cornered rat with a knife. She landed a lucky blow, skewering the creature, and Susanna thought the crisis past, but instead of dropping her weapon, Cecily stabbed the small corpse repeatedly, sobbing all the while. Only the combined efforts of Susanna and Joan finally made her stop.

"Beast! Horrid beast!" The breathy cries were the loudest sounds Susanna had ever heard her make.

"So must all vermin be extinguished," Lady Northumberland declared. "You have done well, Cecily. We must root out all such infestations and leave those who oppose us bloody and mangled in our wake."

Cecily's sudden descent into violence and frenzy shocked Susanna, but the countess's words left her stunned. They were an unwelcome reminder that Lady Northumberland could order the death of a person who stood in her way just as easily as she could give the command to kill the rat.

17

Why am I here? Catherine Glenelg asked herself. She'd been asking the same question for five days, ever since she'd impetuously left Glenelg House in the company of Jennet, Fulke, and a young man called Toby.

Their unexpected arrival had caught her in the middle of the worst quarrel she'd ever had with Gilbert's mother. If she'd stayed in London, she'd have laid violent hands on the imperious old besom by now. She'd only shown common sense to leap at the chance for escape Jennet had offered.

Once she'd heard that Susanna Appleton was in trouble, Catherine had wasted no time. She'd changed into the boy's breeches and thigh-high boots she used for travel, packed a few essentials, left a note for Gilbert, saddled Vanguard, and set off for Yorkshire. She'd had plenty of time since to consider that her departure might have been a bit precipitous, but once committed, she'd had to continue on. Hadn't she?

Why am I here? Catherine asked herself again, sprawling on the bed in their chamber at the George as she watched her companion pace. An hour into their journey, she'd been missing Gilbert and young Gavin, but concern for Susanna, who had raised her from the age of fourteen and taught her and loved her, had kept her moving north.

Catherine understood Jennet's reasons for recruiting her well enough, perhaps better than Jennet did herself. The presence of a lady in their company assured better service on the road—faster horses if they needed to change mounts, more luxurious accommodations, and the right to demand an audience with someone in authority, the lord president of the council in the North himself, if the need arose.

But was there need? Even before they left the home counties, they'd heard rumors of an uprising in the North Riding. That part of Jennet's theory seemed true enough. But there was nothing to indicate Susanna was in any danger or that they could help her even if she was. Indeed, if the rebels heard that Lady Glenelg was asking after Lady Pendennis, that fact might complicate matters for Susanna. Gilbert was known to be a supporter of the Protestant party in Scotland.

"Well, where is he?" Jennet demanded. "We have been here for hours without a sign of him."

Catherine stared at the canopy above her head. She'd held her tongue long enough. Jennet had worked herself into a frenzy of worry and frustration, gnawing at her lower lip until it bled. She attempted a mild reproof. "Master Baldwin cannot have known which day you'd arrive. You must be patient, Jennet. When he hears you are waiting, he will come."

"Inefficient. He named this inn in his letter. He should have left a man behind."

"We made better time than he'd have expected."

The road from London to York was straight and in reasonable repair. Although the days were growing shorter, they'd been blessed with fair weather. The key to their speed, however, had been Catherine's insistence that Jennet abandon her pillion, which she disliked in any case, and ride astride as Catherine did. Reluctantly, Susanna's housekeeper had accepted the horse she'd been offered, but she'd resolutely refused to wear breeches, bunching her skirts up between her legs instead and showing a good deal of plump ankle.

"Inconsiderate." Jennet continued to grumble as she peered out the chamber window, squinting at the street below. "How difficult is it to leave a message?"

"He is wise to trust no one he does not know and Toby was with us." As soon as they'd discovered Nick Baldwin was not at the George, Catherine had dispatched both Toby and Fulke to search the city for him.

Jennet swung around to glare at her. "You are passing calm, madam." Her tone turned the words into an accusation. "Can it be you do not care what happens to Lady Appleton?"

Catherine sat up and glowered back. "Certes, I care! But the Scots have an expression. They say, 'Dinna fash yerself, lassie,' and 'tis good advice." Although she'd be happiest if she never had to set foot in Scotland again, Catherine did like the language.

Jennet's sputter of protest failed to impress her.

"You were to come here, to this inn, and wait. That is what we will do."

"Yes. *I* was to come here. Master Baldwin does not expect you." After a significant pause she added, "madam."

"And it may be that neither one of us is needed. Susanna agreed to pretend to be Lady Pendennis and spy for Sir Walter. Mayhap Master Baldwin exaggerates her need for assistance."

Returning to her post at the window, Jennet turned her back on Catherine. "Faith, I pray you have the right of it."

There had been no mention of meeting Sir Walter in York, which made Catherine wonder if he and Nick Baldwin were working together or at cross-purposes. Perhaps the greatest service she could provide would be to bring the two men together, to point out that, no matter how little they might care for each other, they must put aside their differences for Susanna's sake.

"Do you remember the first time Sir Walter met Susanna?" Catherine asked. "Even though Robert was still alive then, he could not help but fall in love with her."

"He wooed her after Sir Robert's death, until Lady Appleton refused his offer of marriage."

"And then Eleanor—crafty, clever Eleanor—won him. I wonder what will happen now that they are both free to marry again?"

The sound of bootheels on the planks outside the chamber door prevented Jennet from speculating. Accompanied by Fulke and Toby, Nick Baldwin had arrived. To Catherine's surprise, Lionel was also with them.

"I did not expect you, Lady Glenelg," Baldwin said when the first wave of greetings had ebbed.

"I am, I hope, a happy surprise."

They had met before, but only twice and both times briefly. Although Catherine was aware of the extent of Susanna's involvement with this man, she had difficulty imagining what Susanna saw in him. Sir Walter had far more to offer, and Catherine's half brother, the late Sir Robert Appleton, had been much better to look at.

Still, she could scarce question Baldwin's devotion. His fears were writ large on his expressive face, along with everything else he felt for Susanna. "She has no notion that Lady Pendennis's death was anything but an accident," he told them. "She must be warned before she makes some misstep that will get her killed, too."

An hour later, Catherine and Jennet had been apprised of all Baldwin knew of the situation. Catherine did not like any of what she'd heard and was disturbed by three points in particular.

According to Master Baldwin, Sir Walter Pendennis

had not been upset by the news that his wife's death was murder. Indeed, Baldwin seemed convinced he would sacrifice anyone for the good of England. Was that jealousy talking? Or had Walter's affection for Eleanor diminished over the years?

Further, Baldwin believed that the earl of Northumberland had given the order for Eleanor's death, and yet Lionel's report from Topcliffe indicated another possible interpretation of the facts. Lady Northumberland seemed to be the one in charge, and it would have been easy enough for her to have used her husband's signet ring to seal a letter. Had she been the one who suspected Eleanor of deceit? Did she still?

Third, as Baldwin himself continually emphasized, Susanna was in danger as long as she did not have all the facts. She'd gone willingly to Topcliffe to spy on the rebels, but she was under the impression that everyone there trusted Eleanor Pendennis and had from the beginning. Clearly, that was not the case.

The rebels had now left Topcliffe, taking Susanna with them in the guise of Eleanor Pendennis. But Eleanor Pendennis had once been considered a threat, simply because of her connection to Sir Walter. If the earl, or his countess, had any reason to believe she was there to spy on their activities, she could expect no mercy.

"Does Sir Walter have one of his agents with the rebels?" Catherine asked.

"*Susanna* is his agent."

"It is not like him to neglect to send in support." She gave Baldwin a pointed look. "How difficult can it be to pretend to be one of the rebels?"

Leaning back on a stool, both feet extended in front of him and his head resting against the paneled wall, Baldwin's pose was negligent but the look in his eyes was anything but. "Easier said than done, Lady Glenelg, as Pendennis repeatedly reminds me. I could cause more harm than good if I try to reach her. If Susanna recognizes me, she might give herself away without meaning to. As much as I dislike agreeing with Pendennis about anything, he has the right of it. I cannot approach Susanna without increasing her danger."

"Is that why you sent for me?" Jennet asked. She had been silent for a very long time . . . for her.

An embarrassed flush suffused Baldwin's face. "I do not know what I was thinking. It just seemed to me that you might be of some use."

Jennet had used the same reasoning, Catherine suspected, in deciding to stop at Glenelg House. Sound instinct had been at work in both cases.

His facade of unconcern crumbled as Baldwin shifted position. With his feet flat on the floor and his spine stiff, his very demeanor betrayed the depth of his concern. "Pendennis is willing to take risks with her. I am not. You are a woman and a servant, Jennet. Ideally suited to get close enough to tell her that Lady Pendennis was murdered."

"Once Jennet informs her Eleanor's death was no accident, then what?" Catherine awaited Baldwin's answer with considerable interest. His reply would tell her a great deal about how well he knew Susanna.

"I do not hold out much hope that she'll agree to leave the rebels. Not when she is there to fulfill a promise to Pendennis."

Catherine regarded him with greater interest. Perhaps he was not such a bad match for Susanna, after all.

"I can do more than warn her to be cautious," Jennet interjected. "I can stay with her to watch her back."

"And there must be something I can do," Catherine murmured. "Mayhap Sir Walter will have some use for me. Where is he, Master Baldwin?"

"He left York this morning, to meet with Sir George Bowes at Streatlam."

"Then I will go to Streatlam." She was about to say more when she noticed the odd expression on Lionel's face. "What troubles you?" she asked him.

"This talk of servants makes me wonder what happened to Sir Walter's man. He took Jacob Littleton with him when he left England."

Baldwin frowned. "Pendennis traveled alone by the time he came to Hamburg."

Thinking that, most likely, the fellow's fate had naught to do with anything, Catherine nevertheless resolved to ask after Jacob when she next saw Sir Walter. As Susanna was wont to say, one could never tell what small detail might prove significant.

18

The way to Brancepeth Castle wound through mountainous terrain, well wooded with oak trees. On the second day of their journey, Marion stuck to Susanna's side like a burr.

"This is Weardale," she remarked when they came to a place where the road branched. "The border between Durham and Westmorland is that way." She gestured toward the west.

Northumberland, Susanna recalled, was to the north.

A mile below Brancepeth Castle, they reached the ford across the River Wear. The entire entourage halted. The men at arms went first, then the earl and countess. The countess's women had a considerable wait before their turn, time enough to dismount and stretch and unearth a bit of cheese and bread from their packs. Susanna took the opportunity, along with Joan Lascelles and Margaret Heron, to slip behind convenient bushes and relieve themselves.

They remounted a short time later.

The water was exceeding cold, and moving faster than Susanna had expected. Just the sight of it made her queasy. "Onward, Turmeric," she urged her horse, but the mare shied as droplets splashed up by other hooves struck her full in the eyes.

Without warning, the saddle begin to slip. Susanna gasped and flung her arms around Turmeric's neck. As she clung, she felt the leather seat beneath her shift again, until all that held the sidesaddle in place was her own weight. With one knee hooked over the pommel and both feet inserted in a sling buckled to the left-hand side of the saddle, she had little ability to maneuver. She could not even break free of the contraption. If it slid completely off Turmeric's back, she would go with it and be dragged beneath the water by its weight.

Seeing her distress, one of the men-at-arms waded into the river. He seized her about the waist and pulled her from the saddle, which dropped into the water behind them. Ignoring it, he carried her to safety, unharmed and barely wet. One of the others led her horse to shore.

Shaken, Susanna stood on dry land looking back at the ford. A chill swept through her that had nothing to do with the temperature of air or water. Something had caused her saddle to slip, but what? Accidents happened. She knew that. And yet . . .

"Eleanor! You might have died!" Joan Lascelles engulfed her in a warm embrace. "Poor chick!"

She seemed so upset that Susanna ended up trying to soothe her. "Oh, no," she insisted. "A fall would not have killed me."

"A drenching in cold water can be fatal," Cecily reminded her.

Susanna shivered again. She was right. If she'd gotten soaked to the skin in temperatures this cold and been unable to secure dry clothing and get warm again quickly, she might well have died of exposure. But that had not happened. Nor had she been trampled by rebel hooves while caught in her own saddle.

She looked around for her equipment and found Guy Carnaby examining the girth buckle. "A billet strap broke," he informed her when she came up beside him.

"How could that happen?" She bent to examine both

buckle and strap. "Did it fray?" She had owned this saddle for many years.

"If leather is not well cared for, it can become brittle and break. It looks to me as if your man neglected his duties."

Making a noncommittal sound, Susanna allowed Master Carnaby to put her up on a pillion behind one of the men-at-arms. Leigh Abbey's grooms were taught to be diligent; she would have expected her saddle to be so well maintained that such a thing could not happen. But Lionel had only posed as a groom. He'd been trained as a gardener.

"Could immersion in seawater weaken the leather?" she asked.

Carnaby allowed that it could, then issued the order to bring along Susanna's horse and the damaged saddle. They resumed their journey.

Without further incident, they reached Brancepeth. Susanna, Margaret, and Joan had almost finished installing Lady Northumberland's possessions in the chamber assigned to her when Marion reappeared, fresh from her reunion with her own mistress.

"Lady Westmorland sends me to fetch you to her," she told Susanna.

"What does she want with me?"

"You must ask her that yourself." Marion's face was pale, her manner distracted, and as soon as she'd escorted Susanna into the small room where the countess waited, ensconced upon the only chair, she fled.

It was a study, but Susanna had little time to appreciate the abundance of books or the fact that a casket overflowing with letters stood open on a table. One look at Lady Westmorland and Susanna could not blame Marion for making such a hasty retreat.

Where Lady Northumberland's eyes tended to be lit by enthusiasm, this other noblewoman's burned with a darker fire. They narrowed in suspicion the moment they lit on Susanna. In combination with high color and tightly compressed lips, her whole visage gave the impression she was about to explode into some sort of emotional outburst.

"My lady." Susanna made her obeisance, expecting at any moment to be denounced as an imposter.

"You were responsible for my brother's arrest."

Susanna blinked at her in amazement. "Madam, I was not."

"Do not trouble to deny it. I know the truth."

In the face of such an outrageous statement, Susanna could think of nothing to say.

"Six weeks ago, the queen turned against the duke of Norfolk and ordered his arrest."

"Six weeks ago, madam, I was still recovering from a serious accident."

"Before that accident," Lady Westmorland insisted, "you sent word to England of our plans."

In truth, Susanna was not certain of the precise date of Eleanor's death, but something seemed askew in the countess's arrangement of events. Letters *could* travel quickly between merchants abroad and their counterparts in England. It followed that official messages made the journey with even greater dispatch. But without Walter to ask, Susanna had no way to determine if the duke's sister could be right. It did not matter, she decided. She would in no case ever admit that Eleanor, through Walter, might have alerted the queen.

"I know all about you, Lady Pendennis." Bitterness laced Lady Westmorland's words. "You sought out our agent in Augsburg, offered to serve as a courier, then betrayed our plans to your husband."

Eleanor had approached Dartnall? Susanna frowned.

That was not how Walter told the tale. He'd said Dartnall recruited Eleanor.

"I do not understand, madam. I never told Sir Walter anything. Indeed, I knew passing little to tell. To be honest, I saw doing a small service for the earl of Northumberland as the means by which I might escape my husband."

"Why should I believe you?" The countess leaned forward, her face ruddy with anger. "You are wed to a man who has been a thorn in the side of all right-thinking men for years. He has made of our honest plans to advance our interests a seeming treason. He has helped thwart the efforts of anyone outside that sacred circle of advisers to Elizabeth. Why would he hesitate to do so again at my brother's expense?"

"Because he knew nothing of my actions or your plans." Susanna feigned outrage. "Nor did he know that I meant to leave him. I fell into conversation with Master Dartnall and he spoke a little of what was happening in the North. Enough to tell me that I might be able to help him and help myself at the same time."

"Your husband knew naught of these meetings?"

"I took care that he should not."

Abruptly, the noblewoman stood, advancing until she was only a foot away from Susanna. "Marion tells me you were in an accident and that, as a result, suffer holes in your memory. This is passing convenient. Will you now claim 'twas during one of those gaps that you sent word back to England?"

"I did not do so." Susanna was taller than Lady Westmorland and more sturdily built, but she did not feel that gave her any advantage. An almost palpable threat emanated from the smaller woman. "I know where my loyalties lie, my lady. Remember that I did serve as your courier. If I'd betrayed you, if I'd turned that letter over to Sir Walter, you may be sure I would then have stayed as far away from Yorkshire as I could."

"Do you support deposing a heretic queen and replacing her with the queen of Scots?"

"I support the restoration of any church that allows for the dissolution of a marriage."

Susanna spoke the words on impulse, but when the countess was surprised into a laugh, she knew her instincts had been sound. It was one of the world's great ironies that the break with Rome, occasioned by King Henry's desire to divorce his wife, had led to the establishment of a religion in England that made it impossible for anything but death to sever the bonds of matrimony.

With another abrupt movement, the countess of Westmorland resumed her former position in the chair. "You may return to Lady Northumberland."

Concealing her relief as well as the trembling of her hands, Susanna scurried away. If she'd had any idea how to get out of the castle without being challenged, she'd have been tempted to flee into the night, for her close call at the ford had not unnerved her half as much as the interview with Lady Westmorland.

19

DURHAM—NOVEMBER 14, 1569

Nick watched the coming of the rebels with Jennet at
his side. Reportedly twenty-five hundred strong on foot
and horse, they sang as they marched along the route to
the cathedral. There they intended to break the law of
England by hearing Mass.

No one would stop them. The bishop of Durham had
prudently removed himself and his family from the city.
That he'd destroyed all the glass in the cloister, because
it depicted the life of St. Cuthbert, had not endeared
him to English papists.

Nick's sources of information were excellent. The
merchants of York, concerned about the possibility that
rebels might lay siege to their city, had sent men into the
countryside to find out what was happening. Some had
stayed. Others had brought back word that Northumberland was at Brancepeth Castle, three miles from
Durham, and that armed men were flocking to him
there. Gentlemen. Farmers. A physician Nick had met
recently in York. Nick did not need to be a strategist in
order to guess that when the rebels gathered enough
strength they would march against the most convenient
large target.

Most of those filing into Durham appeared to be simple countryfolk, although they did wear crosses on their

chests. In the vanguard rode a cluster of women. Two of them, the countesses, he presumed, had also dressed themselves as crusaders, although they scarce embraced either piety or poverty. Their palfreys were caparisoned in silk and velvet, the saddles decorated with flowers made of gold and pearls.

Their ladies, less colorful, most riding astride, accompanied them.

"Praise God," Nick whispered when he picked out Susanna's familiar form among them and saw that she looked fit. There was no indication she rode with the rebels under duress. That meant her disguise still held.

Pulling Jennet after him, Nick threaded his way through the crowd, getting as close to the women as he dared. He'd not risk speaking to Susanna. For the present it would be best if she did not notice him. But as soon as Jennet warned her he was back in England, there would no longer be a need to keep his distance or worry that his sudden appearance might startle her into betraying herself.

Someone jostled him, hard, in an attempt to steal his purse. "Dragon water!"

At the precise moment he spoke, Susanna glanced in his direction. Nick froze. Their eyes locked. Then, without giving any sign that she knew him, she looked away and did not allow her gaze to stray toward him again.

"She recognized me." Jennet sounded smug. "'Twill be an easy matter now to speak to her."

"Go then, and Godspeed." Nick was tempted to accompany her now that Pendennis's dire predictions had come to naught.

Within seconds, Jennet was swallowed up by the crowd, just one more woman of indeterminate age and middling height, although somewhat too plump and rosy cheeked for the role they'd decided she should play. Nick stepped into a convenient doorway to let the traffic in the street stream past. The smell of rising bread made his mouth water, but he ignored his hunger. When the rebels had all passed by, he returned to the inn where he had earlier bespoken a room. If Jennet could convince Susanna to leave the countess's household, they would meet there, but he did not hold out much hope she'd agree, not as long as her position as Lady Pendennis was secure.

Involuntarily, Nick's fists clenched. The mere thought of Susanna answering to that name made him angry. Although he believed what he'd told Lady Glenelg, that Pendennis would sacrifice anyone, even Susanna, to defeat the uprising, he also suspected that Pendennis intended to set himself up as Nick's rival once the rebellion had been put down.

Susanna had agreed to help Pendennis for the sake of England. Nick knew that. She derived great satisfaction from righting wrongs. But he feared she also enjoyed venturing into the dangerous waters braved by intelligence gatherers.

Pendennis was cut from the same cloth as Sir Robert Appleton. He could offer her excitement, and additional opportunities to do good. In comparison, life with an ordinary merchant would seem passing dull. Furthermore, although Susanna claimed to long for a peaceful existence, she had never yet failed to involve herself in the troubles of those with connections to her late husband.

His thoughts as dark as night in a collier's mine, Nick reached the inn. It was all but deserted, since most of Durham's inhabitants were at the cathedral. When last he'd stayed here, he remembered, he'd been with his father. He'd been a mere apprentice then. In the years since, he'd traveled far and seen much.

That realization stopped Nick in his tracks. If Susanna craved excitement, he could offer her Muscovy. Or, better yet, Persia.

Let Pendennis top that!

A roar of sound—the crowd at the cathedral—
brought him back to the present with a crash. Yes, he
could offer Susanna a whole wide world, but first they
had to get out of Yorkshire in one piece.

20

Her heart had stumbled at the sight of him. As she sat through mass, Susanna was still reeling from the shock of seeing Nick in Durham. Her mind was filled with as much chaos as the street outside.

It seemed impossible. He was supposed to be in Hamburg.

She had only seen him for an instant, and yet, in that suspended moment, she'd absorbed every detail of his beloved face and form. The strands of white in the darker shades of his hair. The velvet brown of his eyes. The broad shoulders that revealed his great physical strength. She'd even noticed that he wore a good black riding coat, fringed, and thick knitted riding stockings pulled up over his boots in the fashionable way that also protected them from the dust and dirt of the road.

And Jennet. It was Jennet's added presence that had made her doubt the evidence before her eyes. Jennet should have been hundreds of miles to the south, in Kent. Why was she here and dressed in plain fustian and in Nick's company when neither of them could abide the other?

A poke in the ribs from Joan Lascelles reminded Susanna to kneel.

Walter had taught her how to use a rosary during the voyage from Hamburg and she no longer felt awkward toying with the beads. She'd been surprised by how easily she'd also become accustomed to hearing Mass and by how little the Catholic church service differed from the English liturgy set out in the *Book of Common Prayer.* Certes, the priests spoke Latin, although most had passing poor pronunciation, and wore more elaborate vestments, but aside from that, and the use of such embellishments as a censer and holy water and music, the content was much the same.

Hearing Mass in the North meant choirs and cornets and sackbuts, too. Susanna quite enjoyed all that. Only an organ remained in Leigh Abbey's parish church, and there had been attempts by some radical reformers to expel it and banish the singing of psalms.

The priest's voice thundered powerfully from the pulpit, preaching against heretics who embraced the New Religion. Susanna. Her family. Her friends. "When Elizabeth Tudor refused to receive the papal nuncio, she became excommunicate and sacrificed the allegiance of her subjects," he declared. "It is not treason to rise up against her." In the rousing sermon that followed this denunciation, he equated loyalty to Queen Elizabeth with certain hellfire . . . or at the least excommunication by Pope Pius V.

This was a message popular with the crowd and when, after mass, the countesses and their ladies adjourned to the safety of the churchyard on the south side of the minster, the earls turned their followers loose. Susanna looked back only once, just in time to see two men tearing pages from the English Bible customarily used from the pulpit. A crash and splintering sound signaled the destruction of the communion table.

"They will light a bonfire," the countess of Westmorland predicted, "to burn the heretic prayer books."

Susanna's stomach turned at the thought of so much waste. Lady Northumberland's bonfire at Topcliffe had been disturbing. This was vile. She glanced at Lady Westmorland with distaste. How could a woman whose girl-hood tutor had been John Foxe, that fiery advocate of the New Religion who in later years had written the volume popularly known as the *Book of Martyrs,* detailing the suffering of those who had been persecuted for their religion under the harsh Catholic regime of Mary Tudor, so easily sanction the desecration of copies of the New Religion's *Book of Common Prayer?*

What irony, Susanna thought, that Foxe's most outstanding pupil should lead a rebellion designed to return England to Mary's faith. Susanna doubted it was done out of any fervent religious belief on her part, which only made the countess's actions that much more reprehensible. Lady Westmorland was prepared to use religious zeal to further her own ends, the restoration of her husband to the position of power and wealth he'd once held in the North and the advancement of her brother, the duke of Norfolk.

The previous evening at Brancepeth, Lady Westmorland had worked the rebels into a frenzy. It had been Susanna's turn to attend Lady Northumberland, so she'd heard every heated word, observed every volatile reaction.

Tempers had been high on the raised dais throughout the evening meal. Everyone expected that the earl of Sussex would send troops to enforce his summons to York. Brancepeth might be strongly positioned, standing on an outcropping of rock and surrounded by higher hills, but it was not prepared for a siege, and the earls and their countesses could not agree on what to do next. No one wanted to submit to Sussex, or flee the realm, but neither of the earls had appeared to have much enthusiasm for open rebellion. There was no sign yet of Alba's armada. The earl of Northumberland, fearing failure that would leave him in even worse straits, had argued for disbanding at once. He seemed to think he'd be allowed to go home and pretend naught had happened.

At this suggestion, Lady Westmorland had become very red in the face. Standing so quickly that she'd overturned her chair, her voice had risen to a shriek of outrage. "We and our country were shamed forever," she declared, "that now in the end we should seek holes to creep into!"

The earl of Westmorland was a young man, no more than five and twenty, and devoted to his slightly older wife. He had not interrupted her as she'd berated the other conspirators, calling them cowards and worse. At one point, in sheer frustration, she'd burst into tears.

It had been a remarkable performance. Even Lady Northumberland had fallen silent before it. Calming herself, Lady Westmorland had spoken quietly to her husband, then briefly left the hall. When she returned, Westmorland had stood. He'd raised one fist and shouted, "A fight to the death!"

His words echoed through the great hall. The battle cry was taken up by a few in the crowd, but enthusiasm was lacking until Lady Westmorland produced the banner of the Five Wounds of Christ. It had been the symbol of the Pilgrimage of Grace, a rebellion that, some thirty years before, had attempted to prevent King Henry from closing the monasteries. It still had the power to stir Yorkshiremen's hearts.

In order to raise the hordes of followers needed to overthrow Queen Elizabeth, Lady Westmorland had embraced a more universal cause than personal gain. A holy cause.

"This time we shall succeed!" The countess of Westmorland's ringing declaration brought soldiers to their feet in the great hall of the castle, cheering and chanting.

"Take up the banner!" they'd cried.

A kind of madness seemed to take possession of all those present. Susanna feared it drove them still. In sunlight, in open air, the continuing sounds of wanton destruction were painful to her ears.

"I believe I will explore the churchyard," she murmured to no one in particular. "There appear to be many old tombs here."

She set a course away from riot and chaos, driven by a need to be alone to think about what she could do to subvert the terrible events Lady Westmorland had unleashed.

Marion followed her. "Some people say that that one came from the consecrated churchyard on the island of Lindisfarne." She gestured toward the tallest of the crosses.

Susanna did not reply, but she recognized the name. She'd picked up quite a few bits of religious lore since her arrival in Yorkshire. Lindisfarne was in Northumberland, near the earl's castles of Alnwick and Warkworth. It was the site of an old monastery dedicated to St. Cuthbert, the same St. Cuthbert who had once been revered here in Durham.

They stopped at the Lindisfarne cross. Susanna touched her gloved fingers to the indentations that were all that were left of what had once been an inscription.

"We've scarce spoken since your interview with Lady Westmorland, Nell. Are you wroth with me?"

"Why should I be? I can scarce blame you because she thought me responsible for the duke's arrest."

"Is that what she accused you of? I did not know." Marion's troubled expression spoke volumes about her own doubts and fears. "She mistrusts most people." After a moment, she added, "She found the setback caused by his arrest most frustrating, the more so because she already blamed him for failing her. When she was told that a message had come from Norfolk, before he was sent to the Tower, advising Westmorland to abandon all plans for an uprising, she flew into a rage. She said her brother was a fool to begin a matter and not go through with it."

They walked on in silence. Lady Westmorland, Susanna

thought, was accustomed to having everything her own way. She'd seen ample evidence the previous evening that the countess had a talent for finding and manipulating the weaknesses of others to achieve her own goals.

If the countess had one weakness of her own, Susanna decided, it was overconfidence. In her study, she kept an ornate casket overflowing with letters. Was there, among them, one that proved the queen of Scots had conspired with the rebels to bring about the overthrow of Queen Elizabeth?

Susanna's hand rested on the surface of yet another monument to the dead. There had been too many deaths, too many wars. She was uncomfortable with the thought that, if she was correct in her assumption, and capable of making off with the prize, she'd be condemning at least one woman to a terrible death. And yet Walter's logic was irrefutable: As long as Mary of Scotland lived, English papists would keep on devising plots to overthrow Elizabeth. Susanna opposed unnecessary loss of life, but the only way to slay this dragon was to cut off its head.

They would return to Brancepeth for the night. When they did, she resolved to find a way to search Lady Westmorland's study.

A slight movement caught Susanna's eye, the flutter of a dark cloak. Someone stood in the shadow of a tomb, waiting. She could guess the watcher's identity. Not Nick. That would be too likely to arouse suspicion. Jennet. Walter had sent Jennet to assist her, and while she deplored the risk her old friend would be exposed to here, Susanna was heartened at the thought of not being alone anymore. She continued to wander among the monuments until Marion lost interest and rejoined the others. Only then did a cloaked and hooded figure step into view.

"Good day to you, Lady Pendennis," Jennet said in a

loud voice. "I doubt you remember me, but I was in service in Lady Quarles's household when you were her waiting gentlewoman. Hired me in London, she did, when the tiring woman she'd brought with her fell ill."

All too aware that the countesses and their women were listening to every word, Susanna stepped closer to Jennet. "Your face is familiar to me." She spoke slowly but her mind was racing. Where was Nick? Where was Walter? Was she supposed to go with Jennet or find a way to take Jennet with her?

"I am Jennet Messenger," Jennet continued, "and I would ask a boon of you."

"Name it, my good woman." In spite of the seriousness of their situation, Susanna had to fight a smile. Jennet had a flair for the dramatic. If women were allowed to act in public in England, as Susanna had heard they did in France, she might have had a career as a player.

"I seek employment, Lady Pendennis. Lady Quarles brought me north with her when she left London. I met a man from Durham and married him, but he is dead now, and so is Lady Quarles, and I am near destitute. Do you need a servant, madam? I am very good at fixing hair and caring for clothes."

"I must have mine own mistress's permission to add another person to her household." She risked a glance at the cluster of women. Marion was the only one looking their way. The countesses were about to leave the churchyard. "Follow me," Susanna told Jennet. In a whisper, she added, "If she refuses to accept you, there's no help for it. You will have to go away again."

Alarm flashed in Jennet's eyes. "I must speak to you in private, madam. Lady Pendennis's death was no accident."

21

In a surly frame of mind made worse by the stale bread and weak ale provided for her supper, Jennet inspected the anteroom attached to the chamber Lady Appleton shared with the other waiting gentlewomen. Here she would spend the night, together with the countess's chamberers. She supposed she should consider herself fortunate to have a pallet and blanket. Most of the newest arrivals had to sleep in the open, or on the floor in the great hall. But what did comfort matter if she did not find a way to rescue Lady Appleton?

There had been no time for Jennet to expand on her terse warning in the churchyard. She wished now she'd simply told Lady Appleton she must come away with her, but she'd been caught up in the role Master Baldwin and Lady Glenelg had created for her. In the blink of an eye, she'd lost control of the situation.

Lady Northumberland had generously allowed her waiting gentlewoman to acquire a personal servant, but there had not been a single moment for private speech between them for the remainder of the day. Toward evening, when the rebel leaders returned to Brancepeth, Jennet had gone with them, but the castle, too, was crowded, making it impossible to exchange any confidence without being overheard.

"I grow too old for all this rushing about," she grumbled as she limped back into the gentlewomen's bed-chamber.

Her feet hurt from the three-mile walk, and she could feel a blister coming up on one heel. She'd had to leave Poppy, the horse Lady Glenelg had given her, in Master Baldwin's keeping. A poor servant woman, down on her luck, would not own such a fine animal. Who would have thought that she, who had always hated riding, would be missing a horse?

Lady Appleton, Mistress Lascelles, and Mistress Heron had returned in Jennet's absence. They all looked up at her entrance.

"You'd best let me take a look at that ankle, Jennet," Lady Appleton said, hurrying across the room toward her.

" 'Tis naught but a—"

"Here, now. Sit by the light and let me see." She all but pushed Jennet onto a stool in one corner of the room. "What did you mean, Eleanor's death was no accident?" she asked in a whisper.

To the head bent over her toes, Jennet explained, keeping her voice low and her account brief. It felt wonderful to have her shoe removed and her foot massaged with skillful, healing hands.

Telling her to stay put, Lady Appleton released it to fetch water, soap, a clean cloth, and a pot of some vile-smelling salve. Jennet wrinkled her nose but did not object to the doctoring.

"I cannot imagine Northumberland sending such an order," Lady Appleton murmured as she worked.

"That is what Lady Glenelg said. She wondered if it might have been his countess who—"

"Catherine is in Yorkshire, too?"

"She has gone to meet with Sir Walter at Streatlam. Master Baldwin says Sir Walter believes all will be well, because you proved your loyalty to their cause by delivering that letter from the duke of Alba, but the message in the letter you took to Topcliffe is one Sir Walter substituted for the original."

"No more than I expected," Lady Appleton murmured.

"Master Baldwin intercepted another copy of the original in Antwerp and worries that there may be a third. He fears your life will be forfeit if it arrives or if there is any suspicion you are disloyal. He wanted you to come away with me. He waits for us at an inn in Durham."

A little silence fell. Jennet wished she could see her mistress's face.

"I believe I am safe enough for the moment." But there was a hint of doubt in Lady Appleton's voice. Before Jennet could take her to task for it, she spoke again. "I had thought to leave here, if a chance presented itself but there is something I must do first."

The approach of Mistress Lascelles put an end to their privacy. "How does she, Eleanor?"

"Well enough."

"You look pale yourself."

"Something I ate did not agree with me. I fear I will need to make more than one visit to the privy this night." Just before she turned away from Jennet, she winked.

The *privy?*

Well, 'twould be private there.

Dutifully, Jennet helped her mistress prepare for bed, then slipped out of the anteroom, her cloak wrapped around her for warmth, to await Lady Appleton. A long, cold hour passed before she appeared. To Jennet's relief, she led the way past the two-hole privy. The odor from the cesspit reached them even through the closed door. A little farther along the passageway, they came to a tapestry that concealed a narrow alcove. It was dark and dusty behind the arras, but they'd be out of sight and able to hear footsteps if anyone came near.

"How did you come into this, Jennet? I left you safe in Kent."

"Master Baldwin sent for me." She repeated his account of murder and conspiracy, then added, "It was my idea to stop in London for Lady Glenelg. Master Baldwin plans to join the rebel army if we do not return to Durham. Toby, too. He's the one Master Baldwin sent to fetch me. Lionel and Fulke have gone with Lady Glenelg to Sir Walter."

There was a catch in Lady Appleton's voice when she spoke again. " 'Tis good to have friends." She cleared her throat. "Is all well at home? Has Rosamond been told of her mother's death?"

At the thought of Leigh Abbey and those she'd left behind, Jennet's chest tightened with emotion. "We told Rosamond nothing, but she wanted to come with me all the same."

The child had been set to throw a tantrum to get her own way. She'd tossed her dark brown curls and pouted when Jennet reminded her she had lessons to do. Before Lady Appleton had left for the Continent, she'd hired a tutor and given him special instructions for the girl to begin the study of Latin and Greek.

"Let Mole do them," Rosamond had said. Spoiled brat. She'd been indulged during the four and a half years she'd lived at Leigh Abbey. In addition, she'd inherited all her father's most unpleasant traits—a wild streak, a quick temper, and a stubbornness that defied common sense.

"His name is Rob," Jennet had said through clenched teeth. She despised the ekename Rosamond had given her son. "He has his own studies at the village school." Jennet had insisted he go there to be taught with other boys as soon as he reached his sixth year. He was a big boy now, she thought with a glow of maternal pride. A day scholar and in breeches, too.

As she'd ridden away from Leigh Abbey, Jennet had been unable to resist looking back. She'd seen Rosamond, red faced, hands on her hips, working herself up to a howl of outrage at being left behind. But when Mark's hand had come to rest on her shoulder, she'd abruptly closed her mouth.

"When my wife returns home," Jennet had heard Mark say, "Lady Appleton will be with her."

As they hid in the stifling darkness at Brancepeth, Jennet prayed he'd spoken the truth.

"Your little ones must have objected to their mother's leaving," Lady Appleton said. "I am sorry to have taken you away from them again."

"They have Mark. And Hester." Rosamond's nursery maid also looked after Jennet's three children.

As soon as Mark had lifted Jennet onto the pillion behind Fulke, eight-year-old Susan, their eldest, had stared at the pack animals with big, sad eyes and, sensing her mother was about to embark on a long and dangerous journey, had started to sniffle. Kate, a year younger, had copied her sister. Rob had struggled to maintain a manly stoicism. He might have succeeded had not Rosamond whispered something in his ear. After that, he'd had to bite his lip to keep from sobbing as hard as his sisters.

"I am surprised Hester did not insist upon accompanying you," Lady Appleton remarked. Jennet could hear the smile in her voice.

"No doubt she'd have liked to." Hester was enamored of Lionel, who ran the other way whenever he heard she was in the vicinity. The woman had a good heart, but it was lodged in a gangly, unfeminine body.

"Well," said Lady Appleton, "there is no more to be done tonight. Get you to bed, Jennet, and to sleep. We will need all our wits about us on the morrow."

22

The advice Susanna had given Jennet had been sound, but she found herself unable to follow it. She lay stiff with tension beside Joan Lascelles, who slept like a dead person—on her back and unmoving—and stared at the tester overhead.

Scenes and images kept rest at bay. The sack of Durham Cathedral. The evening at Brancepeth that had preceded it. Madness, Susanna thought as she made a futile attempt to get comfortable on the lumpy, wool-stuffed mattress: Lady Westmorland was perilous close to it. Worse, it was the kind of madness that inspired fanatic devotion.

What Jennet had said, about orders sent to Dartnall under the earl of Northumberland's seal, also troubled Susanna. It was true Lady Northumberland had access to her husband's signet ring, but Susanna could not imagine why either the earl or the countess would command Eleanor's death. Tell Dartnall not to trust her, yes. That made sense, although Susanna had seen nothing to indicate that either of them suspected Eleanor of anything. Even if they had, would they not have urged Dartnall to retrieve the parcel he'd given Eleanor rather than kill her? If she'd understood Jennet, and if Jennet had been accurate in reporting what Nick had learned from Dartnall, the clerk's commission had been very specific—arrange an accident that would leave Lady Pendennis dead.

Susanna's head began to ache from trying to sort out whys and wherefores. Shivering in spite of the warmth of the covers and the nearness of her bedmate, Susanna's thoughts turned to Lady Westmorland. The second countess blamed Eleanor for her brother's arrest. Could she have sent those orders to Dartnall? Had the seal Dartnall mentioned belonged to the earl of Westmorland rather than the earl of Northumberland? This theory made a certain amount of sense. Lady Northumberland might have a reckless streak in her nature, but it was mild compared to the inherent violence Susanna sensed from Lady Westmorland.

Thinking back on their encounter, Susanna remembered that Lady Westmorland had said Eleanor contacted Dartnall, not the other way around. How had she known that? And what else had she known? Had she been told Eleanor was with Lady Northumberland? Had she arranged for someone to cut partway through that billet strap, causing it to break?

Susanna tried to tell herself she was letting her imagination run away with her, but she could not stop thinking about the way her saddle had slipped when Turmeric shied. What if that had not been an accident? No one else seemed to have the slightest motive to harm Eleanor. Anyone else, suspecting Susanna's true identity, would simply have exposed her, rather than make an attempt to kill her. And now? Was she still in danger? She thought, by meeting Lady Westmorland face to face, she'd convinced her Eleanor was innocent of betraying the duke of Norfolk's plans to the queen.

Well, then, Susanna decided, slipping out of bed once more, she no longer had to worry about her own safety. Perhaps she never had. But she would be wise to fulfill her mission here as soon as possible. If she could get into Lady

Westmorland's study tonight and find an incriminating letter from Queen Mary, then she could plead illness when the rebels set out again. She and Jennet would remain behind, find Nick, and go home. Once the rebellion had been put down, Eleanor's murderers would be punished for that crime, as well as for their treason.

Dressing herself in the dark presented a number of challenges but Susanna deemed it unwise to creep through the sleeping castle barefoot and dressed only in a shift beneath her heavy, dark wool cloak. After a considerable struggle, all her points were tied and she was ready to go. She had marked the way to Lady Westmorland's door and knew there would be enough light from wall sconces to guide her. There were also several shadowed alcoves and concealing tapestries along her route. She could hide herself in a trice if she heard anyone coming.

In the pocket of her cloak was the key she'd taken from the countess of Northumberland's chamber door. She expected Lady Westmorland's study to be locked, but she'd already ascertained that it was secured with a highly decorated plate lock identical to those used for all the principal bedchambers at Brancepeth. She was in hopes a single key would open one and all.

She was denied the opportunity to test that theory. When she reached her goal it was to find light streaming out through the open portal. Wide awake in spite of the hour, the countess of Westmorland sat at her writing table, scribbling furiously on a surface littered with papers. Before slipping quietly away, Susanna caught one more tantalizing glimpse of the casket she had hoped to examine. It had no lock, only a simple latch to hold it closed.

23

While Jennet helped Lady Appleton dress, there were too many other people around to allow for private conversation. Things did not improve as the day wore on. Resigned to spending an indefinite length of time with the rebels, Jennet resolved to throw herself into the role of humble maidservant. Unfortunately, since neither the countess of Northumberland nor any of her waiting gentlewomen wished to soil their white hands emptying the noble chamberpot, that job was the first that fell to her.

The work was hard and there was plenty of it. As long as Jennet did her share, no one questioned her presence at Brancepeth. Even better, the livery she was issued at midday allowed her to blend in with the rest of the retainers. Jennet had to admit a secret liking for the clothes. They were much brighter than those she'd once worn as a tiring maid at Leigh Abbey. Instead of a nondescript blue kirtle, she was given a stammel red frisado skirt fringed with crewel. The bodice, of red kersey, had a fine linen collar. She was also issued several kerchiefs, two coifs, and three bibless aprons.

It was late afternoon before Jennet saw Lady Appleton again. Passing a window, Jennet happened to look into the courtyard, where all the waiting gentlewomen had gathered. Lady Westmorland's attendants had engaged Lady Northumberland's in an archery contest. As Jennet watched arrow after arrow fly toward the butts she realized that even Mistress Carnaby, whose vision was impaired, shot well. Only Lady Appleton was conspicuous in her lack of skill with a bow.

That night a sense of barely suppressed excitement permeated the castle. After supper, the company sang songs in four, five, and six parts. Later the earl's musicians, who were more accustomed to playing taborette and lute and rebec, outdid themselves on Lincolnshire bagpipes to accompany dancing. Perhaps because everyone knew they intended to set out again in the morning, the celebration had a hectic quality that put Jennet in mind of the story of the tarantella, which Lady Appleton had once read to her servants at Leigh Abbey. Poor souls, bitten by the poisonous wolf spider, danced until they dropped in the futile belief their frenzied movements would expel the poison from their bodies.

"We could slip away in all this confusion," Jennet suggested when she found herself standing close to Lady Appleton in the great hall.

"Meet me behind the arras in a quarter of an hour," Lady Appleton murmured, and walked away.

A quarter of an hour after that, Lady Appleton used a key to unlock what turned out to be Lady Westmorland's private study. "There should be a casket here somewhere," she whispered after she closed the door behind them and lit a candle. "Of a size to hold letters."

"Do you have a key to that, too?"

"It is not locked." Disappointment tinged the words. She'd found what she sought, but the ornate metal box was empty.

"It may be just as well, madam," Jennet said. "If there were letters and you took them, Lady Westmorland would be sure to notice. Do you think she destroyed them?"

"No. I think she has them with her." Lady Appleton extinguished the light. Her voice sounded eerie in the darkness. "She'd get rid of them only if she thought she was in danger of having their contents used against her."

"I do not understand, madam."

"I know you do not, Jennet, and there is no time now to explain. I've no idea how to go about retrieving those letters if she's taken to carrying them on her person. Will you stay and help me?"

"I will stay," Jennet promised.

The next morning the rebels were on the move again. Together with Lady Northumberland's chamberers, Bess Kelke and Meggy Lamplugh, Jennet shared a precarious perch atop the rawhide cover that protected a load of featherbeds, traveling chests, and other household goods. It was not the most comfortable way to travel, but Jennet preferred it to walking.

"Great sackless cuddy," Bess muttered as Master Carnaby rode by, his horse's hooves kicking up dirt from the road.

All Northumberland's lesser servants spoke English with thick Northern accents and at first Jennet had not always been able to make sense of their conversation. Now, however, she was becoming accustomed to the way they talked. "Big stupid donkey?" she asked.

"Reet," said the heavily bearded groom perched on the driver's bench. He'd traded his livery for a crusader's cross. To Jennet's mind, one was as bad as the other. The Percy lion engraved upon a badge marked him as the earl of Northumberland's man. The cross identified him as a rebel.

"I dinna ken whe Mistress Standbridge will nivver give ower clamming for him," Bess continued.

"She's always chunteren on, nivver content w' nowt," Meggy agreed.

Since everyone at Brancepeth knew Mistress Standbridge and Master Carnaby were lovers, Jennet supposed Bess meant Carnaby would do well to make his mistress his wife. Unfortunately, no one seemed to know much else about Lady Pendennis's cousin, save that she'd made frequent visits to Topcliffe in recent months, carrying messages from one countess to the other.

"Is Mistress Carnaby Master Carnaby's sister?" Jennet asked. Then she listened in fascination as Bess recounted a long involved tale to explain Mistress Carnaby's widowed state. She sat up a bit straighter when she heard that Ranulf Carnaby had been slain by one of the queen's intelligence gatherers. Caught carrying a secret message to the king of Spain, he'd fought to the death rather than go to London and be tortured for what he knew.

"What man did he fight?"

Bess gave her an odd look. "A divvent knaa his nyem.

Jennet wondered if Guy Carnaby knew it. "How long ago was this?"

"Six years since," Bess thought, but she jabbed the groom in the ribs and asked him for confirmation.

"De'el take ye, what are ye naggin' on at?"

When the two of them began a spirited exchange, half quarrel, half flirtation, Jennet retreated into her own thoughts. Six years ago . . . when Sir Walter Pendennis had been one of the most successful of the queen's intelligence gatherers. He'd been important enough to be in charge of other agents. Had he been responsible for the death of Ranulf Carnaby? Could he even have killed the man himself?

She frowned. If he had, did that mean Master Carnaby had told the earl of Northumberland that Sir Walter's wife might betray them? Or did it mean Carnaby had sent the message to Dartnall himself? As the earl's secretary, he might have been able to steal the earl's seal and affix it to a letter Northumberland knew nothing about. Jennet puzzled over the matter for the rest of the day's journey.

The sun hung low in the sky by the time they reached Darlington and stopped for the night. Absently, Jennet spoke as she clambered down from the cart. "I must see if Lady Appleton needs me."

"Who?" Bess's bewildered question sent Jennet into a panic. How could she have been so stupid as to use the wrong name?

"Lady Pendennis, that is," she blurted, trying to force a laugh through a suddenly dry throat. "Lady Appleton was another young lady in Lady Quarles's service when Lady Pendennis was there. Not that she was Lady Pendennis then. Just plain Mistress Lowell."

Her babbling only attracted more curious looks. Jennet was almost in tears. If anyone had heard of Lady Appleton, the expert on poisons and loyal subject of the queen, there would be trouble.

Thankfully, a distraction presented itself, an excited buzz running through the line of riders as word came that the earls had been thwarted in their wish to hear Mass. There was holy water in Darlington but no vestments. They would have to settle for reading their proclamation of rebellion, something Jennet had heard they intended to do in every place they stopped.

"We, Thomas, earl of Northumberland, and Charles, earl of Westmorland," it began, "most loyal vassals of Her Majesty, to all true believers in the ancient Catholic Church."

Jennet listened in growing amazement as they accused "certain wicked and designing men of the retinue of the queen" of "crafty and malicious wiles" and of persecuting "the true Catholic religion of God" and attempting the destruction of the nobility.

The proclamation went on to spell out the earls' chief demands and vow to restore "the ancient freedom of the Church of God and of the realm." "If we do not this of ourselves," it continued, "we risk to be made Protestants by force, which would be a sore danger to our State and to our country to which we belong."

So much wordiness, Jennet thought, and all it meant was that they wanted to replace the Church of England with the Roman Catholic faith.

She was surprised to hear no mention of the queen of Scots. Master Baldwin had told them Sir Walter believed freeing her was the real goal of this rebellion. The chief objectives, as read out in Darlington, were the reinstatement of what the rebels called "the true and ancient religion," the removal of several of the queen's councillors, the liberation of those nobles who were in prison, notably the duke of Norfolk, and the recall of certain former councillors. Those who had served under the queen's late sister, Jennet presumed. At the end of the proclamation was a demand for general amnesty.

A great cheer went up when the reading was complete. Most of the men who flocked to the earls' cause were armed with guns and halberds, pitchforks and bows, prepared to back up their convictions with force. "Death to the heretics!" some cried. Others shouted, "Take back the monasteries!"

A horrifying vision materialized in Jennet's mind at these words. Until that moment, this uprising had seemed far removed from her loved ones, but Leigh Abbey had once been a monastery. It had been granted to Lady Appleton's grandfather after its dissolution as a religious house. Would her home be destroyed if men such as these had their way? Mark and their children thrown out of their home? It had not been so many years ago that the fires of Smithfield had made martyrs of those who would not give up the New Religion. Jennet knew, only too well, that people who objected to the policies of the Crown ofttimes lost their lives.

"Faith," she whispered. No wonder Lady Appleton had agreed to spy on the rebels. If they were not stopped, they might well destroy all she held dear.

24

Their betters were invited to sup at the house of a gentleman of Darlington, where the earl and countess of Westmorland would lodge, but the waiting gentlewomen and lesser female servants made do with what a harried and overburdened innkeeper could supply for their supper. They gathered in the common room, tired after a long day of travel and upheaval. Spirits were high, for men did seem to be flocking to the cause, but bodies flagged, in dire need of food and drink and rest.

"Turnip soup?" Marion complained, setting her bowl aside untasted. She looked with even less favor on the dark bread she'd been given. Another of Lady Westmorland's gentlewomen was likewise contemptuous of the offering. Both were out of sorts because they had been billeted at the inn while their mistress's two other attendants had beds at the manor.

"I am hungry enough to swallow anything," Joan Lascelles declared, accepting her portion from Meggy Lamplugh. Bess Kelke filled each bowl from a steaming cauldron the innkeeper's boys had brought in, then passed it to Meggy and Jennet to distribute.

Susanna made no comment, simply dipped her spoon in the hot, watery broth and lifted it toward her mouth. The smell reached her a moment before she took the first taste.

"Do not eat of it!" she cried.

Reaching out, Margaret Heron caught Joan's hand. "What is it, Eleanor? What is wrong?"

Cecily Carnaby, startled, leaped to her feet. She collided with Marion in an attempt to reach Joan and in the resultant tangle the cauldron tumbled over, spilling its contents into the rushes.

"Do not let one drop pass your lips," Susanna warned. She dipped a finger into her bowl and at once withdrew it, wincing. She'd not even had to touch one of the thick fleshy roots. The milky juice alone was enough to make her skin tingle.

"Have you burnt your finger?" Jennet rushed to her side. "Oh, madam! The soup was too hot."

Marion, too, came to inspect the damage. "'Tis very pink," she said of the fingertip. "Shall I fetch a house leek?" Its juice was a sovereign remedy for burns.

"The soup was not too hot. It was made with poison." The unpleasant, acrid odor of bryony had warned Susanna in time.

Exclamations of "Poison!" and "How could this be?" greeted her announcement, along with calls for the cook to be brought forth. In the confusion, bowls were dropped and pushed away in haste, until little of the deadly contents remained.

"I did naught!" the cook protested when the men-at-arms the earl had left behind dragged him out of his kitchen. "I did naught!"

"Naught but mistake the Devil's turnip for its harmless cousin. If I had eaten of the soup, my mouth and throat would have blistered, at the least. I might well have died."

"'Twas an honest mistake," the cook whined. "One root for another."

"Show me your hands," Susanna demanded. Her own were shaking.

The plants grew plentifully in the wild and bore some resemblance to the turnip, hence the common name for bryony, but although the Devil's turnip might be pale yellow in color within, it was black on the outside. To make the substitution, it had been peeled and chopped up, and anyone who'd done that with bare hands would have blisters to show for it.

The cook's hands bore several old burns and calluses, but showed no evidence of recent exposure to the caustic juice of a poisonous plant. The men-at-arms searched his kitchen for gloves and found none. The slim possibility remained that the cook was one of those rare people unaffected by the juice, in which case, Susanna reasoned, he *might* have made an honest mistake.

"Were some of your turnips black?" Susanna asked him.

"Were in the ground, madam. Dirt be dark of color."

"Did anyone come into your kitchen who should not have been there?"

"Anyone might have, madam. In all the confusion." His face brightened as he realized he had a way to exonerate himself. "I was gone for some time while the soup simmered," he admitted. "Listening to the proclamation in the marketplace with everyone else."

"An accident," Guy Carnaby concluded when he was called in, but he gave Susanna an odd look. "What else could it be? Why would anyone have tried to poison you women?"

In spite of his calming words, it was some time before the furor died down, although not so late that the countess had returned to the inn for the night.

"Let us leave to chance which one of us waits up for her," Susanna suggested to the other gentlewomen.

She drew the short straw herself and, as she'd expected, Jennet offered to keep her company, claiming she was too distressed to sleep. The two of them adjourned to the privacy of the countess's chamber.

They had plenty to keep them busy there. When the

countess of Northumberland traveled she took with her all her own household goods, including a bed and a portable altar. The mattress and featherbed and curtains had been assembled, but the sheets and coverlets were still to be added.

"Did someone try to kill everyone, or just you, madam?" Jennet asked as she stirred up the fire and set several of the earthenware hot water bottles, known in the North as pigs, on the coals. The fact that these were used to warm beds had given rise to the slander that uncouth northerners slept with their livestock.

"I do not know. By the time I thought to sniff any of the other bowls, most of the soup had been spilt. You do not think it was, after all, just another accident?"

"Too many accidents for my liking," Jennet muttered.

"Yes, and you do not know about all of them." Susanna gave Jennet a concise account of the incident at the ford. "The billet strap could have worn through with age."

Jennet snorted. "Not since Fulke last saw it."

She was right. Fulke was her master of horse, who kept a close watch on every aspect of Leigh Abbey's stable. He'd not have let her take faulty equipment with her to Hamburg.

"Well, then, 'tis possible someone wants me dead. But is it because of who I am or who Eleanor was? And what person here would go to such extremes?" She could not tell now, with all the broken crockery and spilled soup, but that only her bowl had contained the deadly root seemed unlikely. If the poisoning had not been an accident, that someone was willing to endanger all the women to get at her.

"Madam," Jennet blurted, "the murderer is Mistress Carnaby!"

"Cecily Carnaby? Why would she want me dead?"

" 'Tis Lady Pendennis she wants dead. Mistress

Carnaby's husband was killed by an intelligence gatherer. What if it was Sir Walter?"

The story Jennet had heard tumbled out, and it did not take Susanna long to find flaws in her logic. "Ranulf Carnaby's death was a long time ago, and even if his widow does still want revenge for his death, why attack me? Indeed, she has made me most welcome in Lady Northumberland's household. She is even grateful to me for the improvement in her eye. Poor woman. She will be blind in time. There's no hope of saving her sight. Already it makes her clumsy."

"She overset the cauldron on purpose," Jennet muttered.

"She stumbled into it," Susanna corrected her. "Besides, you've just said yourself that it was Guy Carnaby you suspected of telling the earl of Northumberland about Walter's past."

"If he knew, she could have known, too. And as revenge, a spouse for a spouse makes perfect sense."

"Do you mean to say you think she convinced the earl to order Eleanor killed? That she's behind all three so-called accidents?"

Jennet had given up any pretense of making the countess's bed ready for the night. She stood with hands on hips, glaring at Susanna. "She could have sent that letter herself. Stolen the earl's seal. Written the—"

"In code?"

"*Was* it in code? No one's seen it but Master Dartnall and I do not think Master Baldwin thought to ask him about that detail."

"More likely something I have said or done has made someone nervous."

"Master Carnaby was quick to dismiss tonight's incident as mischance. Perhaps he and Mistress Carnaby conspire together to kill Lady Pendennis."

Susanna sighed as she fluffed the pillows. What happened this evening troubled her. That it had been an accident seemed to stretch credulity, but not so much as thinking it had been deliberate. How could a poisoner have known in advance that the cook would serve turnip soup? Although any one of their company could have added that poisonous root to the pot—it would be the work of a moment to step into the kitchen and drop it in—that person would also have had to know how and where to find the Devil's turnip growing in the woods, and dig it up, and prepare it. She supposed they'd have found it easy enough to avoid blisters. The more gently bred someone was, the more likely to wear gloves, even indoors. But Susanna had difficulty seeing how the whole affair could have been planned in advance.

Accident or design? If it had been deliberate, that meant the poisoner was willing to let others suffer and mayhap die to get at Eleanor. She did not want to believe that anyone she'd met here could be that cold-blooded, but she remembered the night Cecily, at Lady Northumberland's command, had slain the rat.

Then Lady Westmorland came to mind. Susanna shook her head. Of them all, Lady Westmorland seemed least likely to have had advance knowledge of the turnip soup. And if, by some wild stretch of the imagination, she'd paid the cook to poison his own dish, surely the fellow would have fled afterward for fear of being hanged for murder.

"Mayhap we are too quick to dismiss Master Carnaby's opinion," Susanna said aloud. "Now that I think about it, the root seems more likely to have got into the soup by mischance."

"Well, then, what of the matter of your saddle? That sounds suspicious to me." Jennet applied the hot pigs with such a will that she imperiled the countess's fine linen sheets.

"If it was cut, it could have been tampered with well in advance."

"Cecily Carnaby," Jennet said, abandoning her task. "Or Master Carnaby. If they blame Sir Walter for Ranulf Carnaby's death—"

"Why take revenge on me if it was Walter who killed Ranulf? And remember, it is pure speculation that Walter was responsible." But she recalled, of a sudden, the tone of voice Guy Carnaby had used when he'd spoken of Walter that first day at Topcliffe. Susanna picked up where Jennet had left off with the pigs. "It makes no sense. Everyone here believes Eleanor left her spouse. Killing her would not punish him, for logic dictates that Walter no longer cares for the wife who abandoned him. Indeed, he might thank the man who freed him to marry another."

"Revenge is not logical. You must watch your back around both of the Carnabys." Jennet shot a worried look in Susanna's direction. "Have a care, madam. If some person does wish to harm Lady Pendennis, he or she may try again."

Susanna sank down on the end of the bed, inexpressibly weary. "I wish I dared make lists. Writing things down makes matters so much more clear."

"We must leave here, madam. Escape before there are any more attempts to kill you."

Susanna ignored the suggestion. Another thought had occurred to her and she knew she might not have a better chance to solicit Jennet's opinion. "Something has been plaguing me ever since my interview with Lady Westmorland. There are inconsistencies in what Sir Walter told me about Eleanor's involvement with the rebels. He said they approached her, but Lady Westmorland seemed certain Eleanor had contacted Dartnall. And Marion told me that her cousin wrote, at least once, to her kinfolk in Westmorland."

"Do you think Lady Pendennis intended to leave Sir Walter? Could the story he concocted for you to tell the rebels have been the truth?"

"If she did mean to leave him, we must ask another question. Did he learn of her activities from her before her accident, as he told me, or only afterward, by going through her effects?"

Jennet's eyes went wide. "Do you mean to suggest *he* arranged her death?"

"I do not like to think so, but Walter's odd behavior has bothered me all along. He is cold and distant when he speaks of his dead wife. And from what you've told me, he had little reaction when Nick told him that Eleanor had been murdered."

"He did not care, Master Baldwin said."

"But we both know Walter loved her deeply when they wed." Susanna closed her eyes. What she was thinking caused her pain, but it had to be considered. "If he discovered she'd betrayed him, betrayed England, could he have lashed out?"

Jennet did not have to consider long. "Yes," she said. "But he'd do it coldly and with calculation, not in the heat of anger."

In her heart, Susanna knew Jennet was right. And for a man with Walter's background, it would not be difficult to forge orders and send them to Dartnall, tricking him into thinking they'd come from the earl. And if Walter had been responsible for killing Eleanor, it followed that the "accidents" here in Yorkshire had nothing to do with what happened in Augsburg.

She would not leave the rebels just yet, Susanna decided. Not until she had completed the assignment Walter had given her, and not until she had ferreted out the truth about Eleanor.

25

When she heard about the poisoned soup, Lady Northumberland gathered all her waiting gentlewomen together and hugged each one of them in turn. "I could have lost you all," she said in a choked voice. "Eleanor, we owe you a great debt."

Jennet watched her mistress struggle for words. She wondered what Lady Appleton would have said if the countess had waited for a response. But Lady Northumberland, who never surrendered for long her position as the center of attention, lost no time regaining it.

"What if we had supped here? The entire cause might have failed because of a root picked in error." Her eyes widened, enhancing the drama of the moment. "*Was* it a mistake? Or has some foul fiend wormed his way into our confidence to kill us all?"

Her women hastened to reassure her, as did Master Carnaby, who arrived to report that a dead scullion had been found behind the inn's stable. "His hands and the inside of his mouth were most horribly blistered," Carnaby declared. "It is plain enough what happened. He added the wrong root by mistake and then, having no notion he'd put poison in the soup, ate of it himself and died."

"A neat solution," Lady Appleton murmured.

Jennet shared her mistress's skepticism. It would be comforting to accept an explanation that did not involve malice. She'd like to believe that billet strap had just worn out, too. But Jennet was not so trusting. She had helped Lady Appleton find murderers in the past. More recently, she and Mark had unmasked a most insidious villain all on their own. Jennet considered herself to be clever at discovering things, almost as good at it as her mistress. She went down to the stable to have a look around.

When she discovered that the body had already been removed, Jennet ventured into the kitchen to ask questions. The inn's servants were glad enough to talk, now that they'd been cleared of suspicion. The scullion had been hired only a few days earlier, she was told. He'd had no family. He'd seemed a clever enough lad, a boy of twelve or so, but everyone agreed he must have been the one who'd made the mistake. Were not those blisters proof of it?

"But where did he get the bryony?" Jennet asked. The inn's garden provided all the turnips anyone could possibly need, even this late in the year.

No one had an answer to that.

She looked again at the garden. She was not known for her ability to tell one plant from another, but there did seem to be a great many turnips. More had already been stored for the winter in a root cellar.

"Why are there so many turnips?" Jennet asked the cook.

His annoyance at her snooping faded and he beamed with pride. "I am famous far and wide for my turnip soup. We serve it at this inn every Wednesday."

26

Catherine repressed a sigh.

Sir Walter Pendennis was not pleased to see her.

It had taken her longer to travel from York to Streatlam than it had to make the entire journey from London to York, thanks to bad roads, heavy traffic—all the Yorkshire gentry flocking to join the earls—and a spate of bad luck. Vanguard had thrown a shoe. Then Fulke's horse had gone lame. Worse, by the time she'd finally arrived at her destination, Sir Walter had already left. He and Sir George Bowes had come here to set up a command post inside the fortified castle Bowes controlled as steward for the queen. They seemed to expect to be attacked by the rebels.

Catherine had been admitted to the premises, but she'd been put off until after supper. Now that Walter had at last received her in his well-appointed living quarters, he greeted her with stiff politeness and a visage that gave away none of his feelings, not even when she offered her condolences on Eleanor's death. He'd changed in the four years since she'd last seen him, Catherine decided. He was colder. Harder. And although it seemed impossible, more secretive than he'd been when he served as one of the queen's intelligence gatherers.

"Have I come at a bad time?" She made no attempt to hide her sarcasm.

"What are you doing here, Catherine?"

"I came to talk with you."

"I mean in the North. It is no place to be a woman traveling alone."

"I am not alone." She drifted across the tower chamber and seated herself by the window. "As you have no doubt been told, Fulke and Lionel accompanied me here. They will keep me safe."

"Did Baldwin send for you?"

"No. He sent for Jennet, who has by now attached herself to Susanna, or rather to Lady Pendennis, as a tiring maid."

She'd managed to surprise him. He seated himself in the chair beside his writing table and gave her an owlish look. "And Baldwin?"

"I do not know where he is." She suspected, however, that Nick was as close to Susanna as he could get. It would not be difficult now to pretend to be one of the many malcontents flocking to the rebel cause.

"Go back to London," Pendennis said.

"I can be of help here."

"There are already too many spoons stirring the pot."

"The last time I saw you," Catherine said slowly, "we were both concerned in the matter of proving Susanna innocent of murder. Her life was in danger. Is it in danger again?"

"No." But he did not look at her.

"Are you certain of that?"

"I am. As long as everyone believes she is Eleanor, she has naught to fear." At last he met her eyes, his gaze bleak and implacable. "Risk enters in when those who know her as herself are near. A slip of the tongue, a careless word . . ." He let his voice trail off suggestively.

"Yes. I see." But she did not. Not entirely. Nick had

told them Walter insisted that "Eleanor" would be accepted by the rebels as one of them, that her arrival with a coded message would assure her welcome. Catherine had found this argument flawed from the first. Someone who had been driven to give an order to kill would not lightly abandon the conviction that such an action had been necessary.

And something had Walter worried. When she'd known him before, he'd covered his true thoughts with a courtier's arts. He was a master at trifling conversation. The thick silence simmering between them was proof there were troubles preying upon his mind. So was the way he twisted the agate ring he wore. She doubted he was aware he was fiddling with it, and that was telling, too. He might, as he said, be afraid that Susanna's friends would accidentally expose her, but Catherine's instincts insisted there was more to it than that.

"I can be of use to you in the North," she informed him. "I can pay a visit to the queen of Scots. She knows me from the time Gilbert and I spent at her court. I will tell her he supports her cause and she will give me information I can pass on to you."

"She might believe you. So might those currently in power in Scotland. You put your husband in peril if they do. Besides, I have spies in her household already. I have no need of another. Go back to London, Catherine. There is naught you can do here."

Back to London? It was tempting. Back to Gilbert. Back to their son. And back to Gilbert's mother. "I am not yet ready to return." If that sounded willful, so be it. "You have been out of the country, Walter. You cannot have that many sources left after so long away. Let me help."

It occurred to her then that here was the simple explanation for Jacob Littleton's disappearance. Walter's longtime manservant must also be an intelligence gatherer. No doubt he'd remained in Augsburg to collect information to use against the rebel leaders when the uprising was over.

"Put me to work, Walter," she said again. "Let me serve as one of your agents." As incentive, she gave him a pithy report on all she'd heard about the uprising during her journey from York. Much of it was useless gossip, more was fanciful rumor, but Walter seemed interested in a few of the gentlemen's names she dropped.

"Egremont Radcliffe? The earl of Sussex's brother?"

"He's gone over to the rebels." Catherine had spoken with him herself. She knew the family, Lancashire land-holders like herself.

Catherine could swear she heard gears whirring inside Walter's head as he left his chair and crossed the room to stand beside her. With both hands braced on the win-dowsill, he stared out at the dark landscape.

"Very well," he said at last. "I do have a use for you, but you must promise to take no undue risks."

Eagerness swept away any hesitation. "I swear it."

He glanced at her, then away. "You need be nothing but what you are, a Scots noblewoman traveling north from London. Rural hospitality will demand that you be offered a bed for the night at any country gentleman's house."

Catherine nodded. The tradition predated the closing of the monasteries, which had also offered shelter for travelers. "Where would you have me go?"

"Penrith. Then Keswick, where Haug and Company operate copper mines for the Crown. Haug and Company," he added, turning to look at her fully, "employs Lucius Dartnall."

"The man who killed Eleanor." She searched Walter's face for some sign of emotion and found none.

"When Baldwin left Antwerp, Dartnall was on his way to Augsburg. He never arrived there."

"Do you mean to say he may be in England? Oh,

Walter! He will recognize Susanna as an imposter!"
Alarmed, she seized his arm. "You must find him."

He patted her hand. "He'll not reach Susanna. The
queen herself authorized me to coordinate the efforts of
all intelligence gatherers in the North. Those who for-
merly reported to her or to members of her Privy
Council now send their news here to Barnard Castle, as
do the men Bowes sent out. All of them have Dartnall's
description. If he makes any attempt to join the rebels,
he'll be caught."

Reassured, Catherine calmed down and considered
what else Walter had said. "You think he'll go to
Keswick."

Walter nodded. "Before I got word of Dartnall's disappearance, I'd pulled the man I had there out of
Keswick. I cannot spare another just now. If Dartnall is
on Haug and Company business, nothing to do with the
rebellion at all, he'll not try to hide his presence." He
hesitated. "What troubles me is that he may attempt to
make contact with Eleanor's mother. Gillingham Place,
the manor belonging to Sir Giles Gillingham, Eleanor's
stepfather, lies near Keswick."

Dismay filled Catherine at the thought that Dartnall
and Lady Gillingham, two people who would know at
once that Susanna was not Eleanor, might . . . what?
Compare notes? "I thought Eleanor and her mother
were estranged."

"Aye. So did I. But if she wrote to her uncle in Westmorland without my knowledge, she may also have
contacted Lady Gillingham. Your task is simple, Catherine. Find out if Eleanor's mother has had aught to do
with the rebels and determine whether or not Dartnall
is in Keswick."

"And if he is?"

"Set Fulke to watch him while you and Lionel bring
word to me here. Do nothing more. Do not attempt to

question or detain him. You should be in no danger. Dartnall chose a coward's way to kill Eleanor, arranging a clumsy, if effective, accident, but I do not want anything to alert him to the fact that he succeeded. His behavior is too unpredictable."

Catherine refrained from pointing out that Dartnall had, with his own hands, killed the driver of the wagon that had run Eleanor down. If Walter remembered that, he might forbid her to go. Not that she'd obey him. "How will I know Dartnall?" she asked.

"He is a bookish fellow, thin and stoop-shouldered, with a mole on the left side of his neck. It is partially hidden by lank, brown hair. I met him once only," he added in response to Catherine's questioning look, "but it is my business to remember faces."

"Did you ever encounter Lady Gillingham?"

"No, and I have never written to her, either. She should be in ignorance of her daughter's accident, unless Dartnall *has* contacted her."

"You had better tell me a bit more about Eleanor's family. Was Eleanor an only child?"

"Yes. Eleanor was descended from a cadet branch of the Cholmeley family. Their seat is in Westmorland, where Sir Roger Cholmeley still lives. His brother George, now deceased, was Eleanor's grandfather. George had one daughter, Philippa, now Lady Gillingham. Sir Roger's youngest brother, Alan, died at the time of the Pilgrimage of Grace. He also sired just one child, Mary, who wed Arthur Standbridge. And once again, the only offspring was a female."

"Marion Standbridge. Lionel mentioned her."

"Let us hope nothing makes her suspicious of Susanna's impersonation."

"And Marion's parents—where are they?"

"Dead and buried. Since Sir Roger never married, there are now only four surviving members of that entire branch of the family—Philippa, Marion, Eleanor, and Sir Roger himself."

"Three surviving members," Catherine corrected him. She found it disconcerting when, for just a moment, a look of confusion appeared on Walter's otherwise inscrutable features.

27

From the same window where they'd stood together the previous evening, Sir Walter Pendennis watched Catherine Glenelg ride away from Barnard Castle. Her scent, violets, seemed to linger in the chamber, but it was not her feminine side that made him nostalgic for the past. It was her resemblance to her late brother.

How Robert would have enjoyed following the progress of Walter's scheme. They'd have laughed together at the news that a rebel troop had been dispatched to Hartlepool to wait in vain for the arrival of Alba's armada. Robert had once been Walter's closest friend. Like him, Catherine was impatient and headstrong. Imagine leaving a child who could not be more than six months old to gallivant around the countryside attired in boy's clothing!

Walter had persuaded her to tarry long enough in Penrith to acquire a more appropriate wardrobe. Any delay involved in having clothes made, so that she would be dressed as befitted her rank when she arrived at Gillingham Place, would put off the moment when she began to suspect he'd deceived her.

It was for her own good, he told himself. He'd had to do something to prevent her from making a foolhardy attempt to ingratiate herself with the queen of Scots. And he'd only stretched the truth, not lied outright. Dartnall *had* been dispatched to England, his destination Keswick. According to the last report Walter had received from his agents, the fellow was at Haug and Company's headquarters in London. Walter expected at any moment to hear he'd been taken into custody there.

When Catherine and her two henchmen, or rather Susanna's two henchmen, had disappeared from view, Walter returned to the stacks of reports on his writing table. It was fortunate, he thought, that Susanna was a resourceful sort of woman, since he'd failed to establish contact with her. His first messenger, the one who'd taken the second copy of the duke of Alba's letter, had been turned away at Topcliffe without penetrating the guard around the countess of Northumberland and her women. After that, the man Bowes had placed at Raby Castle had seemed an ideal candidate for the job. As captain of the guard, he'd have experienced no difficulty speaking with one of the countess of Northumberland's women . . . if the earl of Westmorland had made Raby his headquarters. Unfortunately, Westmorland had chosen Brancepeth instead. Bowes's man had been ordered to stay where he was. He'd returned Walter's agate ring two days ago, with that message.

Walter had confidence in Susanna's ability to cope with rapidly changing circumstances. She was an altogether remarkable woman. A pity he'd not kept that in mind instead of letting himself be seduced by a pretty face. He'd been too quick to accept Susanna's refusal to marry him. A faint smile flitted across Walter's face as he picked up a list of the earl of Northumberland's holdings. When this was over, he would try again to win Susanna. At the least, he could make certain Baldwin stayed out of her life. She was too good for the likes of him. Let the fellow return to Hamburg and stay there a good long time.

Although Walter tried to focus on an analysis of the best way to bring the uprising to a rapid and ignominious end, his thoughts soon drifted to Baldwin again. As he traced the facets of the glass inkpot with one idle finger, he began to devise a quite different scheme, a plan for dealing with an interfering merchant. Baldwin's meddling annoyed him beyond reason. There had been no need to send for Jennet, let alone involve the wife of a Scots peer in this business. That there might be some basis for the fellow's panic over Susanna's safety only made his interference more intolerable.

Such grim ruminations were interrupted by Sir George Bowes, his face flushed from running up the stairs. "New information!" He waved a sheaf of papers. "The latest reports give the rebels sixteen thousand men in arms, including four thousand horsemen."

"Yesterday's rumors had them at five thousand strong, one thousand horse and four thousand soldiers." No one could guess how much of the populace would rise up in support of the earls of Westmorland and Northumberland, but Walter found each new set of numbers more suspect than the last. Even if they were accurate, that many men could not all be trained and armed. He'd seen the most recent muster rolls for Yorkshire and Durham, drawn up to evaluate the state of preparedness in those counties to repel foreign invaders. They'd shown the entire region woefully unready, a fact the earl of Sussex had used as his excuse not to call up troops.

Before the rebellion began, Sussex had convinced himself that the earl of Northumberland had no stomach for rebellion. This furor, he'd insisted, would die down if left to its own devices. When the earls did rise up, he'd changed his tune. Now he claimed he dared not risk a muster for fear half the men he armed would promptly desert to the rebel cause.

The man was a fool, though likely not a traitor. In most circumstances, Walter agreed that caution was a virtue. In this instance, however, if Sussex had acted quickly, the rebellion would have been over by now. Walter's scheme to trick the rebels into jumping the gun would have been a resounding success. Instead, what he had most hoped to avoid, a civil war, had come upon them.

All was not lost, he reminded himself. His plan would still work . . . just more slowly than he'd anticipated. And Susanna, trapped in enemy territory, would have to stay there a bit longer. At least he'd sent Lady Glenelg out of harm's way, he reminded himself. "Any further word from Lord Hunsdon?" Hunsdon was gathering troops in the south, whence they intended to march into Yorkshire, rally whatever men were still loyal to the queen, and rout the rebels.

"God willing, they will be here within two weeks."

"A great deal can happen in two weeks."

"Aye."

Walter felt confident that between now and then, Susanna or one of his other agents would uncover proof that the queen of Scots was directly involved in the earls' treason. When Hunsdon's army triumphed, she would be executed right along with them, removing forever the threat she posed to the realm. The movement to restore Catholicism in England would likewise receive its death blow. There would be no more uprisings against Queen Elizabeth.

To achieve that end, Walter was willing to sacrifice as many lives as necessary, even his own.

Even Susanna's.

28

Susanna awoke with the dawn, threw aside the covers, and braved the cold floor with her bare feet. Jennet was already up, as were Kelke and Lamplugh, which prevented any personal exchanges. This same situation had frustrated her for days.

Privacy had been a rare commodity of late. Only the earls and their countesses could achieve any semblance of it, and then only by ignoring the presence of their body servants. It was unusual, Susanna had discovered, for the nobility to be truly apart from others at all. Since joining the Northumberland household, she'd overheard far more than she wanted of the activities pursued by the earl and his countess behind the curtains of their bed.

Immediately after the incident with the turnip soup, the two earls had separated, each taking a different route south, while a third contingent marched to Hartlepool to wait for the duke of Alba. With Lady Westmorland gone, Susanna could no longer hope to obtain Queen Mary's letters. Jennet wanted her to leave, but she continued to refuse. For one thing, they'd seen no sign of Nick or Toby. For another, the earls would eventually join forces again. When they did, she'd have another opportunity to end this madness.

"I believe I will take the air," she announced when she was dressed. "Will any of you join me?"

Joan groaned and pulled a pillow over her head. "Not when we can sleep late for a change!"

Concerned for his wife, who'd had an alarming pallor for the last two days and wore the tight-lipped look of one suffering from a throbbing head, Northumberland had consulted neither priest nor secretary but made his own decision, electing to remain here in Boroughbridge until Westmorland's forces arrived.

Susanna had applauded his stand. In summer, the hardships of travel were bearable, although it was never easy to rise day after day at dawn and be given only time enough to gulp down a bit of bread and ale before an early start. The cold made everything worse. Even she, who had always enjoyed rude good health, save for the occasional bout of seasickness, felt tired and sore and out of sorts. They'd all have fallen sick if their breakneck pace had continued much longer.

Cecily smothered a yawn. "Best take someone with you," she murmured in a sleepy whisper. "A gentle-woman should not wander about alone when there is an army camped nearby."

"I will take my tiring maid." Susanna held her breath, but Cecily was no more inclined to rise and accompany her than Joan. Margaret Heron was on duty with the countess.

A few minutes later, Susanna and Jennet had left the inn and were breathing in crisp, cold air permeated with the smell of snow to come. They walked briskly through the small village, for Susanna had already selected a place where they would be able to talk undisturbed.

Boroughbridge lay on Watling Street, the main thoroughfare to London. It had one outstanding feature, four massive stones, their tops formed into points by ancient workmen, which stood in three separate fields.

This site was Susanna's destination. Superstition had kept anyone from camping near the megaliths.

"I looked for Master Baldwin ere now," Jennet said, surreptitiously crossing herself as they approached the first of the giant monuments, "but even he would think twice about meeting us in a place like this."

Susanna disagreed. If Nick or Toby had been watching their movements, this was the exact location they'd look to. If they wanted to make their presence known, here was their chance. "I have seen no sign of a man from Sir Walter, either," she said aloud.

Fascinated, she stared up at the first stone giant. It was at least twenty feet high and perhaps eighteen in circumference. Roughly square in shape to about half of its height, it fluted to a point above that. From the amount of millstone grit littering the field and the uneven look of its top, the obelisk had once been taller.

"How hard can it be to show themselves?" Jennet grumbled.

"Getting out is easier than getting in and even that would have been difficult." The countess of Northumberland's ladies moved as a unit, almost always in her company and constantly in each other's pockets. The earl had made it passing difficult for anyone to come near his wife and that had meant no one could reach her attendants, either.

"I do not like this place." Jennet shivered and cast a nervous glance over one shoulder.

"It is very old, I think." Susanna regarded the next two monuments, which stood within six feet of each other, a bow shot away from the first. One was bigger than the other. A fourth pillar, the largest of them all, rose up out of a third field a stone's throw from the second.

"I've learned nothing new," Jennet said. "Have you?"

The last tidbit she'd unearthed, about the cook's habit of making turnip soup every Wednesday, had provided

Susanna with food for thought but had not narrowed the field of suspects. Nor was she yet convinced the incident had been intended to kill her. Nothing untoward had happened since.

"When last I spoke to the earl of Northumberland"— she'd given him an infusion of cowslip juice for his wife, cautioning him to administer it drop by drop into the nostrils, not have her drink it —"I said I was grateful to him, that he had been most kind to me in spite of what he must have been told about Sir Walter's activities. I do not believe he understood what I meant. The more I see of Simple Tom, the less likely it seems to me that he could have ordered Eleanor's death."

Susanna leaned in close to examine the deeply seamed and moss-covered surface of the standing stone. She saw no inscriptions and wondered if there had once been some. Weather, she knew, could wear words away. She supposed the Romans had left these monuments behind, as they'd left the roads, but she doubted anyone would ever unravel the mystery of their origin. She was beginning to wonder if they'd have any greater success solving more recent puzzles.

"Come and sit, Jennet." Susanna settled herself on a large rock beneath the standing stone.

Reluctantly, Jennet perched on a second rock, but not before she looked over her shoulder once more.

"We are in the middle of a field, out of earshot. This monolith hides us from the village and no one can approach us in the other direction without being seen." Susanna waited until Jennet met her eyes. "And there are no ghosts."

They spent the next half hour reviewing everything they knew, but came to no new conclusions. Finally, too chilled to sit still any longer, Susanna rose from her rock to wander in the direction of the second and third megaliths.

"Do the rebels have any chance of success?" Jennet fol-

lowed, clutching her cloak close as the breeze that earlier had only made the cloth ripple, now caused it to
billow out like a sail.

Susanna paused beneath the second standing stone,
her gaze on the third field, but in her mind were pic-
tures from the last few days. She saw scores of followers,
poorly organized and provisioned, crusaders' crosses fly-
ing above them. But religious fervor could carry men
only so far. They needed to win a battle or see the
queen's men in retreat or have some other spectacular
success. Destroying prayer books in towns where they encountered no resistance could not long sustain
enthusiasm for rebellion.

With this realization, Susanna experienced a surge of
relief. She turned impulsively to Jennet. "They will not
win."

At the same moment, she heard an odd noise from
the direction of the first field and something flew past
her head, passing so close she felt the rush of air.

Jennet gave a startled cry.

Susanna jumped back.

An arrow imbedded itself in the cold ground just beyond where they stood. It had come within a
hairsbreadth of piercing Susanna's throat.

29

"There!" Jennet cried, and took off at a run after a cloaked figure just leaving the shadow of the first monolith.

She heard Lady Appleton's uneven gait behind her and stumbled herself as she tried to race across treacherous, half-frozen clods of earth. Lady Appleton was further impeded by her voluminous skirts. The ladies left off their farthingales when they traveled, but were still encumbered by yards of fabric. In contrast, Jennet's garments were simply cut and easier to hike up out of the way, but by the time they reached the giant pillar, the archer who had fired at them from behind it was long gone. On this side of the fields, both houses and hedgerows provided cover for the villain's retreat.

"That was no accident." Panting, Jennet leaned against the stone.

Lady Appleton's face was flushed with exertion. "No. Not this time."

"Oh, madam. Someone tried to kill you."

"What did you see? Did you recognize him?" While she caught her breath, she massaged one leg with strong, sure fingers.

"I cannot even say it was a him. Cloaked that way, the archer could have been a man or a woman." Jennet examined the ground, but it was too hard to show footprints.

"He, or she, took the bow away. I wonder if we can tell

anything from the arrow." At a slower pace, they retraced their steps. Lady Appleton pulled the shaft from the ground, but when she saw it was fletched with brown, her face fell. "It is a very ordinary sort of arrow. I'd hoped it might be one of the distinctive sort the countess's ladies use to shoot at targets."

"We must leave here at once, madam," Jennet urged.

But Lady Appleton shook her head. "No. This gives me even more reason to stay. It proves there is one among us who wants Eleanor dead. And I do not believe it is because someone fears she is a spy. If that were the case, or if my true identity had come to light, I'd have been locked up or left behind and that would have been the end of it. No, Jennet. This arrow suggests none of the accidents have had to do with the rebellion. And if that is true, there is no longer any certainty that the person responsible will be punished when the uprising is put down."

"Mistress Carnaby," Jennet muttered.

With reluctance, Lady Appleton nodded. "Mayhap. Let us return to the inn and see if my bedmates still sleep."

Jennet's suspicions seemed confirmed when they asked Bess Kelke if she'd seen anyone up and about.

"Mistress Carnaby left the inn ahint ye," Bess said. "She's nee come back."

Mistress Lascelles was still abed, but had she been there all along?

"There are other suspects," Lady Appleton murmured, ticking them off on her fingers. "Carnaby. Sir John the priest. Margaret Heron. The earl. The countess. It must be someone present at the ford and in Darlington."

At that moment, Mistress Carnaby, fully dressed and with her cloak over one arm, reappeared. "Back so soon from your walk, Eleanor?" she inquired in a soft, cheerful voice.

"It was . . . eventful."

Jennet realized, too late, that she was still carrying the arrow. It had been beneath her cloak when they'd questioned Bess, but Jennet had removed her outer garment when they'd entered the bedchamber.

Mistress Carnaby squinted at the weapon. "Where did that come from?"

"Someone shot at us," Lady Appleton told her.

Jennet's gasp was louder than Mistress Carnaby's. She'd not expected her mistress to reveal that information.

"Have you been gone long, Cecily?"

"I could not sleep after you left. I went out to use the privy."

A location difficult to verify, Jennet thought.

Mistress Carnaby stared at the arrow, transfixed with fascinated horror.

Mistress Lascelles, awakened by their voices, rolled over, took in the scene, and mumbled, "Lady Northumberland should be told of this."

"Yes," Mistress Carnaby whispered. Before anyone could stop her, she seized the arrow and whisked it out of the room.

By the time Lady Appleton gathered her wits, and Jennet, and followed her, she'd barged in on the countess of Northumberland. The earl had already left their chamber. Mistress Heron, helping the countess dress, was as startled as her mistress by the sudden invasion. For several minutes, confusion reigned, until Lady Northumberland grasped the salient facts.

"Someone has tried again to harm one of my women!" Enraged, she shook Mistress Heron off. Lady Appleton stepped forward to help tie her sleeves in place while Mistress Carnaby tried to attach the ruff. "Intolerable! Give me that arrow. I will discover to whom it belongs."

"It is not the first time," Mistress Heron said.

"The poisoned soup—"

Mistress Heron dared interrupt the countess. "There was an earlier accident. When we forded the river near Brancepeth."

Jennet, watching Lady Appleton's face, saw the moment she made her decision. Giving an admirable impression of a reluctant desire to unburden herself to her mistress— Jennet could have done no better herself—she told them about the first accident, in Augsburg.

"Mayhap I am just unlucky," she demurred.

The countess was not fooled. "Or someone has been trying to kill you for some time now. I wonder why?"

"I do not know, madam." She grimaced. "Or I cannot remember." She explained that the first accident had left gaps in her memory. To Jennet's surprise, no one doubted this claim. "How did I win approval, madam? To be a courier, I mean?"

"Why, that is simple enough. Your uncle vouched for you. After you approached our agent in Augsburg, he requested authorization to use you. Knowing your family background, I sent to Lady Westmorland for information. She had already heard of you from Sir Roger Cholmeley, a loyal supporter of our cause, and sent word back that you could be trusted."

Lady Appleton looked thunderstruck but was able to take advantage of Lady Northumberland's delight in holding center stage to press for more answers. "You authorized Dartnall, then? Sent him word I was to be employed to bring the packet to England?"

"Aye. Oh"—she waved one hand dismissively—"the order went out under my husband's seal. I have the keeping of it."

"You did not know, then, of my husband's sentiments?" Lady Appleton managed to look downcast. Jennet was proud of her. She'd improved mightily in her ability to deceive. "You did not send a second order to Master Dartnall, revoking your support?"

"No, indeed. I did not know of your husband's politics, or his former career, until after you arrived here with the duke of Alba's letter." She leaned close to Lady Appleton, prepared to continue her confidences, but what else Lady Northumberland might have disclosed, her ladies and Jennet were not to learn. Guy Carnaby chose that moment to bring the news that the earl and countess of Westmorland would arrive within the hour. They had spent the previous night only a few miles away.

"Mark my words, madam, it is one of them," Jennet whispered an hour later.

From an upper window, she and Lady Appleton watched the earl of Westmorland's entourage clatter into the inn yard and be greeted by the earl and countess of Northumberland and their attendants. Master Carnaby was there. As Jennet watched, Mistress Standbridge joined him. Apparently, she had once more been the one Lady Westmorland sent ahead with messages.

"I wish I knew more about Eleanor's uncle Roger," Lady Appleton murmured, "but if I ask too many questions I will arouse suspicion."

"Mistress Standbridge seems to accept you as her cousin."

"There are moments when she looks at me oddly. And she does not like to discuss Uncle Roger. He is intent, I think, on marrying her to someone she does not like." Lady Appleton sighed. "More and more often, of late, I wish I could confess this whole deception and be done with it."

"You might be safer then."

"But of no more use to Sir Walter. And the revelation would not be well received. Better to have Lady Northumberland as my champion than mine enemy."

"She can keep you safe from Mistress Carnaby," Jennet

agreed as that gentlewoman appeared below in the company of the countess of Northumberland.

"Cecily Carnaby is half blind," Lady Appleton protested.

"Him, then." Jennet jerked her head toward the burly figure of Guy Carnaby.

"Because of what Walter may or may not have done years ago?" Lady Appleton shook her head. "There has to be more to it than that."

"Orders from Lady Westmorland?" The countess had discarded her crusader's cross for warrior's garb. A sword hung from her belt. A quiver of arrows and a bow were strung across her back. "You did say she blamed you for her brother's arrest."

Lady Appleton looked thoughtful. "She could have ordered someone else to act for her, I suppose. But the timing seems wrong. It would help if I knew exactly when Eleanor was killed. I am not even certain just when she first became involved in this treason." A little laugh escaped her, devoid of humor. "There are still pieces missing from this puzzle, Jennet. That is the only thing of which I am certain."

A moment later, her breath caught.

Jennet followed the direction of her gaze and recognized another familiar face in the crowd of new arrivals below. She sent a quick prayer of thanks heavenward. At last, Master Baldwin had come. Perhaps now Lady Appleton would agree to leave . . . before whatever person was trying to kill her made the next attempt.

30

The arrival of the earl of Westmorland's troops strained Boroughbridge to the breaking point. There were men billeted in every corner and more in the open countryside beyond the town. It did not take Nick long to realize that the only place no one dared make camp was in the shadow of what locals called the Devil's Arrows, four ancient monuments built to commemorate some long-forgotten pagan deity.

It seemed logical to him that Susanna Appleton would fix on this as their meeting place. He had seen her during the confusion of the earl's arrival and knew she'd spotted him, but there had been no opportunity to get close to her. At dusk, he left Toby behind and went forth alone. He'd waited close to an hour before he caught sight of a solitary female form gliding past the first standing stone.

A brief moment of joy was followed by a stab of disappointment. All delight departed when he realized it was Jennet who'd come to meet him, not Susanna. The moon was nearly at the full, but the sky was overcast. Wet snowflakes had fallen earlier in the day. Still, he had enough light to see that Jennet was not happy.

"Where have you been?" she demanded as soon as she reached his side. "I looked for you days ago."

"Where is Susanna? Why is she not with you?"

They glared at each other. Stubborn woman. Would she refuse to answer his question until he'd responded to hers? Aye, she would. Rather than waste more time, he drew her into the shadow of the monument.

"I was all set to call myself James Leastways, gentleman of Lincolnshire, and claim to have lived for the last ten years in London. The gentry flocking to the rebel cause should have accepted me and my manservant without question, but the first person I encountered in the rebel camp was Dr. Grant of York. I had the misfortune to meet him when I first arrived in that city, at the house of a fellow merchant. He knew me at once and, further, remembering that we had talked of remedies used in Muscovy and Persia, insisted upon keeping me with him. Thinking I would have a better opportunity to enter the inner circle of the earls and their countesses in his company, I agreed, but when the two earls separated their troops, Dr. Grant accompanied Westmorland. I had no choice but to go with him."

Jennet looked as if she did not believe a word of it. Nick's jaw tightened. If Susanna needed explanations and apologies, he'd make them to her. "Where is she, Jennet?"

"With the countess. It is her turn to attend Lady Northumberland."

"No one suspects she is not Lady Pendennis?"

A moment's hesitation told him Jennet was not as sure of that as she'd like to be. "It appears not, in spite of what happened here this morning." She gave the surrounding area a look of extreme distaste. "Someone shot at her with an arrow. Came near to hitting her, too."

"An arrow?" Incredulous, he gaped at her.

"Shot from behind this very stone. We stood there." She pointed to the next field.

"Did you see the archer?"

"Only a glimpse. A figure in a cloak. It could have been a man or a woman." She gave a short, ironic bark of laughter. "All the gentlewomen practice with arrows."

"Dragon water." In growing alarm, Nick listened to Jennet summarize two earlier incidents.

"I do not believe either was an accident," she said when she'd finished her account, "but Lady Appleton is not convinced."

Nick swore creatively in three languages. "We must get her out of here."

"She'll not leave, not until she has proof the queen of Scots has been hand in glove with the countess of Westmorland from the beginning."

"What proof?"

"A letter in Lady Westmorland's possession. She also feels responsible for Lady Northumberland's care. The countess has been ailing."

"Perhaps she will welcome Dr. Grant's help," Nick mused.

He took heart from one part of Jennet's report. The inspiration for many, early on, had been the countess of Northumberland. She'd ridden up and down the ranks, encouraging the soldiers. The countess of Westmorland's exhortations, on the other hand, had begun to grate on her followers. Many had become disaffected in recent days. Nick had done his best to add to the discontent, even starting a rumor about an outbreak of the sweating sickness among Northumberland's men.

"Lady Appleton wants to know if it could have been the earl of Westmorland's seal on the second order sent to Master Dartnall."

"No." Nick had a clear memory of Dartnall in his cups, muttering *Thumberland's seal.* But Jennet's question provoked others. How long had passed between the first order bearing Northumberland's seal and the second? *Had* the letters been in code? In the same handwriting? He'd never thought to ask any of those things.

"Lady Westmorland blamed Lady Appleton, that is to say, Lady Pendennis, for her brother's arrest. If it is possible Sir Walter had time to send word to England of the plot, causing the duke of Norfolk's arrest, then Lady Westmorland might have heard of it in time to order Dartnall to kill Lady Pendennis for betraying them."

Nick felt his brow furrow in concentration as he searched his memory. He was good at recalling numbers, and dates were numbers. "Dartnall told me he left Augsburg a week after Lady Pendennis's accident. That must mean she was killed around the middle of September. All English ports were temporarily closed on the twenty-second and the militia put on alert, although I do not believe the duke was detained until the end of the month. The uprising, from what I have heard, was originally to begin on October sixth, but on the first Norfolk ordered Westmorland to call off their plans."

"So, Lady Westmorland could not be the culprit. Lady Pendennis was already dead by the time the duke was arrested. The countess could scarce have given the order afterward to have Lady Pendennis killed." Jennet sounded discouraged.

Nick did not blame her. Eliminating one suspect did not move them ahead. There were too many remaining.

"Do you think Sir Walter could have killed his wife?"

Nick stared at her, unable to believe he'd heard correctly.

Seeing him so taken aback, Jennet brightened. "If Lady Pendennis meant to do what Sir Walter asked Lady Appleton to pretend to do, act as a courier for the rebels, it is possible he found out about it and stopped her himself, then made up the story he told Lady Appleton."

Betray her country? Her husband? Yes, that might have provoked a man like Pendennis to murder. And if he had killed his wife, then it also made sense that he'd be certain Susanna would be safe with the rebels, as long as she was not revealed as an imposter. The more Nick thought about it, the more appealing he found the idea of his rival as cold-blooded killer. He had no doubt that Pendennis was fully capable of sending Dartnall a false, coded message, ordering him to do the deed and putting the blame on Northumberland.

"You think it possible, too." Jennet's sharp eyes had tracked his every emotion.

"It is possible," he agreed, "but if no one among the rebels ordered Lady Pendennis's death, why does someone keep trying to kill Susanna?" If Jennet's account was accurate, Susanna had come close to death three times since joining the countess's household. Much as Nick might like to blacken Pendennis's name, he could not blame those attempts on him. "The idea of two separate killers at work, both bent on killing the woman who calls herself Eleanor Pendennis, stretches the bounds of credulity."

"Sir Walter is no fool, and he knows Lady Appleton well. If he suspects she's guessed what he's done, if he *did* do it, then he knows she will not rest until she has brought him to justice for his crime."

Long after he and Jennet parted company, Nick was haunted by her words. If Jennet had the right of it, Susanna's good friend Sir Walter Pendennis could also be her most dangerous enemy.

31

KESWICK—NOVEMBER 22, 1569

"There." Fulke pointed down into a valley nestled between the hills, his lugubrious expression giving way, for an instant, to a flicker of relief.

Catherine followed the direction of his finger. The sight would have been a joy to behold in another season, but now everything seemed passing damp and dreary. Still, it was good to have arrived at last. She had sent Fulke ahead while she and Lionel tarried in Penrith, acquiring the clothing Sir Walter insisted she have. A great waste of time, Catherine suspected, but Sir Walter had more experience than she in this business of ferreting out information. She had decided she'd best follow his instructions. For the nonce.

From Penrith she'd also dispatched a messenger, paying him the exorbitant fee of four pounds to take her letter to her husband in London and return with Gilbert's reply.

In high summer, carriers regularly plied the road from Barnard Castle to the copper mines at Keswick. Even with the delay, Catherine had arrived within a week of leaving Sir Walter. "I am told Keswick was naught but a small, impoverished market town before the German miners came," she remarked to Fulke as they began their descent to the village.

He nodded. "I had not time to learn much, madam, except that here German is spoken as often as English. Everyone's livelihood depends upon Haug and Company."

Fulke Rowley was a good listener. That was his value. He talked more to her, Catherine knew, than to any other person on earth. When she'd been a girl, he'd been a groom of the stable at Leigh Abbey. He had taught her most of what she knew about horses.

"Did you hear any talk of the uprising?"

"Folk here are more concerned about renegade Scots than rebel earls."

The following day, Catherine put on her best noblewoman airs and paid a visit to Haug and Company. She presented herself as an English-born Scot with money to invest and dropped the earl of Northumberland's name.

Once she'd convinced the company's representative, Master Loner, that she was a vapid, uneducated Englishwoman with more money than she needed and too much time on her hands, he willingly displayed entries in various journals and account books. Anxious to make a good impression, he assumed she would not understand what she saw. He was right. Most of the records were written in a beautiful, legible hand . . . in German. Fortunately numbers did not need translation, and proper names were easy to pick out.

Catherine found little of interest on the double-page sheets marked RECHNUNG WEYHENNACHTEN, the Christmas term's reckoning to date. Likewise, much of a summary of the previous months dealt with supplies purchased and ore mined. Loner called her attention to expenses for the building of a men's bath above the smelthouse and the purchase of a watchdog, collar, and chain.

Dealings with a number of prominent Englishmen and women had also been recorded. There were rents paid to a Lady Radcliffe—kin to the earl of Sussex? she wondered. There were notations concerning Cuthbert

Musgrave, last year's sheriff, and Simon Musgrave, who had just taken over the post. She also saw that, since the beginning of the year, the earl of Northumberland had been paid for 1,200 seam of charcoal. The purchase appeared to be legitimate, even though only 444 seam had so far been delivered. Another entry revealed that Northumberland's forester had felled 360 oaks in the Vorwold and a number of birches in the Bradelaw to fulfill part of the bargain.

This was not sufficient income to fund an uprising. If it had been Dartnall's plan to funnel money to the earl through the copper mines, he'd apparently failed to put the scheme into effect. Or else he had devised some means to hide the transaction. A list of travel expenses on a separate page caught Catherine's eye. The dates were very recent, and the stops for the night followed a route from London to Keswick—St. Albans, Northampton, Derby, Buxton, Haslingden, Lancaster, Furness Abbey.

"A messenger?" she asked.

"Our messengers travel faster than that," Loner protested. Then he flushed, realizing he'd revealed more than he'd intended.

Catherine smiled and delayed asking the question she most wanted answered. "Do you use more than one regular courier?"

"We use two men, John Grave and Robin Fletcher."

"English?"

He nodded.

"Haug and Company is most forward-looking to employ native Englishmen. My dear friend the earl speaks of another, a Master Dartnall, most warmly."

"Master Dartnall was here in Keswick not long ago." Apparently deciding Catherine was harmless, Loner chuckled and flipped over the page she'd been looking at. "See. Here is the proof of it." Entered in a concise and readable hand were entries for the first part of his journey, indicating it had cost him two pounds one and six for his passage from Antwerp to Calais and as much again to reach Dover. Then he'd had to pay customs sixteen shillings and another sixteen had gone to rent a horse for the trip from Dover to Gravesend, where he'd boarded a tilt boat for the rest of the journey into London.

"Where is Master Dartnall now?" she asked. "I would like to talk to him before I make the final decision about investing in Haug and Company's mines."

"I do not have a precise itinerary, but his intent was to visit investors here in the North."

"He chose a poor time if he meant to go into Yorkshire." Her heart beat faster as her concern for Susanna increased. Walter had assured her his men would catch Dartnall before he could get near the rebels, but Walter was not infallible and neither were his agents.

"He went to Westmorland."

Catherine graced the German with her most charming smile. "Do you, perhaps, recall a name?"

"Cholmeley! Sir Roger Cholmeley! But there were others he meant to visit, too, and I do not know when he will be back, nor what route he followed. It would be futile to go after him."

"Perhaps Master Dartnall will return before I must leave Keswick," Catherine suggested. Would Walter want her to wait for him or go on to Gillingham Place? "I wonder," she mused aloud, "if you know whether Master Dartnall meant to visit a Lady Gillingham?"

Loner beamed. "He intends to go there after his trip to Westmorland, Lady Glenelg. I remember now. But he will come here again first."

With no more ado, Catherine made her decision. She would remain in Keswick until Lucius Dartnall returned. What she did after that would depend upon him.

32

Lady Northumberland's desire to keep one of her gentlewomen safe cost Susanna much of her freedom. For four days after the incident at Boroughbridge, she insisted Susanna ride at her side and sleep in her chamber, reasoning that no one would make another attempt when she was close at hand. Lady Northumberland did not, however, make any effort to discover who had shot that arrow and soon she was distracted by her own troubles. The rebels were plagued by delays, desertions, and disappointments. The support they'd expected from abroad had not materialized at Hartlepool.

Susanna's plans to search Lady Westmorland's possessions were likewise thwarted. Equally frustrating was her inability to speak privately with Nick even though she saw him every day. Nick and his friend the doctor were welcomed by Lady Northumberland, who still suffered from periodic headaches, but Susanna had no chance to talk to him about anything other than herbs and cures.

By the time they entered Tadcaster, the rebel army had begun to shrink. When Susanna looked back, she still saw men streaming out behind them like the tail of a comet, but where once eighty gentlemen of substance had ridden there, commanding at the least seven thousand soldiers, twelve hundred of them mounted, now there were no more than a few hundred followers.

First the earl of Sussex had promised a free pardon to everyone who returned to his home and stayed there. Then rumors had spread that twelve thousand of the queen's men were on their way north. Word that Alnwick, Warkworth, and Newcastle had fallen to those loyal to Elizabeth had further sapped morale.

The rebels' last hope of success faded when an advance troop, which had crossed the Ouse and gone as far as Selby, brought word back to Tadcaster that Queen Mary's jailers had removed her to a more secure prison farther south.

Early the next morning, Susanna and Jennet hurried through the predawn darkness toward the meeting she'd at last been able to arrange with Nick. Overnight, the weather had deteriorated. During the march south they had been blessed, for the most part, by bright sun and clear, moonlit nights. Now a damp chill penetrated her cloak and shards of snow stung her face.

Just as they passed the stable, Margaret Heron emerged from its shadowed interior. She was leading a horse and all her possessions were bundled up behind the saddle. She exchanged a startled look with Susanna but did not speak. They both continued on.

Tadcaster's bridge was a fine one, with eight stone arches. Nick and Toby sheltered beneath it holding four horses. Susanna checked as she recognized Turmeric. "Do you mean to abduct me?" she asked.

"I *have* missed you, *mitgeselle.*"

"And I have missed you, Nick. But I cannot go with you. Not now."

"The rebellion is collapsing. Come away with me. Let me keep you safe."

"I still have reason to stay." Although Lady Westmorland's behavior had been increasingly erratic and volatile, Susanna did not think she'd destroyed any letters. Not yet. She reached out with gloved fingers to touch the side of Nick's face. "My honor demands I see this through, both Walter's assignment and the matter of murder."

For a moment, Nick looked as if he might clout her on the chin and carry her off unconscious. He kissed her instead. "How can I help?"

"Go to Walter. Take word that he must go at once to Wressel, southeast of York. Northumberland's daughters are there. The rebels will march north, but they mean to make that one detour first. They'll be vulnerable there."

A part of her writhed at betraying the countess. Lady Northumberland had, after her own fashion, been good to Susanna. But the only alternative was to let traitors escape. If the earls were not stopped, they would regroup abroad to plot more treason. There would be no peace in England until they had been captured and imprisoned, and their wives with them.

"Go, Nick," she whispered. In spite of the swirling snow, the day grew brighter with every passing moment. "I will be safe enough here. I have Jennet." She managed a brave smile.

He did not accept her decision without argument, but in the end she prevailed. "I have other information the queen's men should have," he admitted. "And if I leave now, I can return the sooner."

He turned over Turmeric's reins and mounted his own horse. For a moment, Susanna was reminded of all the old stories she'd heard in which the fair lady offered her departing knight a stirrup cup. She shook her head to dispel the image.

"It is best this way," she murmured as the two men rode across the bridge. "I could not live with myself if he were taken for a rebel and killed."

Jennet snorted. "'Twould have been *best* to go with him, but there's naught to be done about it now."

They took Turmeric and the horse Nick had brought for Jennet back to the stable, then returned to Lady Northumberland's chamber. They found her engaged in a bitter quarrel with the countess of Westmorland.

"I have four children of my own," Lady Westmorland declared, "but I'd not forfeit our last chance of success just to fetch them. Your daughters are safe enough where they are. Send for them anon."

"I'll not risk their safety, not now when all turn against us. If the duke of Alba failed us, how can we count on anyone?"

"You should have thought of them sooner! We've no time for sentiment now. The weather grows worse with every hour we delay." Outside the inn, the wind screamed like a woman in childbed.

Jennet, who with Bess Kelke had been told to disassemble Lady Northumberland's traveling bed, caught Susanna's eye. This disagreement between the two countesses boded ill for her plan that Walter capture the rebel leaders at Wressel.

"It is not far out of our way," Lady Northumberland protested.

"We must go direct to Topcliffe, where you still have tenants loyal to you, and then to Brancepeth to gather our followers." Lady Westmorland's face was flushed, her eyes overbright. "Meanwhile, the men who were to have met the duke at Hartlepool will strike at the queen's man in the North."

Lady Northumberland spoke in the choked voice of one fighting tears. "Oh, yes. I have heard what they intend. Petty vengeance of their own against Sir George Bowes. How does that help us?"

Susanna barely contained a sound of alarm.

"Would you put your daughters above your husband?"

Lady Westmorland demanded, ignoring the countess of Northumberland's question. "You risk his freedom to dally near York. Keep him safe and you can always have more children. After all, those you are so concerned about are only girls."

Yet more vileness, Susanna thought. How could any woman, any mother, say such a thing? She thought of Rosamond and, when Lady Northumberland began to sob, was close to tears herself.

Nothing less than her fear of losing the earl could have swayed the countess of Northumberland, but she could not bear the thought of leading her husband into mortal danger, especially when she'd been the one to urge him to rebel in the first place. In the end, she agreed to do as Lady Westmorland wished, and the victorious countess swept out of the chamber.

"Well-bruised rue steeped in vinegar," Susanna muttered. She set about making a poultice with which to anoint her mistress's temples. Applied twice a day, it could relieve most headaches. She was about to fetch a red silk bag filled with crushed lavender flowers, bay, betony, red rose petals, marjoram, clove pinks, and nutmeg blossoms, soothing scents even if they did not do much to ease pain, when Cecily Carnaby burst into the chamber. She stopped short when she caught sight of Susanna and her face lost every bit of color the wild weather had given it.

"You are here! Then who . . . ?"

"What ails you, Cecily?" Joan Lascelles demanded.

"They've found a body. A woman. I thought . . ."

The need to take charge snapped Lady Northumberland out of the misery into which she had sunk. She issued a series of terse orders and within a quarter of an hour had the answers she sought.

The dead woman was Margaret Heron. She'd broken her neck in a fall from her horse while attempting to desert the rebel cause.

"A tragic accident," Guy Carnaby declared.

Jennet and Susanna exchanged a look.

Another accident, Susanna wondered, or another murder?

33

"During the time you wasted in York," Pendennis said in a cold, uninflected voice, "the rebel force dwindled to the earls, their countesses, a few of their women, Susanna among them, and about forty other followers."

Nick said nothing. He knew now that it had been a mistake to go to the earl of Sussex, but his distrust of Pendennis went deep. He'd thought to save time, York being so much closer to Wressel than Barnard Castle.

Instead, he'd been delayed by bad weather and detained by a suspicious lord president of the council in the North, whose inability to make a decision had not stopped him from locking Nick up while he considered the information he'd brought. Finally, Sussex had decided to dispatch Nick here. In the interim, all chance to intercept the earls had been lost.

"Well?" Pendennis demanded.

"If you know so much, why did you fail to stop their retreat?"

Only the presence of Sir George Bowes kept the two men from going for each other's throats. "I do not see what difference it makes," Bowes complained. "They will be captured. It is only a matter of time. I'll wager they will end up at Brancepeth. We will lay siege to the castle."

"Even the earls are not such fools as to let themselves be trapped there," Pendennis snapped.

Nick was forced to agree with him. "They know their lives are at stake. They will continue northward and seek sanctuary in Scotland. I heard talk while I was with the rebel troops that Northumberland is owed a favor by a Scot named Hector Armstrong."

"You heard they meant to to go to Wressel, too, and they did not."

Susanna had been wrong. The earl of Northumberland had abandoned his own children.

"Northumberland's tenants care only about saving their own skins," Pendennis added. "They ignored his efforts to rally them. I doubt Westmorland will have any better luck."

"What else did you observe while you were with the enemy?" Bowes asked.

Nick answered, then detailed his dealings with the earl of Sussex. "You have the right of it, Pendennis." Although Nick begrudged the admission, he could no longer withhold it. "I should have ridden here as soon as I learned where you were, or at the least sent my man, but I believed I could persuade Sussex to act."

"Hah!" Bowes exclaimed.

Pendennis's smile was derisive.

"There is another matter I would discuss with you," Nick added. "Privily, I think."

The smile became even more unpleasant. "Leave us, Sir George, if you will."

Bowes looked as if he wanted to protest, but something in Pendennis's expression warned him off. As soon as they were alone, Nick provided a second summary, this time including everything he knew about the attempts to kill Lady Pendennis.

"Three attempts to kill Susanna?" Pendennis did not show his emotions, but they might run all the deeper for being constrained. Nick was certain he heard a thread of concern in the other man's voice.

"The first two might have been accidents, but that arrow was deliberate."

"A warning, mayhap, rather than a true threat? You did say even the women are expert archers. If one of them wanted to kill Susanna, she would be dead."

"Warn her of what? Either they suspect she is not who she says she is, or they have some reason not to trust your wife. Either way, it cannot be wise to let Susanna remain with the rebels."

"Is any place safe now?"

Pendennis's attitude annoyed Nick. Obtaining an incriminating letter from Mary of Scotland to Lady Westmorland apparently mattered more to him than Susanna's life. "There seems to be some confusion about your wife's recruitment to the rebel cause." In spite of his growing irritation with Pendennis, Nick chose his words with care. "You told Susanna that Lady Pendennis was approached by Dartnall. The rebels appear to believe she contacted him."

"My wife was no traitor, Baldwin." The voice was still uninflected, but Pendennis's eyes burned with such hatred that Nick took an involuntary step backward.

A sudden conviction made mincemeat of all Nick's previous speculations. If Pendennis had been given proof of his wife's betrayal, he would have strangled her with his bare hands. Devious as he might be when it came to planting spies and untangling conspiracies, he'd never have arranged a clumsy accident at second hand, an accident that might as easily have left his wife crippled as dead.

"What your wife did or did not do," Nick said, "is of no interest to me. All my concern is for Susanna. If the numbers with the earls are as depleted as you say, then let us take a troop of men from here and ride after them.

Let us end this now. Seize any letters for yourself, before Lady Westmorland decides to destroy them."

To Nick's surprise, Pendennis nodded. "Yes. I believe you may be right. We will leave first thing in the morning." Although Nick chafed at further delay, the advantages of waiting for dawn seemed obvious. It was already late afternoon. Tomorrow they would be able to set out with well-rested men and horses, and with fresh intelligence concerning the whereabouts of the earls.

He woke early, ready to ride, only to be faced with an unforeseen setback. Pendennis's spies had failed him. Under cover of night and inclement weather, a large band of rebels, motivated as much by their extreme hatred of Sir George Bowes as by any real hope their uprising could now succeed in overthrowing the queen, had laid siege to Barnard Castle. All those within, including Pendennis and Nick, were trapped for the duration.

34

Lucius Dartnall returned to Keswick on the last day of November. In his absence, although she'd chafed at the delay, Catherine had not been idle. She'd learned everything there was to know about Northumberland's connection to Haug and Company. She had also managed to question Robin Fletcher and John Grave without, she hoped, arousing any suspicions as to her motives. Both messengers had made journeys from Topcliffe to Augsburg at the beginning of September.

The timing struck Catherine as peculiar. Fletcher had left within a day of Grave, although the second message had not been delivered until more than a week after the first, due to the vagaries of travel. The second message must have been of vital importance to warrant sending a special courier, and yet Fletcher insisted that no fuss had been made over its dispatch. Indeed, it had not even been given to him by the earl's secretary, as was usually the case. That letter, and a generous bonus for leaving at once, had been delivered to him by one of Topcliffe's many pages.

"Did the lad say he was sent by the earl?" Catherine had asked.

"He did not say otherwise," had been Fletcher's reply.

Master Dartnall, she now discovered, gave the same sort of answers. The present, unsatisfying inquisition had ensued when he arrived at the inn where she was staying, the

Red Lion, to make the same case for investment in the mines that he'd carried to the county of Westmorland. Catherine longed to ask him what other business he'd had with Sir Roger Cholmeley, but she bit back the words and pretended to be fascinated by his discussion of ore production and the need for more charcoal burners.

"I am most intrigued by what you say," she assured him when he paused for breath, "but I have been in Keswick too long already. I am told you mean to travel in the direction of Penrith, where I am bound. Might we not journey together, that I may hear more of this?"

He fell in with her suggestion at once.

Two days later, her discussions with Dartnall en route having been most illuminating, they arrived together at Gillingham Place. Catherine had contrived to reach there just at dusk, when country custom demanded she be invited to spend the night. She hoped, through simple conversation, to solicit additional useful information. Since Dartnall had so recently paid a visit to Lady Gillingham's uncle, it seemed likely he'd speak of it. She'd not counted on their hostess's aversion to any mention of Roger Cholmeley.

"We are estranged," Eleanor's mother informed Dartnall, "and I have no desire to mend fences."

Lady Gillingham was an older, more brittle version of her daughter. Although she offered the travelers food and lodging, she was frugal with information. She admitted that her husband was not at home, but said no more about him.

Catherine abandoned subtle probing. "Does he ride with the rebels?"

"That is no business of yours, madam."

Dartnall winced at Lady Gillingham's sharp tone. Catherine sipped from a plain glass beaker containing beer spiced with cinnamon, resin, gentian, and juniper. "I ask only because I know your daughter is now in Lady

Northumberland's service." She felt a twinge of conscience that she could not tell Lady Gillingham the truth, that Eleanor was dead, but the older woman's attitude soon relieved her of any sense of guilt.

"We will not speak of her, either."

How much, Catherine wondered, did Lady Gillingham know of recent events? She bided her time, waiting only until Dartnall left them to pursue the subject.

"A few weeks ago," she said, "Sir Walter Pendennis returned to England with his wife. May I ask, madam, when you last heard from her? You do *know* Eleanor wed Sir Walter, I presume?"

Lip curled in disdain, Eleanor's mother spat out her answer. "I know, but I have neither seen nor heard from that ungrateful harpy since I arranged for her to go and live with Lady Quarles."

Catherine's brows lifted at the bitterness that laced her words. She considered her own brief acquaintance with Eleanor. What she could recall of the woman did not generate any fond memories, and she'd thought at the time that Susanna was too trusting where Eleanor was concerned. Walter, in a manner quite out of character for him, had been blinded by love. "Is it Sir Roger Cholmeley who keeps you informed?" she inquired. "Did he also tell you she has a child?"

The news that she was a grandmother did nothing to warm Lady Gillingham's manner. Catherine wondered if Eleanor would have become as cold and aloof as her mother if she'd lived. She had a feeling the answer was yes, in which case Walter had been fortunate in his escape.

"This child is nearly seven years old," Catherine said. Lady Gillingham's thin lips pursed in disapproval. "Her father was my half brother, so you will understand that I have some interest in her welfare. That is connected to the uprising in Yorkshire, for Eleanor is with the rebels. So, I understand, is her cousin, Marion Standbridge"

"You know more than I do, madam."

Not enough, Catherine thought, and set out to be even more provoking. "Why do you suppose Eleanor would write to her uncle and not to you?"

Lady Gillingham's sardonic expression gave Catherine chills. "I have no money. Uncle Roger's fortune is pledged to the female relative who makes the best marriage." Lady Gillingham looked as if she'd bitten down on a sour grape. "He disinherited me long ago. He did not approve of either of my husbands, or of certain other misadventures he learned of some years back. He will not change his mind. He never does."

"So Eleanor is his heir?"

A wicked gleam came into Lady Gillingham's eyes. "Only as long as she can conceal the existence of her bastard child."

"Your grandchild," Catherine reminded her.

Lady Gillingham paid her no mind. "He'll disown her when he knows. Serve her right. An eye for an eye. She played telltale tit on me. Now 'tis my turn." She strode purposefully toward the door and bellowed for a servant to bring pen and ink and paper.

Stunned, Catherine gaped at her. "You mean to write to Sir Roger to tell him about Rosamond, hoping he'll disown Eleanor because of the child? But why? If I understood you correctly, Mistress Standbridge is the only one who can benefit from such a betrayal. You will not profit."

"No matter. My daughter set Uncle Roger against me. I do but return the favor."

Repulsed, Catherine left Lady Gillingham to her revenge. And what sort of man was Sir Roger, she wondered, to be so unforgiving? When she left here on the morrow, she decided, she would attempt to learn more about him from Dartnall . . . both before and after she informed the fellow he was her prisoner.

Her plan was simple. With Fulke and Lionel to guard him, she meant to take Dartnall to Walter, thus ensuring that Dartnall could not cause any problems for Susanna. And during their journey back to Barnard Castle, she would do her best to discover what role Sir Roger Cholmeley had played in the events leading up to Eleanor's death.

35

The second time the countess of Westmorland ordered Marion Standbridge to bring Lady Pendennis to her study at Brancepeth for a private interview, Susanna thought herself prepared for whatever the volatile noblewoman might say to her.

She was not.

"Your husband is the queen's man," Lady Westmorland declared. "You will go to him now and take us with you."

The expression of shock and dismay on Marion's face gave ample proof that Eleanor's cousin had not expected this, either. Instead of leaving them, she remained in the room. Lady Westmorland did not appear to notice.

"Madam," Susanna said, "I am the last person Sir Walter will be inclined to help. It will do you no good to use me to get to him."

"You underestimate yourself Lady Pendennis. Use your womanly wiles and he'll be glad enough to take you back. He has influence. He will convince the queen I had no part in this foolish rebellion."

Susanna felt her mouth drop open.

Lady Westmorland lowered her voice to a confiding tone. "He is an intelligence gatherer. A vile schemer who sends men throughout England, and other places, too, in order to find out what the queen's enemies do plot.

Such a man has the power to keep me out of prison. We will leave here at dusk. Is he in York or in London?"

Susanna thought quickly. She had no idea where Walter was. Moreover, she had no desire to travel through a winter's night in the company of a mad countess. There was only one place she could think of that would deter Lady Westmorland. For all she knew, she might even be speaking the truth. "He is at Barnard Castle."

"Devil take it!"

"The siege continues, then?"

"Aye. Sir George Bowes has made many enemies hereabout. One faction will fight against him long after they've ceased to support our cause."

"Then we must remain at Brancepeth." It was Susanna's fervent hope that the queen's men would soon arrive at the castle gates.

"No one stays here, and my lord means to go to Scotland. Scotland! Barbarous place!" She lowered her voice. "They have reason to hate me there."

The countess's comments, a mixture of the astute and the irrational, left Susanna in a state of confusion. Her gaze strayed to the ornate casket she'd noticed before. Did it once again hold letters? Was one of them from the queen of Scots? Her fingers itched to reach out and discover those answers for herself.

"My ancestors, the dukes of Norfolk, have led many a campaign against Scotland." Lady Westmorland glanced over her shoulder as if she feared being overheard. "I have here in this room a book the first duke took with him on campaign. Eighty years ago, that was." She rambled on about her family, alternately deriding the Scots and cursing her husband for a fool. "I am determined to throw myself on the queen's mercy," she declared. "My high rank will protect me. I will go to court. I will plead my case. Elizabeth will see reason."

Queen Elizabeth, Susanna thought, would at the least

throw Lady Westmorland into the Tower of London to keep her brother company. Treason was not, could not be, taken lightly. The only leniency someone of Lady Westmorland's rank and sex could expect was a clean death by the headsman's ax rather than the horror of being hanged, drawn, and quartered.

While Marion attempted to calm her mistress with words, Susanna searched the chamber for something more effective. She found it in a small, wooden box— poppy syrup, used to cure insomnia—and poured a generous dose into a cup of wine. She gave it to Marion to press upon the countess, and when they were both distracted, Susanna picked up the casket and left the study.

Since their return to Brancepeth, Jennet had slept on a truckle bed in the chamber Susanna shared with Joan Lascelles and Cecily Carnaby. She was there when Susanna returned, and for once they had the room to themselves.

Jennet gasped when she noticed the casket. "The letters?"

"Let us see." Susanna drew out one piece of parchment, unfolded it, and studied what was written there. She did not know whether to be elated or downcast. "A cipher."

No one put communications in code unless they had something to hide. But how, she wondered, could anyone prove a letter had come from Mary of Scotland? There were five missives. None bore any seal and none was signed. Each consisted of rows of uppercase letters. The top line of one read: YASISSREINFRTH.

"Walter will have to decipher these," Susanna decided.

Holding a page this way and that, Jennet squinted at the columns. "There must be some way to read them."

With a sigh, Susanna took the paper back. "You know how complex the codes Robert used were. They required a key to interpret."

"Are there no simple ciphers?"

"Some secret messages are disguised as ordinary lists. Common words are assigned other meanings. The correspondents use code names. In other cases, the message becomes clear by reading every third letter, or every eighth. You get the idea. But this . . ." She stared at the page in frustration.

Y	A	S	I	S	S	R	E	I	N	F	R	T	H
T	N	S	W	E	T	E	T	L	H	N	O	H	J
S	D	E	A	N	O	H	I	U	E	E	M	G	U
U	W	T	I	I	E	E	C	F	R	E	W	I	L
R	E	N	T	L	X	H	T	T	I	U	I	E	Y
T	L	U	O	O	C	T	O	H	T	Q	N	R	R
T	L	O	N	H	O	E	C	G	A	R	G	O	E
H	B	C	L	S	M	T	L	I	N	U	F	N	G
G	E	D	Y	I	M	A	A	R	C	O	I	A	I
I	L	E	F	H	U	C	I	Y	E	Y	E	M	N
R	O	V	O	R	N	I	M	M	A	S	L	D	A

"Is Regina a name?" Jennet pointed to the bottom half of the last column.

"It means queen." The letters, which had seemed incomprehensible a moment before, abruptly shifted into focus. "I have been making this too difficult," Susanna murmured in amazement. "The message is meant to be read up one column and down the next."

Using one finger to follow them, she decoded a simple yet damning message. "Right trusty and well beloved countess. I wait only for His Holiness to excommunicate the heretic to claim my rightful inheritance as your queen. From Wingfield Manor, eighth July. Regina."

The other messages were similar. Thoughtfully, Susanna returned them to their casket and placed it in the bottom of the chest in which she stored her belongings. She could not bear to look at them, for they were more than mere messages. They were the death warrants for two countesses and a queen.

"We can do nothing more about this until late tonight."

"Then we will leave here?"

"We will try." First she had supper to get through, and she was expected to attend Lady Northumberland.

Susanna laid her plans with care. A judicious combination of bribery and sleeping draughts seemed best. She would not have to drug Joan, who would not wake if there was an explosion, and it was Cecily's turn to spend the night at the countess's beck and call. That would keep her out of the way. But if Margaret Heron had been murdered and her killer was watching them, they would need to use extreme caution. That person, Susanna believed, was Guy Carnaby, although Jennet continued to suspect Cecily was behind all the accidents. Jennet was certain Cecily's poor eyesight had led her to mistake Margaret for Susanna.

During the journey to Brancepeth, Susanna had reviewed all she knew about the attempts on Eleanor's life and realized that only three people had easy access to the earl of Northumberland's seal, the earl, the countess, and the earl's secretary. Guy Carnaby enjoyed the trust of the other two. He must have known of the plan to use Lady Pendennis as a courier. When Lady Northumberland wrote to Lucius Dartnall, Carnaby had been in an ideal position to send the second order to Augsburg, the instructions to arrange an accident for Eleanor, revenge for Walter's involvement in the death of Ranulf Carnaby. Guy Carnaby had also been on the scene of every accident Susanna had suffered since her arrival in Yorkshire.

Unfortunately, Susanna had not a shred of evidence against him and was unlikely to discover any at this late date. Short of catching him in the act of yet another attempt on her life, she'd never prove he'd arranged

Eleanor's death or murdered Margaret Heron by mistake. She hated the thought of letting a killer go free, but she consoled herself with the certainty that Guy Carnaby would be among those caught and executed for treason. It was time to cut her losses and escape, getting both herself and Jennet to safety before the queen's army laid siege to Brancepeth.

No one remarked upon Lady Westmorland's absence from supper in the great hall. Even her husband seemed relieved not to have to deal with her erratic behavior. After the meal, Susanna accompanied Lady Northumberland back to her chamber, where Cecily and Joan joined them a few minutes later. Jennet slipped into the room soon after, her gaze darting first to Susanna and then, once she'd reassured herself that her mistress was safe, to Cecily, whereupon her eyes narrowed with suspicion and she began to gnaw on her lower lip.

Dear, predictable Jennet, Susanna thought, and allowed herself for the first time in weeks, to focus on going home to Leigh Abbey. A lovely daydream was well advanced when Marion burst into the chamber.

"She's gone! Lady Westmorland is gone!"

"When?" Susanna demanded.

"An hour or more past. She was asleep. I thought it safe to leave her."

"Where has she gone?" Lady Northumberland asked.

"I do not know." Marion sent a quick, warning look in Susanna's direction. "She took a chamberer and two henchmen but she left these behind." From the concealment of her voluminous skirt she withdrew a handful of letters, offering them up as she threw herself to her knees before the countess. "Let me stay with you, Lady Northumberland. We will not be in exile long. We will gather allies. Return. Triumph. Restore life in the North to the way it was before King Henry's heresy."

Susanna stared at the five coded messages with a sink-

ing heart. Marion must have seen her take the casket
from Lady Westmorland's study. It appeared she had un-
derestimated Eleanor's cousin and put far too much
faith in her own cleverness. She wondered what else
she'd been wrong about.

36

"Master Baldwin?" Toby sounded hesitant.

Nick stood on the ramparts, studying the ragged army outside Barnard Castle's triple walls. The fortress stood high above the River Tees, guarding a three-arched bridge that crossed from Durham to Yorkshire. The rebels held the bridge. They had no siege equipment, but that had not prevented them from imprisoning the entire garrison—nearly eight hundred men—for two long weeks. They waited to attack only until the food inside ran out, which it would do before much longer. Barnard Castle had been poorly victualed to begin with.

"What is it, Toby?"

"Some of the men have deserted."

That got Nick's full attention. There had been mutinous rumbles for days, even talk of surrendering Sir George Bowes to the enemy, since he was the one whose policies had provoked the wrath of these armed malcontents. "How?"

"The only way—over the wall. The first man landed safely. The second broke his leg."

It would require a leap of faith as well as of body in order to get away, Nick realized. The rebels, in spite of their stand here, were losing the war. They had no reason to be merciful to men who'd fought on the other side.

As the day progressed, more men tried to escape. For every five or six who managed to land unscathed, one was severely injured. Sir George kept a tally of broken legs and necks and announced that any fool who wanted to kill himself was welcome to join the ranks of the deserters. Nick considered the odds. The rebels seemed to welcome those who survived unscathed. If he jumped, he could be on his way to Susanna by nightfall.

She was in danger; he could feel it. And he'd become more certain with each passing day at Barnard Castle that it would be wise to put as much distance as possible between himself and Pendennis. Even Toby had noticed the calculating way the other man watched them, as if he itched for an opportunity to do harm.

Toby jumped first. Nick breathed a sigh of relief when the lad landed without harm. He'd just steeled himself to follow when he felt a hand press against his shoulder. In the next instant he was tumbling from the heights, arms flailing wildly. Nick had no control over his fall. He heard the snap of bone before he felt it, as he struck the castle wall during his descent. Then the ground rose up to meet him, knocking the wind out of his lungs and stunning him senseless. He lost consciousness for a moment, only to be revived by a wash of pain.

Toby's face swam into view. "Master Baldwin! Are you dead?"

"Not yet. Get me away from the castle." Nick spoke through gritted teeth. Even with Toby to support him, every movement was agony. Fire erupted from his ankle. His left arm hung limp as a spitted game fowl.

"I saw Sir Walter up there behind you, Master Baldwin," Toby said.

Nick's jaw was clenched too tightly to allow any reply. After what seemed like an eternity, Toby got them both behind the rebel lines. Safe, he thought. Free to do something to help Susanna, even if it was only to send

Toby to her. But his optimism came too soon. A familiar form made its way to his side to study his injuries.

"Well, well," said Dr. Grant. "Master Baldwin, who deserted our cause in the dead of night. And what, I wonder, were you doing inside Barnard Castle with our enemies?"

37

Catherine Glenelg's journey back to Barnard Castle took twice as long as she'd expected. Her party was brought to a halt for almost a week at Penrith by a fall of snow that made the roads impassable. By the time she got close to her destination and heard about the siege, it was already over. So, apparently, was the rebellion of the northern earls. They and their few remaining followers were reported to be fleeing toward Scotland. Even those few hotheads who'd wanted Sir George Bowes's blood had realized their cause was futile. The terms of Barnard Castle's surrender had granted his release. Together with some four hundred men still loyal to the queen, he'd marched out of the castle and set off for York unmolested. The victors, after looting their prize, had scattered.

"We will follow Sir Walter and Sir George," Catherine decided. She intended to turn her prisoner over to the proper authorities. Besides, she could not be certain Susanna was still with the rebels. There was no point in chasing after the earls if she did not need to.

In York, she found Walter at the King's Manor, preparing to set out again to track down the rebel leaders. "I have brought you a present," she announced. Fulke and Lionel followed her into the room, marching a sullen Lucius Dartnall between them.

Walter's reaction was most gratifying, a moment of

profound shock, but the exchange of information that followed left much to be desired. So did Walter's accusation that Dartnall was behind several recent attempts to kill Susanna.

As Catherine struggled to take in the fact that there had been more "accidents" to Eleanor after her arrival in England, Dartnall blinked at them in confusion. She had not told him Eleanor was dead, only that Sir Walter wanted to question him about the accident in Augsburg. Dartnall was not very clever, but even he had sense enough to stop talking when he was trussed up and forced to accompany her to Yorkshire.

"I went nowhere near Topcliffe," he protested, "nor Brancepeth nor Darlington nor Boroughbridge!"

Belatedly, Catherine found her speech. "He'd have known she wasn't Eleanor, and besides, he is not the kind of man who takes risks. That is why he let Nick Baldwin bring the second packet to England. Only after he arrived in Keswick did he see any advantage to raising more funds for the rebellion. That is why he went to visit Sir Roger Cholmeley."

"I went there for Haug and Company," Dartnall insisted.

Catherine almost felt sorry for the fellow. It had not taken her long to decide he was a poor judge of other people, a sad disadvantage in someone ambitious to make a fortune. He was the sort who did what he was told without stopping to question his orders. Even now, he was passing slow to understand what serious trouble he was in.

"Where is Susanna?" Catherine asked, once Walter had turned Dartnall over to some of the earl of Sussex's men.

"God only knows. The rebel leaders left Brancepeth before our troops could trap them. She's still in the countess's retinue."

"Scotland, then." Catherine heaved a deep sigh. She'd

hoped to avoid returning to Gilbert's homeland. "Very well. I leave this afternoon for Carlisle. Send a messenger after me if you discover Susanna has gone elsewhere. Otherwise, I will contact certain friends in Scotland."

"Once the rebels cross the border, they will not be easy to locate."

"It takes a reiver to find a reiver, and a Scot to deal with a Scot."

"You are as English as I am," Pendennis reminded her.

Catherine fought an urge to stick her tongue out at him. "Have faith in me, Walter," she said in deceptively mild tones. "This time I am the one with influential friends in the right places. I carry a passport signed by the regent of Scotland."

She'd received Gilbert's reply to her letter during her second sojourn in Penrith. His letter had contained two enclosures he thought she might find useful. Bless him. Gilbert, who had his own sources of information about the activities of the northern earls, believed in her ability to act on her own. And he'd understood why she'd abandoned him and their child in London to rush to Susanna's aid. Few husbands would have.

"I do not like this, Catherine," Walter said.

"And I do not like knowing that Susanna is still with the rebels. Why hasn't she left them, Walter? What holds her there, especially when someone has been trying to kill her?" She did not give him time to answer. "She's still trying to do something you asked of her. That's why she remains. She keeps her promises, no matter the risk."

"I have firsthand knowledge of Susanna's stubbornness," Walter said stiffly, "and it does not surprise me that both you and Jennet seek to emulate her, but there are times when I understand why Robert claimed to find Susanna so annoying."

"That is a dreadful thing to say!"

Walter was silent for a long moment, his expression as

enigmatic as ever. Then he shrugged. "Go if you must. It scarce matters now."

Fuming, Catherine left the King's Manor. She would collect Fulke and Lionel and leave York at once. A great many things were clear to her now. Walter had not sent her to Keswick to find Dartnall. He'd thought Dartnall was somewhere else and had packed her off into the Cumbrian Mountains to get her out of the way. He was allowing her to go to Carlisle for the same reason, giving her a pat on the head like a child and telling her to toddle off and play!

She was so angry that at first she did not recognize the third man waiting with her escort and the horses. When she did, she let out a cry of pleasure. "Toby! What news have you?"

"All bad," the lad said.

A short time later, Catherine sat in Nick Baldwin's chamber at the George. Nick lay on the bed, a wooden box around his left arm, which had been broken in two places. His right ankle was swathed in bandages and elevated.

"Why were you so desperate to escape?" she asked him.

"There seemed to be no end in sight for the siege. And I felt—I still feel—that Susanna is in danger."

"Yes. I sense it, too."

Baldwin scowled at his man. "I have tried to persuade Toby to go after her."

"You need me here." Toby's beardless chin jutted out. "He may try again."

"He does not even know I am here."

"He?" Catherine asked. "Pendennis?"

Baldwin looked startled by her perception but nodded. "Pendennis is unimportant. Susanna is the one I am concerned about."

"I saw him—"

"Enough, Toby."

"Saw what?" Catherine fixed Toby with a look that had made lesser men tremble. "Saw who?"

"I saw Sir Walter push Master Baldwin off the wall."

"You saw him at my side. You saw him touch my shoulder. You did not see him try to kill me."

"Dr. Grant thought he meant you harm, too," Toby grumbled, "and a good thing he did. The rebels could as easily have killed as treated you."

Nick shifted his implacable gaze to Catherine. "The rebels realized, soon after I landed in their midst, that their cause was hopeless. I was in no real danger from them. And now that you are here to protect me from Pendennis, Lady Glenelg, perhaps we can persuade Toby to go after Susanna. Her safety is what matters most."

"I will go after Susanna," she informed him. "I have a good idea where the rebels are bound and the safe conduct necessary to reach that place."

"The border?"

"Aye. Liddesdale, to be precise." No other place would serve, not now. Liddesdale was a no-man's land, the haunt of outlaws and masterless men.

Baldwin nodded. "I heard talk when I was with the rebels of ties to the Armstrongs. But, Lady Glenelg, what can you do when you get there?"

She patted the splinted arm as she rose to leave. "A good deal more than you."

38

The face of the man shouting curses at them from the ramparts of Naworth Castle was as twisted as his body. "Crookback Dacre," the countess of Northumberland muttered. "I thought he'd gone to London."

"It appears, madam," Marion said, "that he has returned. And from his refusal to grant us hospitality, I warrant he won himself a fat settlement from the Crown in his dispute with the duke of Norfolk."

Susanna watched and listened as the earls exchanged loud, heated words with their former ally. "A dangerous enemy," she murmured to Jennet. "We are only eight miles from Carlisle, an easy march for troops garrisoned there."

The earls had ridden as far into Northumberland as Hexham, then skirted the Pennines to reach Naworth, in the north part of Cumberland. All along the way, their numbers had continued to shrink. Even the countess's chamberers, Kelke and Lamplugh, had made off on foot when they got close to their homes. Sir John the priest had deserted, too.

Cecily's horse danced closer to Turmeric. Her vision continued to fail but she squinted toward Dacre, her face hard. "He was no help when Ranulf needed him. I am not surprised he refuses to help the earls."

Susanna stared at her. Dacre and Ranulf Carnaby? Something Walter had told her when they were still aboard the *Green Rose* came back to her. He'd had dealings with Dacre some years ago, he'd said. Dacre had provided intelligence to the queen but had not quibbled at betrayal.

If Ranulf Carnaby was the one he'd betrayed, and Cecily knew of it, did she also know of his connection to Walter? "I was told your husband was killed through the treachery of one of the queen's intelligence gatherers," Susanna blurted. "I thought it must have been my husband who betrayed him."

"Whether your husband was involved or not, Dacre was the one who sent Ranulf to his death." Susanna had to strain to hear as she added, "Guy told me so, and he would know."

If that was true, Susanna thought, then neither Cecily nor Guy had any reason to kill Eleanor Pendennis. If neither Guy nor Cecily blamed Walter for Ranulf's death, she no longer had any plausible suspects in the "accidents" that had plagued her since she arrived in Yorkshire. Did that mean they had been accidents, after all? Even the stray arrow? Even Margaret's death?

Did it mean *Walter* had been responsible for what happened to Eleanor?

Before Susanna could question Cecily further, the earl of Westmorland gave the signal to ride away from Naworth. Lady Northumberland slumped in her saddle, drawing the attention of all her waiting gentlewomen. She could not go on much longer without a place to rest and recover her strength. In truth, they were all in sad condition. Endless days in the saddle and endless nights of rough sleeping had taken a terrible toll.

They'd followed the old Roman roads thus far, but rain and snow had turned the stone surfaces slick and treacherous. Now they set out along a track that was narrow and muddy, led toward the border by the aptly named Black Ormiston. Their guide's full black beard and long hair surrounded as vile a countenance as Susanna had ever seen. He took them along narrow passages customarily used by raiding expeditions, trails unsuitable for the army the earls were certain was in pursuit.

Without warning, the Picts' Wall rose up before Susanna's eyes. She'd heard of this towering structure that ran across the north of England, but she'd never supposed that she would see it close at hand. A spurt of energy had her looking for the herbs she'd been told had been planted along its length back when the Romans occupied England. She glimpsed no trace of them as she urged Turmeric between two broken columns. It was winter, after all, and when she saw what lay on the north side of the great wall, her spirits drooped further. Miles of hard and lonely upland stretched out before them, its only signs of life a flock of carrion crows and a merlin just striking at a meadow pipit.

Onward they went at a bone-jarring pace. They crossed no discernible border, but once they were west of the Cheviot Hills and north of the Liddel Water, Susanna knew they were in Scotland. The rough, hilly track became not so much high as steep and contained sections that dropped off suddenly, sending her heart into her throat. Soon bleak sward and rough grass gave way to worse— bare branches and a sharp ridge of treetops and a continual cold breeze that cut through the warmest clothing. Small valleys ran every which way but offered no relief from the barren melancholy of the region.

Susanna tried and failed to imagine the area in spring, when it might have some hope of a stark beauty. She began to regret she'd not heeded Jennet's plea to desert along with Kelke and Lamplugh, but she had not yet regained possession of the letters. Stubbornness, she thought grimly, was a failing as well as a virtue.

Finally, long after Susanna had begun to wonder if they were being taken out into a wilderness only to be abandoned, they came in sight of human habitation, a stone peel tower, three stories high, with a dwelling house attached. The whole was surrounded by a wall more than two feet thick and at least seven feet high. Compared to a proper castle, it was a poor place, and overwhelming in its smell of smoldering peet, but they spurred their mounts toward it, grateful to have found refuge at last.

"Who is laird here?" Lady Northumberland asked.

"Jock of the Side," came the reply.

"An Armstrong," she murmured. "That is good."

They were made welcome, but this was no earl's castle. Even the last inn they'd stayed in, which had boasted only six beds, seemed spacious in comparison to the dwelling house of Jock of the Side. A simple cottage, it was too small to accommodate them all, even with their numbers so greatly reduced.

Jock of the Side was an even greater disappointment. "You must leave my land within twenty-four hours," he told the earls, although he assured them that the others in their retinue were welcome to his hospitality.

"You cannot leave me!" Lady Northumberland clung to her husband's arm. "I will go with you."

But even the earl could see that his wife was not strong enough to ride on. Neither tears nor recriminations swayed him.

The countess's women gave them what privacy they could for a final night of farewells. Then, in the predawn hour, both earls rode west across a desolate moss called Tarras, seeking the protection of Hector Armstrong, who owed Northumberland his life and would be inclined, so the earl hoped, to return the favor.

Standing in the crisp morning air, watching them ride away, Susanna shivered convulsively. "I do not trust Jock of the Side," she whispered to Jennet. "Or Black Ormiston."

Jennet answered with one of the expressive snorts that seemed to have become habitual of late. "Fear not, madam. The earl has kindly left Guy Carnaby to guard us."

39

Lady Appleton had been right not to trust Black Ormiston, Jennet thought as she watched him make off with all their horses. At the first report of an army advancing toward Jock of the Side's peel tower, he and his followers were abandoning the countess and her few remaining attendants. They took with them their household goods and cattle and, to prevent the destruction of the tower, had stuffed it full of smoldering peet. This, Jennet was told, would burn for days, preventing anyone from laying gunpowder charges to destroy the structure. When the borderers returned, they'd have to repair the woodwork, but the stone frame would still be intact.

Better, Jennet thought, to have allowed those left behind to defend the place. It had been built to be held, its sole entrance through a double door at ground level. The upper floors used as living quarters could only be reached by a narrow, curving stair called a turnpike. Once inside, even womenfolk could hold out against a great many attackers, firing at them through arrow slits and shot holes and hurling things down from the roof.

But the Scots did not see matters that way. They were *de'els*, as the Northumbrian folk would say. Savages. Jennet watched them flee, her lip curled in distaste. Barefoot, most of them, even in this cold, although a few had odd-looking shoes made from the hides of red deer.

They wore them pulled up to the ankles with the rough fur side out. Barbarians.

The women were dressed in coarse wool garments that hung loose from their shoulders and cloaks in two or three colors of checkerwork on top, and the men . . . well! Jock of the Side was distinguished from his followers only by his short yellow jacket. Under mantles, the rest wore saffron-colored pleated linen smocks that ended at their knees and left their legs bare.

"We could follow the Armstrongs and hide in the mosses," Master Carnaby suggested.

"We would not know where to go without a guide," Lady Appleton objected, "and I am loath to move the countess."

Lady Northumberland had been prostrate with grief and worry ever since her husband's departure. When he left her behind, it had been as if all the life went out of her.

"What, then?" Carnaby demanded. "Wait for the Scots army to come? This place is not safe. This country is not. I'll not breathe easy until we've reached the coast and found a sturdy ship to take us to the Continent."

Lady Appleton did not argue further. When she went back inside the smoke-filled hovel where the countess lay, Jennet followed. It was a pitiful place, unfit to house a gentlewoman, let alone someone nobly born. The "bedchamber" was no more than a recess in the wall.

Worse, in such surroundings, Jennet's skills were useless. She could not hide herself to listen to other people's conversations. There was nowhere to hide. And she was no longer overlooked as a mere servant. With so few followers left, even Lady Northumberland knew her name.

"That the Armstrongs fear whatever troops are advancing toward us does not mean they are our enemies," Lady Appleton said to the countess. "These borderers are all outlaws. They feud with their neighbors as well as their government."

"The Scots regent will hunt us down like animals," Lady Northumberland predicted. With her listlessness had come a fatalism most unlike her normal outlook. "Since Queen Mary's abdication, he has ruled Scotland in the name of young James the Sixth."

James was Mary's baby son, Jennet recalled. Some said he would one day be named Queen Elizabeth's heir, as well.

"The regent, Queen Mary's bastard half brother, wants his sister dead," Lady Northumberland continued. "He wants the heretic queen to execute her."

"Whatever troops come," Lady Appleton said in a soothing voice, "we will reason with them. Come, madam, it is not like you to despair. You must exert your famous charm and win new champions among the Scots."

Eyes shining with moisture, Cecily Carnaby abruptly left the house. Jennet was torn between following her and staying to discover what Lady Appleton had in mind. Speaking in a low voice, the latter continued to encourage the countess to reclaim her leadership of their little band.

Jennet compromised by watching Mistress Carnaby from the doorway. She and her former brother-in-law spoke together. Plotting? Jennet wondered. She was about to move closer to them when a new note in the countess's voice caused Jennet to turn and stare.

"I must persevere, she declared. "For my children." One hand rested protectively over her womb, making Jennet suspect she believed herself to be with child once more. It was a powerful reason to keep fighting, to stay free.

At that moment, they heard the first thundering of distant hooves.

Lady Appleton touched the countess's sleeve. "Your greatest danger lies in the letters you carry upon your person. Burn them before they can be seized."

Jennet sucked in a startled breath. After all Lady Appleton had risked, remaining with the rebels in the hope of getting hold of those letters, how could she suggest destroying them? Or was this but a trick to regain possession of the damning documents?

"They will help us win support abroad," Marion objected.

"Only if they do not fall into the wrong hands first." Jennet heard the tremor in Lady Appleton's voice. Whatever her intent, it cost her to deceive a woman she admired.

The hoofbeats came closer.

With a quiet dignity in no way diminished by the fact that her velvet cap was askew, Lady Northumberland levered herself up from her pallet. After fumbling beneath her bodice for the letters, she held them crushed in one hand to totter from the bedchamber alcove to the hovel's only chair, which had been drawn up close to the smoky fire.

Lady Appleton knelt beside her. "They are too dangerous to keep, my lady."

A sound from without warned of the imminent arrival of a troop of mounted men. Momentarily distracted, Jennet glanced away from the countess. She saw dozens of armed figures riding hard toward Jock of the Side's holding—a raiding party, not an army.

She turned to tell the countess, but the words died on her lips when she saw the tableau before the hearth. Three women stared at the flames as the letters were consumed.

Jennet blinked. Who had thrown them into the fire? Lady Northumberland? Or Lady Appleton? There was no opportunity to ask. The riders were reining in right in front of the door.

She stepped outside just in time to see a familiar figure in boy's breeches throw herself from the saddle of an equally familiar horse and race toward the burning peel tower. "Lady Glenelg!" Jennet shouted. "Stop! We are here and unharmed."

Jennet was given her own mount for the trek along a narrow, hilly track through a forest and into the bleak and melancholy Cheviot Hills. After a seeming endless journey filled with inconsequential chatter—Lady Glenelg expounding upon the fact that in Scotland the condition of the roads was too poor to allow wheeled traffic and that Scots horses were only shod on their forefeet, as if Jennet cared!—they emerged on the road to Jedburgh and were taken to the relative luxury and security of Ferniehurst Castle.

"The Border is in a tickle state," Lady Glenelg said as soon as she and Lady Appleton and Jennet were alone in the chamber Sir Thomas Kerr had assigned to her. "The Kerrs of Ferniehurst supported Queen Mary when few others would, just before her flight to England, and are in sympathy with the earls, but for all that, Sir Thomas rescued the countess because he owed my Gilbert a favor."

"Do you trust Sir Thomas?" Lady Appleton asked.

Lady Glenelg chuckled. "Kerr read the letter I brought him from Gilbert, which he sent to me along with a safe conduct guaranteed by the Scots regent, then paid my husband exaggerated compliments and made me blush with a few well chosen remarks about my sterling qualities."

Kerr was a very handsome fellow indeed, Jennet thought. And he'd mustered his men to ride into Liddesdale. But trust him? It seemed not.

"The Armstrongs of the Side are notorious outlaws," Lady Glenelg continued, "but the Kerrs are not much better."

"At least the accommodations are an improvement."

Jennet examined a tray containing cheese, oatcakes, and bread, a pitcher of weak barley water, and another of ale. She poured out three cups of the latter and distributed them.

Lady Appleton, she thought, looked almost as worn out as Lady Northumberland. In contrast, Lady Glenelg was bursting with good health. She had an air of contentment about her that made Jennet think, in spite of the very different ways the two noblewomen showed it, that Lady Glenelg might be in the same interesting condition as the countess.

"Lady Northumberland is convinced Sir Thomas acted out of some chivalrous instinct when he heard of her plight." Lady Appleton sipped and grimaced. As Jennet had already discovered, Scots ale was brewed stronger than the English variety.

"Let her have her illusions, poor lady. She will have few enough when she hears that her husband has been turned over to the same regent of Scotland who guaranteed my safe passage from Carlisle. He coerced Hector Armstrong into betraying Northumberland."

"And Westmorland?" Lady Appleton asked.

"Still free."

For a moment there was silence.

"I have more news," Lady Glenelg said. "I believe I have uncovered the identity of Eleanor's killer."

Blue eyes bright with interest, Lady Appleton lifted a brow. "Indeed? Tell us more."

Jennet moved closer, anxious not to miss a word of this exchange.

"Sir Roger Cholmeley." Lady Glenelg launched into an account of her trip into Cumberland, her capture of Lucius Dartnall—a personable but thick-witted fellow, to hear Lady Glenelg tell it—and her visit to Lady Pendennis's bitter and unforgiving mother. "Sir Roger is very wealthy, a source of funding for the rebels, and he takes personally any insult to the family honor. Would he not be doubly angry if he thought Eleanor had set out to deceive him with letters from abroad?"

"How could he send orders to Augsburg? He never leaves Westmorland."

"But he had contact with Topcliffe," Lady Glenelg reminded them. "Easy enough to hire someone there to send it on. Or order some other relation, one who stood to inherit if Eleanor was dead, to do it."

"The attempts on your life, madam," Jennet said thoughtfully, "all took place when Mistress Standbridge was nearby. Even the arrow could have been her. She arrived soon after the incident, in advance of Lady Westmorland."

"I noted this Marion during the journey from Liddesdale," Lady Glenelg said. "She rode next to Master Carnaby. She seemed the frail and helpless sort and Carnaby, for all his bulk and bluster, appeared to be devoted to her. Protective."

"Marion is less fragile than she looks," Lady Appleton said, "and capable of putting off her uncle when he wanted to marry her to a man of his choosing. I had the impression she pacified him by entering Lady Westmorland's service and had some hope of holding out until he died of old age, after which she would wed Carnaby. But murder Eleanor for him? That is difficult to accept. And how could she send orders to Augsburg? She was in the service of the countess of Westmorland then."

"She might have been visiting Topcliffe," Jennet argued. "She'd brought messages before. And do not forget Master Carnaby was and is her lover. She might have used her woman's wiles to get the earl of Northumberland's seal away from him."

Lady Glenelg smiled. *"Cherchez l'homme,"* she murmured.

"Carnaby could have devised the plan to kill Eleanor," Lady Appleton suggested, "if he knew Eleanor's death would make Marion her uncle's heir. Greed is a fine motive for murder. He'll profit if she inherits and they wed." She glanced at Lady Glenelg, who was steadily working her way through the cheese. "Why did Sir Roger disinherit Lady Gillingham?"

"She did not say, only blamed Eleanor."

Lady Appleton looked thoughtful. She had long suspected that Master Carnaby might be behind the attempts on her life. She'd attributed to him another motive, one that had proved false, but now she had reason to reconsider what she knew of him. Jennet hated to give up her own pet theory, but even she had to admit that Guy Carnaby made a more logical suspect than his former sister-in-law.

"If you mean to accuse anyone here of Eleanor's murder and the attempts on you," Lady Glenelg declared, "you had best do so with dispatch. We cannot remain in the countess's company much longer. I will not take the risk that Gilbert could be accused of treason because of my presence at Ferniehurst, and I do not intend to return to England without you."

Lady Appleton sipped more ale and again made a face. "Well, then we must do something to force the killer's hand. We must set a trap."

"For what person?" Jennet asked.

"We have three choices." Lady Appleton ticked them off on her fingers. "One: Sir Roger wanted Eleanor dead and paid some unknown person to do his bidding. Two: Guy Carnaby orchestrated a series of accidents in the hope of marrying Marion and getting his hands on whatever fortune she inherited, by default, from Sir Roger. Or three: Marion herself was behind these so-called accidents. I am inclined to prefer Master Carnaby as a suspect. If he did not act on his own, then he may well be the one Sir Roger employed. Just because the old man does not approve of him for a relative does not mean he'd not have made use of him. And Carnaby may have thought to win Sir Roger's favor, and Marion's hand, by doing his bidding."

Clearly, Lady Appleton liked this solution, and Jennet could find no fault in it. That did not stop her from worrying that her mistress might take one too many risks to prove her theory. "Madam," she ventured, "there is no need to place yourself in danger. Simply tell everyone that the real Eleanor Pendennis is dead."

"She has the right of it," Lady Glenelg agreed. "There is no reason now to hide your true identity."

Lady Appleton continued to look thoughtful.

"What are you plotting?" Lady Glenelg inquired suspiciously. She spoke but a moment before Jennet could ask the same thing.

"'Tis true 'twould be safer now to be myself and telling that truth may also produce the answers we need. Here is what I propose. I will go to Marion and tell her that Eleanor is dead. I will also warn her that she is in danger. I will point out that if Guy Carnaby killed Eleanor in order to secure Marion's inheritance, then there will be nothing to stop him from disposing of her once he has her money in hand."

"She will not believe you." Jennet had seen the way Mistress Standbridge looked at Guy Carnaby.

"No," Lady Appleton agreed, "but she will go to Carnaby. Confront him. And we will be close at hand to hear what he says."

"What if she was behind all the attempts herself?" Lady Glenelg objected. "Do you expect her to confess?"

"One or the other of them, I do think, will be surprised by my revelation into saying more than he . . . or she . . . intended."

"And if one or both of them decide killing you will solve all their problems?"

"That, Catherine, is where you and Jennet, and Fulke and Lionel, too, come into my plan."

40

Susanna was not as calm as she pretended to be. If her plan went awry, she could end up dead, never to see Nick or Rosamond again. But she had to try, had to make one last effort to achieve justice for Eleanor, and for Margaret Heron, and for the unknown driver of that wagon in Augsburg.

"I am not Eleanor Pendennis," she announced as soon as Marion joined her in Catherine's chamber. Catherine and Jennet had gone ahead to implement the next part of the scheme. "My name is Susanna Appleton. I was sent to Topcliffe to discover what person was responsible for your cousin's death." She told the lie easily, surprising even herself.

Marion's face lost every trace of color. "Nell is . . . dead? When? Where?"

"She was killed—murdered—in Augsburg. It was meant to look like an accident, but it was not. A man in the employ of Haug and Company arranged it on orders sent by someone in England."

"I do not understand. How do you know this?" Marion sank down on the window seat, looking small and lost and helpless.

Susanna's heart went out to her. "I know you do not understand. That is why I felt I must warn you. The person who could most easily have arranged Eleanor's

death and who most stood to profit by it is Guy Carnaby.
I believe he has also tried to kill me."

"No!"

"Yes. Because of you, Marion. You are your uncle's sole
remaining heir. When Sir Roger dies, all Guy has to do is
wed you to claim your inheritance. And once he has it,
he'll no longer need you. I have seen this desire to marry
for gain before. Carnaby is not the first to plan to kill an
unwanted spouse for profit." She'd encountered just such
a situation a few years earlier, and in that case, too, the villain had been careful to counterfeit fondness for the
intended victim, seducing that poor pawn—

"No!" Marion sprang to her feet.

Susanna called after her as she rushed toward the
door. "Did he warn you not to taste the turnip soup?"

Marion's wail of despair seemed answer enough.

Catherine had arranged with Sir Thomas Kerr that
Carnaby should be writing letters for the countess in a
tower chamber. This room could be reached in two ways,
by a door at the top of a winding stair and by a privy entrance from the anteroom that adjoined it. As soon as
Marion left her, Susanna met Catherine and Jennet.
They waited until they heard Marion knock, then crept
inside by the back way. They were shielded from the man
at the desk and the woman beside him by a heavily cur-
tained bed, but they could catch glimpses of what was
going on through gaps in the hangings, and they could
hear everything that passed between the two of them.

"My cousin Nell is dead," Marion told her lover. Her
voice still trembled but was stronger than it had been a
few minutes earlier.

"What? How?"

"It appears she has been dead for some time. She was
killed in an accident in Augsburg."

Anger, Susanna thought. That was what she heard.
The injustice of her cousin's murder had overcome any

trepidation Marion might feel at facing Eleanor's killer. She wanted answers. Susanna hoped she'd get them before Carnaby turned violent. If he'd been acting on Sir Roger's behalf, as Catherine had suggested, Susanna expected him to defend himself by saying so. If her own theory was correct, the outcome of this confrontation was less predictable.

Carnaby sounded confused. "But who has been calling herself Lady Pendennis?"

"Some woman named Appleton. She is not important."

"Not—"

"You must get rid of her, Guy, before she accuses you of murder."

Peering around the edge of the bed curtain, Susanna caught a glimpse of Carnaby's face. He looked thunderstruck.

"She knows Nell was murdered," Marion continued. "She thinks you arranged it."

"But you just said your cousin's death was an accident."

"It was meant to *look* like an accident. That fool Dartnall mishandled his assignment."

Susanna's hand went to her throat. She exchanged a startled look with Catherine. She'd not mentioned Dartnall's name. There was only one way Marion could know it, if *Marion* had sent the order to kill her cousin. With sick certainty, Susanna realized she'd misjudged both parties in the drama playing out on the other side of the hangings.

Carnaby heaved himself out of his chair, catching his mistress by the shoulders. "Speak sensibly, woman."

"I did it for us, Guy. So Uncle Roger will make me his heir. So we can marry."

"What did you do?" He sounded as if he were strangling.

"Killed Nell."

"How can you have—?"

"I used the earl's seal to send an order to his man in Augsburg. What choice did I have? Eleanor would have returned to Westmorland and ingratiated herself with Uncle Roger."

Susanna winced at the irony of Marion's logic. Even if that had been Eleanor's intention, she'd ultimately have failed. Once Sir Roger had discovered she'd borne a bastard child, he'd have disowned her. If only Marion had realized Rosamond was not Walter's daughter, she'd have known she had no need to kill Eleanor.

None of the deaths had been necessary.

Carnaby's voice conveyed the same anguish Susanna felt. "You convinced Master Dartnall that the earl of Northumberland wanted your cousin dead?"

Marion's eyes gleamed with a wild light. "What else could I do? But I was clever about it. I used the information you'd given me about Sir Walter Pendennis. And I told him to make it look like an accident. He did what I wanted. She died. But then her husband covered it up and found this Appleton woman and sent her here in Nell's place." A burst of hysterical laughter escaped her. "She thinks *you* were responsible. For all the accidents. She warned me against you."

"What more have you done?" Carnaby shook her until she flopped like a straw poppet in his big hands. "Tell me."

She slapped at him. "I damaged her billet strap to make the girth on her saddle slip. What else could I do? She talked of going to visit Uncle Roger. She'd have told him we were lovers. He'd have cast me out."

"She nearly fell into the river near Brancepeth." Carnaby set Marion back on her feet, but he did not relax his grip on her arms.

"Yes. Worse luck, someone came to her rescue."

Carnaby released his mistress to rake trembling hands over his face. "You poisoned the soup."

"I bribed that scullion to do it, a half-wit stupid enough to afterward eat of it himself."

Susanna had thought she could not feel more repulsed. She'd been wrong. Marion sounded pleased by the boy's death.

"You might have killed everyone."

"Only Lady Northumberland's women." In a peevish voice she added, "It is harder to kill someone than I'd imagined."

"You shot an arrow at her and missed."

Marion folded her arms beneath her breasts and glared at him. "With you to help me, we'll do it right the next time."

"This is madness."

"What I did, I did it for us." Marion jabbed him in his massive chest with one delicate finger. "You are as much to blame as I, and if you do not help me finish it now, you are the one who will be blamed. The woman pretending to be my cousin is convinced you are guilty."

Carnaby sank into his chair. "Did you kill Margaret Heron, too?"

"Margaret?" Marion sounded surprised.

"Has life come to mean so little to you that you cannot remember the names of your victims?" He looked away from her in disgust and his eyes met Susanna's. The torment she saw there convinced her of Carnaby's innocence.

"Oh. Margaret." Marion's tone was dismissive. "That really was an accident. No doubt she was riding too fast, bent on abandoning the countess. I am sure it happened just as you surmised. Her horse stumbled and she fell off. It was her own fault that she broke her neck."

Susanna stepped out of hiding. "I have wronged you, Master Carnaby." She called for Fulke and Lionel, who had been stationed on the other side of the outer door.

"You!" Marion flew at Susanna, fists flailing.

Carnaby caught her, holding her with less effort than he'd have needed to restrain an irritated lap dog. He had no trouble restricting her movements, but he could not stop her words. Tears streaming down her face, she railed at Susanna. "You can prove nothing against me. I will say you lie. You are a spy! A heretic! No one will believe you!"

"They will believe me," Carnaby said.

Several hours later, the three of them stood before Lady Northumberland. Earlier, she had been told of her husband's capture. She listened, her expression vacant, to two versions of events that had little to do with the rebellion. Although it clearly broke his heart to do so, Carnaby was true to his word. He refused to support Marion's claims. Instead he repeated everything she had confessed to him.

"So you are Lady Appleton, not Lady Pendennis," the countess of Northumberland said after a lengthy silence. "The name Appleton is not unknown in the North."

"It is common in most places, my lady." Susanna did not like the way the countess looked. She'd had one too many shocks and showed it. "It derives from *apple tun,* an old word for 'orchard.'"

"Where is your family seat?" A barely discernible flicker of interest put life back into the countess's eyes.

"My late husband came from Lancashire, madam. My family's land is in Kent."

"Is the child you bade me send for real?"

"Yes, madam. Eleanor Pendennis's daughter by my late husband. I am her foster mother and love her as dearly as if she were mine own."

Lady Northumberland leaned forward. "So, you are a widow. Have you wealth?"

"A modest estate."

The countess squared her shoulders and sat up straighter. "I need money," she said baldly, "to ransom the earl. You have, I think, denied me Sir Roger's resources."

Susanna was not so certain of that, but she did not argue the point. She knew what Lady Northumberland wanted. "I will contribute what I can." She did not like the thought of either the earl or his countess in the hands of the queen's men.

"I believe you mean that."

"As much as I must abhor civil war, I understand why you felt driven to restore the Percy to their former glory in the North. Exile is punishment enough for your rebellion against our rightful queen." She moved a step closer. "You will not be allowed to return to England. I will send funds sufficient to let you live in comfort on the Continent, but not enough to allow you to launch an invasion."

"Yes, I will have to go abroad," the countess agreed, "but do not be so certain of the rest. We have powerful supporters in the Low Countries."

"The duke of Alba?" Susanna asked.

Lady Northumberland ignored the jibe and shifted her attention to Guy Carnaby. "Joan and Cecily have promised to accompany me into exile. Will you come with us?"

"My place has always been at your side, my lady," Carnaby avoided looking at Marion.

"Take me with you, madam," she pleaded. "I have been loyal to the cause. My cousin Nell was a threat. It was necessary that she die."

Only the slight flaring of the countess's nostrils gave away her revulsion. "I cannot yet tell how much harm your actions caused our forces, but I do know you have been no help to us." She stood to signal the end of the audience. "Take her back to England with you, Lady Appleton. Turn her over to her cousin's grieving widower and let him decide what's to be done with her."

41

Walter found Nick Baldwin in the same small chamber at the George where they had met once before. One foot was propped up on a stool and an arm was swathed in bandages, but he looked in remarkably fine spirits.

"I understand it was Dr. Grant who set your broken arm and saw to it that you were transported safely back to York."

"A fair exchange," Baldwin said. "He found himself in need of a pardon."

It had been granted, too, reviving all Walter's questions about the source of Baldwin's influence.

"Is the guard necessary?" He nodded toward Baldwin's man.

"Toby feels I need one." Baldwin's voice was bland and uninflected. "I am less certain. You tell me, Pendennis. Did you intend to wish me well in my search for Susanna, or was that clap on the shoulder on the wall of Barnard Castle an attempt to kill me?"

A spurt of uncontrolled anger forced Walter to take a deep breath before he answered. "If I'd decided to kill you, Baldwin, you'd be dead."

"As I suspected." But the manservant continued to look skeptical and did not leave the chamber. "I sent a message asking you to come here to the George," Baldwin continued, "because I have received a message from

Susanna. She is safe and well. More of her whereabouts anon. There is another matter we must discuss first."

"News of the rebels?" Typical of this entire campaign, the leaders of the queen's army had lost track of them. Only gradually had word filtered back to England that Northumberland was a prisoner of the Scots regent while his wife had been taken in by Sir Thomas Kerr at Ferniehurst. Westmorland was on the loose in the Debateable Land.

Baldwin held up two letters, one folded smaller than the other and still sealed. "This came addressed to you, Pendennis, enclosed in a note from the man I left behind in Hamburg."

Puzzled, Walter took the proffered parchment and broke the seal. He glanced first at the signature, which was that of his manservant, Jacob. "Impossible," he whispered as he read the message.

"The letter I received confirms what is written in yours." Baldwin's knowing expression made Walter's hackles rise.

"This is a trick."

"A trick of fate, mayhap, but none of my doing." He produced a third letter. "This is the note I spoke of earlier. From Susanna, sent when she passed by York earlier today. In it she suggests we both come after her. Her destination is not far from here. Even I will be able to ride the distance. When we arrive, Pendennis, you will share with her the news Jacob Littleton sent."

"Damn you, Baldwin." Walter could only seethe with impotent fury.

"If you do not," the merchant said with a complacent smile, "I will."

42

Walter and Nick arrived at Wressel together, though scarce in charity with one another. Susanna ignored the tension between them. She had more important things on her mind.

"The countess's daughters were abandoned." The horror of her discoveries still made her voice shake. "Two little girls, unable to fend for themselves, were left to their own devices for a week or more. The castle had been ransacked. Not a bit of food was left. They were nearly frozen and half starved by the time we arrived. All the servants who did not flee had been executed. They'd been left hanging from trees by marauding troops. Their own or the queen's, I know not, nor do I care."

"Would you rather the raiders had carried the children off? Or murdered them as they did the servants?"

Shocked by Walter's callous comment, Susanna stared at him. As usual, an unrevealing expression kept his feelings secret.

"I will take them back to Leigh Abbey with me," she declared.

"I doubt Rosamond will be pleased by that arrangement," Nick said in a mild voice.

Walter's words were sharp. "The court of wards will deal with them, Susanna. I will arrange for them to be taken to York and turned over to the earl of Sussex. This is his responsibility, not yours."

"I promised their mother I would make sure they were safe and well." Lady Northumberland had called her back, just before she'd left Ferniehurst and taken the old Roman road called Dere Street back to England, to ask that one last boon.

Walter said nothing, but his implacable manner convinced Susanna she would not get her way in this matter. She sighed. She would have to contact Lady Sussex. With her help, she'd at least be able to keep the countess informed as to the health and whereabouts of her children.

There was something peculiar about Walter's demeanor, Susanna decided. He held himself stiffly, as if he were the one who had been injured at the siege of Barnard Castle. A quick, surreptitious glance at Nick's arm and ankle reassured her that he was mending well. Later she would examine the damage more thoroughly.

"I understand now why you came here," Walter said, "but why send word to us to follow you?"

Susanna signaled to Jennet to fetch Fulke and Lionel and their prisoner. Catherine, who had revealed during the journey south that she believed she was expecting another child, had taken charge of the two little girls. "I have something to tell you, Walter."

"And he has something to tell you," Nick said in a low voice.

Before he could elaborate on this statement, Marion burst into the room. Fulke's firm grip on her arm did little to restrain her. "Which one of you is Sir Walter?" she demanded.

Nick indicated Walter.

"I am falsely accused of murder. I have done nothing."

"Who are you?" Walter asked.

"Marion Standbridge."

"She sent the order for Eleanor's death," Susanna said.

Walter sighed. "Release her, Fulke. She did not kill anyone."

Susanna gasped. "Did you not hear me? She stole the earl of Northumberland's seal and sent Dartnall that second message. She also tried, three times, to murder me, thinking I was Eleanor. How can you—?"

"She did not kill Eleanor." This time it was Nick who spoke. He fixed Walter with a stern look. "Tell her the entire story now, or I will." He drew a piece of thrice-folded parchment from inside his doublet, as if to offer it to Susanna.

A letter? She glanced at Walter. He produced a similar missive, turning it over in his hands and staring at it with a bleak expression on his face. "Eleanor is not dead," he said at last.

Everyone asked questions at once—Marion, Jennet, Susanna, even Fulke and Lionel. Walter waited until the furor died down.

"I did believe she was." He met Susanna's puzzled gaze, torment etched into his face. "She was near death when last I saw her. I left my man Jacob with her, giving him instructions for her burial when she did pass on. But she refused to die. Soon after I left them, she recovered sufficient strength to insist that Jacob take her on to Hamburg, to Baldwin's house. This letter is from Jacob, written from that place."

"My man wrote at the same time," Nick put in, "to send on the same news."

"I do not understand," Susanna protested. But she was afraid she was beginning to.

"It is simple enough. I thought myself a widower. I did not know she was still alive. I did not lie to you, Susanna."

"Not about that, mayhap, but neither did you tell me the truth about Eleanor's involvement with the rebels. I know of it now, Walter. She wrote a letter to her uncle. Without mentioning it to you, I think."

He no longer seemed capable of keeping his expression blank. The torment writ upon his face confirmed her guess. Eleanor had contacted Dartnall, not the other way around.

Susanna's probing gaze shifted to Eleanor's cousin. Marion had realized she was not guilty of murdering "Nell," after all, and she'd never felt any sense of responsibility for the deaths of the wagon driver and the scullion. A calculating gleam came into Marion's almond-shaped eyes, and she smiled.

Walter did not notice. He seized Susanna's arm and pulled her after him into a window embrasure. "I do not wish to be overheard by the others." His voice was low and pained.

When Nick would have followed, hobbling to her side on crutches, Susanna waved him away. She seated herself on the bench in front of the window and arranged her skirts with exaggerated care. She was not sure she wanted to hear any more confessions, but Walter had been her friend for a long time. She owed it to him to listen.

"Eleanor thought she was dying. She confessed she had betrayed England. She killed any love I might have had for her with those words. When I set out from Augsburg with her and my man and her maid, I expected the rough roads to finish her off. I felt no pity for her suffering, and when she was still alive two days later, I considered strangling her with my own hands, but I could not do it."

Although profoundly shocked by what he'd just revealed, Susanna put one hand on his arm in a gesture of comfort and forgiveness. "Certes, you could not. You loved her once."

He drew in a strengthening breath. "After we took the road north out of Frankfurt toward Hamburg, I found a place to hide her and left Jacob and the maidservant to care for her. I gave him enough money to support them in comfort, still certain it was only a matter of time before Eleanor succumbed to her injuries. When I told you she was dead, I believed she must be by then, for she was most horribly injured."

"But she did not die."

"No." He managed a wry smile. "Jacob writes that she began to regain her strength the moment I abandoned them. She remains disfigured and she will never walk again, but it appears she will live for many years yet."

"And you will be tied to her for the rest of her life." There was no possibility of divorce in the Church of England.

"Yes."

"Oh, my dear," Susanna murmured. "What a tragedy." She thought for a moment. "There is no need for anyone else to know the unfortunate details."

"Baldwin is aware of most of them."

"He will keep silent if I ask it of him." She ignored Walter's grimace. "But we cannot let Marion go free. Not only would she talk, but she deserves some punishment for all she's done. And what about Dartnall?"

"Dartnall has been dealt with." Walter's mask was back in place and his demeanor discouraged further questioning on that subject, but she could tell he saw the sense in silencing Marion. "A trial will serve no one's interests," he mused, "unless it is the trial of Mary of Scotland. Did you—?"

"No. There were no letters or documents."

She lied without a qualm. When she had deciphered the messages from Queen Mary to Lady Westmorland, she had realized that, for all their wrongheadedness in seeking to overthrow the rightful queen of England, they were in truth only women like herself, who could be driven to desperate measures by circumstances beyond their control.

Mary of Scotland had not asked to be born with a claim to England's throne, or to be raised Catholic. The two countesses had done naught but attempt to right old wrongs, to restore their husbands' honors, denied them because of the way they chose to worship. Susanna did not condone treason, but neither could she allow herself to be the direct cause of Lady Northumberland's execution.

The letters addressed to "beloved countess" might have been used against either noblewoman. Susanna did not regret taking them from the countess's hands and throwing them into the fire. If the approaching riders had been the regent's men instead of Kerr's, they'd have imprisoned Lady Northumberland as they had her husband.

Walter stood staring out the window, lost in his own dark thoughts. He started when she addressed him.

"What became of Lady Westmorland?"

"She was captured."

"Will she be executed?"

"No. The queen has already decided on confinement for life." Walter grimaced. "Unlike her father, Queen Elizabeth appears to have an aversion to beheading noblewomen."

Perhaps, Susanna thought, because one of the great ladies King Henry had decapitated had been Elizabeth's own mother, Anne Boleyn. Whatever her reason, Susanna was glad she had decided to be merciful. After all, Lady Westmorland had not killed anyone.

"I have a suggestion," she ventured. "I understand why Marion cannot be held responsible for the deaths of the wagoneer and the scullion, but is there any reason she should not share her old mistress's imprisonment?"

Walter very nearly smiled. "If what I've heard about Lady Westmorland's temperament is true, that seems a most fitting punishment."

"Then we've only Eleanor's fate to decide."

"I will exile her to my manor in Cornwall."

"Nonsense. As soon as she is able to travel home from Hamburg, she must come to me at Leigh Abbey. I may not be able to heal her injuries, but if there are any medicines that can help, I will find them." And with Eleanor at Leigh Abbey, Rosamond would stay on there, too.

Reluctantly, Walter agreed. Susanna did not give him any choice. In time, she hoped he would find it in his heart to forgive Eleanor and reconcile with her. If he could not, he faced many long, unhappy years ahead.

When Walter went off to make arrangements for Marion's incarceration, Susanna turned her attention to Nick. He had been watching them, a worried look on his face.

A tender kiss reassured him.

"I have missed you," he said after a gratifying interlude.

"And I, you, my dearest."

She cared for Walter, but Nick was the man she loved. Even more important, he was the one person she could count on to have her best interests at heart.

TO THE READER

In *Treason in Tudor England: Politics and Paranoia* (Princeton University Press, 1986), Lacey Baldwin Smith argues that deficiencies in the sixteenth-century Englishman's diet may have been responsible for the sheer stupidity of some of the treason plots concocted during that era. There were many of them, and, despite appearances, the uprising that is the foundation for this book was not the most harebrained of the lot. Whatever the reasons for their erratic behavior and love of intrigue, a number of Elizabeth Tudor's subjects attempted to topple her from her throne. The rebellion of the northern earls has always fascinated me because it should, by rights, have been called the rebellion of the northern countesses.

There is conflicting information in contemporary accounts concerning the movements of the rebels and the dates of various occurrences during the uprising of 1569, but to the best of my ability I have created my fictional tale within the bounds of historical fact. When there were contradictions, I made what seemed to me the most sensible choice, although that, of course, may not have been the one made by the earls and their countesses. Many of their actions defy logic.

Scholars generally agree that the two countesses were "stouter" than their husbands, riding with the troops and urging them on when they faltered. Lady Westmorland's remarks about her brother and the comments she makes to the conspirators when they contemplate calling off the rebellion are taken from contemporary sources. The earl of Northumberland was tricked into ringing the bells at Topcliffe to signal the start of the uprising. He was tricked again at its end by Hector Armstrong, who turned him over to the regent of Scotland.

After her rescue by Sir Thomas Kerr, Lady Northumberland fled to the Continent, hoping to raise enough money to ransom her husband. Another daughter, Mary, was born just nine months after the rebellion began. Meanwhile, Northumberland was held in Scotland for seventeen months, then returned to England, where he was executed. The countess of Northumberland remained an exile until her death of smallpox in a convent at Namur in 1591.

The earl of Westmorland also escaped. He lived in the Low Countries and collected a pension from the king of Spain until his death in 1601. It is not clear precisely when his countess abandoned him or where she went, but she does not seem to have gone to Scotland. She did pen frantic letters to the queen, begging permission to come to court and plead her case. "Innocency and the great desire I have had to do my humble duty to her Highness," she wrote, "emboldeneth me to continue this my suit." She was sent to one of her family's houses, Kenninghall, and lived there as a virtual prisoner until her death in 1593. Her brother, the duke of Norfolk, was executed for treason in 1572.

Hundreds of the common folk who rallied to the earls' cause were also executed, including that Christopher Norton who courted Mary Seton, Queen Mary's lady-in-waiting, in order to open communications with the queen of Scots. Leonard Dacre, as everyone suspected, had his own agenda. He turned traitor after the main uprising was over, seizing two castles. When his effort to hold them failed, he fled abroad and died in exile in 1573.

Pope Pius V finally got around to excommunicating Queen Elizabeth, thus absolving her subjects from their allegiance to her, in February of 1570. The papal bull was not published in England until that May, far too late to help the rebel cause. The duke of Alba never had any intention of invading England. He had troubles of his own in the Netherlands.

Mary, queen of Scots, did not actively encourage the uprising of 1569 and may even have tried to dissuade the earls from carrying out their plans. She did communicate with and exchange presents with the earls and their countesses and consider marrying the duke of Norfolk if Queen Elizabeth approved, but there were no letters in an ornate casket for Susanna to steal. That is not to say that Mary did not use secret codes. She was at the center of one clandestine plot after another throughout her imprisonment in England. In 1571, she received a letter from Spanish supporters that was written in invisible ink. It had to be held to the fire to be read. She answered it in kind, unaware that her reply went straight to the English authorities. As the result of another casket full of letters, confiscated nearly two decades after the events of this novel, Mary was finally executed for plotting treason against Queen Elizabeth.

And then there is Sir George Bowes. The rebels burned his home at Streatlam on their way to Barnard Castle. Suffice it to say he was not well liked by his neighbors. During the siege, he kept a tally of desertions. Of 226 men who jumped off the excessively high wall of Barnard Castle during one twenty-four-hour period, Bowes methodically recorded that 35 broke legs, arms, or necks.

ABOUT THE AUTHOR

Kathy Lynn Emerson lives in Wilton, Maine. She has written many novels, including romantic suspense and children's mysteries. You can visit her website at www.kathylynnemerson.com.

More By Best-selling Author
Fern Michaels

__Kentucky Rich	0-8217-7234-1	$7.99US/$10.99CAN
__Kentucky Heat	0-8217-7368-2	$7.99US/$10.99CAN
__Plain Jane	0-8217-6927-8	$7.99US/$10.99CAN
__Wish List	0-8217-7363-1	$7.50US/$10.50CAN
__Yesterday	0-8217-6785-2	$7.50US/$10.50CAN
__The Guest List	0-8217-6657-0	$7.50US/$10.50CAN
__Finders Keepers	0-8217-7364-X	$7.50US/$10.50CAN
__Annie's Rainbow	0-8217-7366-6	$7.50US/$10.50CAN
__Dear Emily	0-8217-7316-X	$7.50US/$10.50CAN
__Sara's Song	0-8217-7480-8	$7.50US/$10.50CAN
__Celebration	0-8217-7434-4	$7.50US/$10.50CAN
__Vegas Heat	0-8217-7207-4	$7.50US/$10.50CAN
__Vegas Rich	0-8217-7206-6	$7.50US/$10.50CAN
__Vegas Sunrise	0-8217-7208-2	$7.50US/$10.50CAN
__What You Wish For	0-8217-6828-X	$7.99US/$10.99CAN
__Charming Lily	0-8217-7019-5	$7.99US/$10.99CAN

Call toll free **1-888-345-BOOK** to order by phone or use this coupon to order by mail.

Name _____

Address _____

City _____ State_____ Zip _____

Please send me the books I have checked above.

I am enclosing	$_____
Plus postage and handling*	$_____
Sales Tax (in New York and Tennessee)	$_____
Total amount enclosed	$_____

*Add $2.50 for the first book and $.50 for each additional book. Send check or money order (no cash or CODs) to: **Kensington Publishing Corp., 850 Third Avenue, New York, NY 10022**

Prices and numbers subject to change without notice. All orders subject to availability. Check out our website at **www.kensingtonbooks.com**

Thrilling Romance from
Lisa Jackson

__Twice Kissed	0-8217-6038-6	$5.99US/$7.99CAN
__Wishes	0-8217-6309-1	$5.99US/$7.99CAN
__Whispers	0-8217-6377-6	$5.99US/$7.99CAN
__Unspoken	0-8217-6402-0	$6.50US/$8.50CAN
__If She Only Knew	0-8217-6708-9	$6.50US/$8.50CAN
__Intimacies	0-8217-7054-3	$5.99US/$7.99CAN
__Hot Blooded	0-8217-6841-7	$6.99US/$8.99CAN
